# The Viking's Chosen

## By: Quinn Loftis

FOR ALL MY MEN, COULDN'T DO THIS WITHOUT YOU.

THE VIKING'S CHOSEN
Copyright ©2018 Quinn Loftis Books, LLC
All rights reserved.
Printed in the United States of America
First Edition: February 2018

WWW.CLEANTEENPUBLISHING.COM

SUMMARY: Torben, a Viking general, is prophesized to take a foreign bride—and not just any—but a seer and healer like his mother. Allete Auvray of England is said to be just such a woman. Too bad his orders are to pillage her kingdom, and that she's already pledged to marry the king of Tara. Two worlds collide in this epic historical fiction centered on a chemistry that smolders against all odds.

ISBN: 978-1-63422-274-7 (paperback)
ISBN: 978-1-63422-273-0 (e-book)
COVER DESIGN by: Marya Heidel
TYPOGRAPHY BY: Courtney Knight
EDITING BY: Cynthia Shepp

COVER ART
© ULIA KOLTYRINA / FOTOLIA
© RAZUMNIK / FOTOLIA
© EVILKHAN / FOTOLIA

Young Adult Fiction / Historical / Medieval
Young Adult Fiction / Romance / Historical
Young Adult Fiction / Royalty
Young Adult Fiction / Fantasy / Historical

# content
# disclosure

For more information about our content disclosure, please utilize the QR code above with your smart phone or visit us at WWW.CLEANTEENPUBLISHING.COM.

# Prologue

THE HAND FELL TO the ground with an audible thud, accompanied by a scream from its previous owner. Hager was the third man to lose a limb or appendage in a fortnight. Such a staggering casualty of limbs was understandable during war time, but the Hakon clan—my clan—was between raids. Instead of spending this brief respite of peace at home with his loving wife or in the alehouse guzzling his weight in mead, Hager was now lying on the ground, writhing in agony.

I turned away from the bleeding man. The blood didn't bother me, of course. I'd seen much worse on the battlefield. Neither did the brutality of the punishment, which I had been tasked with administering. I was sick and tired of seeing my countrymen—fine warriors and assets to our clan—punished so severely based upon the word of one soldier. Wasn't a man supposed to have a say in his own defense? Didn't he have a right to confront his accuser or see the evidence presented against him before judgement was passed?

But Jarl Magnus gave his clansmen no such chances. The jarl commanded absolute obedience, and anyone suspected of being less than completely loyal was dealt with swiftly and severely.

I had been the jarl's hersir—chief general—for a mere three months and I'd already severed a dozen limbs at his command. I'd crippled a dozen men, so they could wield neither plow nor sword—no longer able to defend or provide for their families.

I could handle cleaving an axe through human flesh. At times, I confess, I might even have enjoyed it, especially when the victim had the audacity to invade my homeland of Ravenscar, threatening my brothers and sisters—my clansmen. I could handle the screams. I could handle the blood. But I couldn't handle knowing that I'd weakened my clan. I couldn't handle knowing that I'd wet my blade with the blood of my clansman without tangible cause. Such was not our way—or at least, it shouldn't have been.

But that was exactly what I had to do. Many others in the clan would've killed for my job, and they may yet. Magnus, childless, had no heir, making the clansmen become restless. They could feel a storm brewing on the horizon. All-out war was coming—the Oracle predicted as much—but whether from within or without, we didn't yet know. The jarl being heirless only exasperated the feelings of unease. If the jarl died without a successor, the strongest of those who remained would take over. A civil war would no doubt follow. Clan Hakon would weaken, distracted by infighting and vulnerable to invaders. If things worsened further, the clan could splinter, collapsing from within. The Oracle, my mother, prophesied that unseen enemies threatened Clan Hakon, and that the clan was more vulnerable than it had been in a hundred years.

My appointment as hersir was greatly protested, many decrying my age, as I'd only reached my twentieth winter. Indeed, the Oracle reckoned I was the youngest hersir in the history of the clan. They did not think that I was strong enough to serve in such an important and sacred role. It was as though they had forgotten that I was raised a Norseman warrior and would do whatever was necessary to see my clan survive. And, though it was not my desire, tradition often saw the hersir ascend an heirless jarl's vacant throne, but never without a fight. But I did not know what I would do if such things came to pass.

Regardless of what storms were on the horizon for Clan Hakon, I only wished for the strength and vitality of my clan. Whatever it took for those things to remain, I would do. I would see clan Hakon survive generation after generation. I would see the strength of clan Hakon echo throughout the hall of Valhalla, so the even the gods themselves would take notice.

# CHAPTER One

IT IS FORTUNATE TO BE FAVORED WITH PRAISE AND POPULARITY.
IT IS DIRE LUCK TO BE DEPENDENT ON THE FEELINGS OF YOUR
FELLOW MAN.

~THE HAVAMAL, BOOK OF VIKING WISDOM

M Y ATTENTION WAS DRAWN from my troubled thoughts by
a voice that reminded me of the scraping of an axe
on a grinding wheel—a voice I'd come to despise.

"Torben, meet me in the training yard," Magnus
commanded.

Swallowing down the contempt I felt toward my king,
I followed him to the fenced-off area where my warriors
practiced and readied for battle. I stood silently by his side
while he watched the men run through countless drills—
drills not typical for our people. Most clan warriors were
merely converted farmers, laborers, or skilled workers. It
wasn't common for a clan to train its warriors so rigorously,
continuously honing their fighting skills. Such practice
took away from time spent hunting, fishing, or farming.
But these sacrifices strengthened the clan as a whole, and,
I believe, were well worth the time spent. This regimen
was put in place by my predecessor, who was a wise battle
strategist. We'd won many wars under his command. I
trusted his judgment; so, after he died and I ascended to

the rank of hersir, I continued the program.

We watched the warriors sparring in tense silence. Brant, one of my most trusted warriors and kinsmen, was engaged with two green recruits. A mountain of a man, Brant bellowed to the heavens and then swung his huge war hammer in a giant sideways arc. The rightmost recruit held up his shield in a feeble attempt to ward off the blow. With a yelp, the man's shield splintered, the force of the blow sending him flying backward into his companion, sending them both toppling.

"Ha! A game of Kubb with greenhorns. This is fun! Who's next?" Brant let out a hearty chuckle, holding his hammer high while scanning the crowd for another challenger. Finding none, his shoulders slumped and his face fell comically.

"Perhaps they're more scared of your breath than your hammer, Brant. I don't think any of them want to get within a sword's reach of you for fear of the smell," I yelled across the training ground to the huge man who was now leaning easily on the haft of his hammer.

"I'll take any advantage I can get on the battlefield," he responded, still chuckling.

"Go grab a drink in the mead hall before you kill all our recruits. I'll meet you there in a little while. And try not to drop your hammer on anyone's foot again. I need these men in fighting shape."

The other warriors seemed to take this as their cue that training was over for the day. The luckier of the two defeated recruits, the one who'd been pushed off-balance by his comrade rather than Brant's hammer, helped his partner back to his feet. After picking up the pieces from the shattered shield, the pair followed their fellow warriors toward the armory to stow their equipment.

Magnus and I leaned against the wooden perimeter

of the grounds, watching as the warriors departed. The king, who was almost as large as Brant and certainly just as fierce, had not engaged in the open banter with one of his strongest warriors.

"It's time we went on another campaign," Magnus said, finally breaking the tense quiet. "We've been idle long enough."

"Have you decided on a direction?" I asked, careful to respond without hesitation. I had been expecting this—yet another reason why I didn't need Brant maiming any more of my recruits. If we were going on a raid, we'd need our warriors at full-strength. As it was, Magnus had incomprehensibly wounded enough of his own people lately with his maniacal campaign for 'justice'. He'd been carrying out his vigil among the clan ranks, ensuring he had absolute loyalty from his subjects, even if such loyalty was encouraged by the point of a sword.

Raiding right now was folly, and everyone in the clan knew it. Why Magnus couldn't see this, I couldn't begin to guess. Our men needed rest and recuperation. Our last raid was but a mere three months ago and the lives of countless good men had been lost. The remaining clansmen didn't need to be tossed back onto unfamiliar grounds where they would be required to fight for their lives. And their reward? Glory and riches for Magnus and more toil and loss for themselves.

"I think it's time we visit our friends, the English," Magnus replied. If he sensed my unease, he made no note of it as he continued. "News has reached me that a royal wedding is on the horizon. The English king is marrying off one of his daughters to the king of Tara. Weddings require gifts, of course, meaning riches will be transported between two kingdoms. It is the perfect opportunity to strike."

"It also means the two kingdoms are uniting, which could result in creating a larger enemy to fight," I said, pointing out the tedious fact. My reasoning was sound. Surely the king would see the error in kicking the English hornet's nest, especially during a time when they were forging allies with their neighbors, growing in strength while we felt the lingering effects of raid after raid.

"We will be doing things a little differently this time," Magnus said, staring at me but not seeing me. He was lost in his thoughts. "The courting period for the princess's hand will span a month's time. At the end of that month, the two kings will hold a ball to celebrate the engagement. The wedding will occur in Tara. This presents us the opportunity to surprise our enemy instead of attacking them head-on. We will be as ghosts among the English's soldiers and King Cathal's court. While we are infiltrating them, we will also take the opportunity to loot but don't be blatant about it. We are trying to keep from engaging them until I have decided exactly what my intentions are. We will be able to do this during the month-long courting period, so we have time. We will infiltrate the castle guards, replacing the English king's men with our own." As he paused, I had a moment to consider his plan, which could lead to fewer casualties for both sides than our normal, brutish strategy.

"We will lay in wait until the engagement party. Then, we will strike in full-force, take what we want at the point of a sword, and then leave. By the time they know what occurred, it will be too late."

We were quiet for a few minutes after he explained the plan. It was too simple for Magnus. As I considered my jarl, I got the distinct impression he was hiding something from me. I had long ago realized that no matter how much power Magnus had, he would still crave more. And no matter how much gold he brought back from the civilized lands, he would never have enough. His lust for battle was never sated, nor was his greed. While Magnus revealed how he would acquire riches on this endeavor, the strategy to obtain power was yet to be seen.

"When do you wish to leave?" I asked, mentally preparing for the worst.

"How soon can you have our troops ready?" It was the answer I knew was coming. I thought long and hard before I spoke again, knowing Magnus would not accept a lengthy delay. His mind was made up. Any opposition on my part would only result in provoking his temper.

"Our warriors are strong, but our new recruits are more adept at wielding a hoe than an axe. Still, if Odin is with us, I think I can get everyone ready in a fortnight."

"Make it a week." He growled. Without waiting for my counter, he stalked toward his hut.

I sighed as I stared at the jarl's back as he tromped away. *Well, at least Brant will be happy*, I thought to myself. While Brant wasn't as bloodthirsty as Magnus, and he didn't kill other men for sport, I knew he enjoyed cracking a few skulls for the glory of his gods. He would probably run the mead hall out of ale this evening when I told him. I was in for a long night.

SMOKE WAFTED FROM THE sturdy hut that stood about a quarter mile away from the rest of the village, resting on a small knoll overlooking the crags of the Skagerrak bay. The smell of stew and freshly baked bread reached my nostrils, making my stomach growl. Having no doubt I would be offered a bowl, I resolved to eat as much as I could—I'd a full stomach if I wanted to stay on my feet.

Brant wasn't going to leave me alone until I'd drunk at least as much as he had, and his tolerance of libations was legendary. He was probably already crooning *the Lament of Ymir* and the sun hadn't even set.

I pushed open the door without knocking and found my mother standing with her back to me, humming to herself as she slowly stirred the contents of a small iron pot hanging on a tripod stand over a low-burning fire. She preferred to live alone in her small house, rather than with one of the large families in a longhouse, even though she would be more than welcome. My mother was small for a Norsewoman, but now she looked even smaller. She stood slightly hunched, a sign not only of her advanced age, but of the toll her visions had taken upon her. Her long silver hair was woven in a braid, which looked like a worn and frayed rope that trailed stiffly down her back.

"When do you leave?" she asked, breaking off her humming without turning around.

"I...we...how did you know?"

"You grew up in this house, and yet you ask me that? A mother doesn't have to be a seer to know when her son is troubled."

"Still, it's... unsettling. I just wish you'd let me actually *tell* you some news once in a while."

"Ah, but you have already told me. It's written all over you, boy."

"You can't even see me, Hilda." I growled, moving to the cupboard, I took out two bowls and placed them roughly on the table. Years ago, my mother had insisted I use her proper name rather than calling her Mother, even when we were alone together. She said that it was important for the clan members to see her as the Oracle first and foremost, and that anything else she might be, including my mother, was secondary. I knew, however, she didn't feel that way in her heart. She had foreseen early on that I would achieve remarkable things and I would have to grow up much faster than the other children. If the clan heard me call her by her name or by her title, they would be more likely to accept me—as a man, a warrior, and a leader.

"I see you more clearly than anyone, even yourself. You can't come stomping up my walkway without giving yourself away—you never could. It's in the way that you move, the way you carry yourself. The shuffle of your feet might as well be a war horn sounding your troubles, and I know what troubles you; you think our warriors aren't ready."

"I *know* they're not," I responded, pouring us each a cup of water from a pitcher on the table. "I see there are two cups on this table. You were expecting me."

"Of course I expected you. Shouldn't an old woman expect her son for dinner? What's wrong with that?" The corners of her mouth quirked upward as she continued stirring.

"Don't give me that *old woman* crap, Hilda." I barked. "I know you've had a vision. That's how you knew we're about to go on another invasion."

"You didn't answer my question," she pointed out, ignoring my sore attitude.

"We leave in a week." I finally sighed as I pulled out the chair that seemed much too small to sustain my weight and sat down ungracefully. "Will you be going?" I asked as I leaned my forearm against the table and pressed my forehead to it. My mother was the only person I would allow to see the taxation the jarl's obsessions were taking on me.

She grinned at me. "Of course I will be going. When has he ever left me behind?"

"What are you so happy about?" I asked, staring at her with a puzzled look on my face.

"That is not enough time for your troops," she responded, ignoring my question, "but that is not for me to say; I'm no battle priestess. It is, however, the appointed time that I foresaw. It is the time frame you must adhere to. You mustn't be late, or early, for that matter. Rather, you must arrive precisely at the appointed time, or you will lose her. The arrow that does not fly true, the scorned seeking revenge, and the greedy who is never satisfied. You *must not* be late."

It was clear that I was in the presence of Hilda, the Oracle rather than Hilda, my mother. Many of our conversations evolved in such a manner—she would slip into seer mode and start spouting prophecies, telling me that our clan must do this or that. Sometimes she made sense, most of the time, however, I had no idea what she was talking about.

"Meet who, Hilda?" I asked, not sure if I wanted the answer. I felt a heavy, foreboding presence fall over me, like a tunic that was much too tight. It made me feel exposed and vulnerable.

As I waited for her reply, she shuffled over to me and, to my surprise, smacked the back of my head. I ducked and frowned. "What was that for?"

"Do you ever listen when I speak, boy?" she huffed. "I have already told you about the prophecy many times. You are the one who chooses not to listen. In order to protect our clan, you must take a foreign bride. Up until now, I wasn't sure, but with the upcoming raid it has been made clear to me your bride just so happens to be from England."

I wanted to groan, but I didn't want to be smacked in the head again, so I held it in. Apparently, she was speaking as both seer and mother this time.

# Quinn Loftis

"That is one prophecy that cannot come to pass, Oracle. Our clan would never accept an outsider, neigh, an *English* princess at that, to become our queen. They would not respect her—they would consider her weak and simple-minded—it cannot be."

As she filled our bowls with the stew she'd prepared, I watched her lips pinch in frustration. Her eyes, always cloudy, were shadowed, and she appeared weighed down by some unseen force. "It is not up to you, Torben, my son. No matter what you think, it is what needs to—no—what *must* happen. If we do not change, if this clan doesn't turn away from the old ways, we will destroy ourselves. The world is changing, becoming smaller. We must be ready; we must adapt."

"Tell me the prophecy again." I held up my hand to stop her. "I know you've told me before, but I want you to tell me again."

I watched as my mother's eyes became unfocused and she seemed to slip into a trance just before she spoke. *A young warrior, who is just, fair, and wise beyond his years, will take his rightful place as leader of his people. As he makes his ascension, he will not be alone. The warrior-turned-king will take a bride, not of his people, but from across the sea with a new vision for the Hakon Clan. She is a warrior in her own right and a healer—a rare kind for her race—but she keeps the skill hidden from her people. They fear it instead of embracing the gift that it is. Together, they are a catalyst for the change that will save Clan Hakon. Without their union, the Clan will be snuffed out, ground into nothing. We will be forgotten, a people lost to history."*

"I suppose you believe *I'm* this young ruler?" I asked. Once she'd returned to herself, she wordlessly took the seat next to mine, said a quick prayer to the gods, and began to eat. I did not repeat the question; there was no point. She would answer when she was ready.

Several bites later, she decided to speak. "It does not

take a vision to see that you will be the next king of this clan. But, then again, you somehow manage to bury your head in the ground when something is staring you in the face."

Whatever else she might be, my mother was honest. "Am I to marry this foreign bride—to bear offspring with her?"

"What?" Her piercing gaze met mine and mischief danced in her eyes. "Do you think her body will somehow be inferior to those of the women in our clan? Do you think she will repulse you? Perhaps she's deformed in some way because she is not a Norsewoman, with three eyes, six breasts, and a forked tongue. Is that what you fear?"

"Damn, woman, you have a sharp tongue." I choked as I tried to swallow the bite I'd taken before she'd begun gushing her nonsense. I took a quick sip of mead to clear my throat, and then, because I am my mother's son, retorted, "You know I do not think such things as well as you know any warm-blooded male would be thrilled to find out his wife has six breasts. He wouldn't even notice the forked tongue or the third eye."

Cackles of laughter rolled out of my mother as she covered her mouth with her apron. She shook her head at me, and then she patted my hand. "I am hoping she can match your wit and stand up to your pigheadedness. Having a sharp tongue would probably serve her well also."

"You are cruel, Mother. If a sharp tongue and stubbornness is what you desire in a daughter-in-law, I might as well marry one of our own clanswomen. I don't have to look far to find those things."

She stood and took our bowls to the wash bin and began cleaning them. Her back was to me, but I could see the tension in her shoulders. "A Norsewoman is not what you need—not what *we* need. We need a healer, not a conqueror."

"I will not wed a woman I do not love," I told her as I stood and walked over to her, setting my cup on the counter next to the wash bin.

"Can you not love an Englishwoman?" She pressed.

"Why do you insist she will be English?" I narrowed my eyes at her. It wasn't uncommon for the Oracle to move people around like a chess game in hopes of bringing her visions to fruition. My mother wasn't simply a messenger; she was sometimes a meddlesome instigator, if she thought her prophesies were not coming to pass quickly enough.

"The winds tell me there is a young English princess born with the ability to heal. Now, you come to me, telling me you are leaving to invade England in a week's time," she said coyly as she turned her head and raised her brow at me.

I didn't have to respond. We'd already hashed out the coming campaign. She'd made her point. Unfortunately, her most recent revelation left me unsettled. I was supposed to be getting my soldiers ready to storm a foreign land. There were drills to be done, weapons to be maintained, provisions to be packed. I didn't need any distractions right now. Not to mention that, when the fighting commenced, I was going to need my attention fully on keeping us all alive. I wasn't going to have time to search for some princess healer amid the chaos. Diverting my attention on the battlefield would be utterly mad, tantamount to suicide. I could have told Hilda this, but I knew it would garner me no sympathy. So instead, I leaned down and pressed a kiss to her forehead, then bowed to the Oracle. "Peace to you this night, seeress. Thank you for the meal."

"And to you, brave warrior. May the gods bless your battle with victory."

I left the warm familiarity of the hut and stepped out into the cool fall air. Winter was coming—a change of season. Apparently, it was not the only change our clan needed to prepare for.

# CHAPTER
## Two

"MANY PEOPLE THINK BEING ROYAL IS A PRIVILEGE, A GIFT
GIVEN ONLY TO A LUCKY FEW. IN SOME WAYS, I'M SURE THEY
ARE CORRECT. BUT, MOST DO NOT REALIZE THE RESPONSIBILITY
THAT COMES WITH THE BIRTHRIGHT. PLEASE DON'T THINK ME
UNGRATEFUL, BUT OH HOW I WOULD LOVE TO WALK IN THE
SHOES OF A COMMONER AND BREATHE IN THE FREEDOM OF
THAT STATION. TO BE ABLE TO LIVE WHERE I CHOOSE, MARRY
WHOMEVER I LOVE, AND BE MYSELF IS A DESIRE BURNING SO
STRONGLY INSIDE ME THAT I FEAR IT WILL CONSUME ME."

~DIARY OF PRINCESS ALLETE AUVRAY

A S A PRINCESS, THE oldest of three sisters, and future
queen of England, I, of course, did the mature thing
when my parents told me I was to marry the King of Tara—I
ran. Allete Auvray, noble-born heiress of the Britannia
Empire, ran. Now, I did not run *away*. There would be no
point in that. My father would have sent guards searching
for me like crazed hounds to drag me back before I even
made it to the borders of our land. I ran only as far as my
familiar old oak tree—the ancient tree that had become a
sanctuary to me and my cousin, Thomas, when we were
children—our place of refuge. Disregarding the fact that
I was clothed in one of my finer dresses, I hoisted myself
up on to the lowest branch. Then, I continued, up and up,

until I was sitting high enough that I could see the whole of my father's lands spreading out before me like a giant green picnic blanket. Ours was a beautiful and bountiful kingdom for most, but it was but a gilded cage for me. The day I had dreaded had finally come, even though I had always known I would be married off to a nobleman. As the oldest, it was my duty to either marry a nobleman worthy of becoming king of England or marry another king in order to secure an alliance beneficial to our empire. Every decision for my family was about power—how to gain it and how to keep it. Throughout all the kingdoms, the ruler who held the most land and possessed the largest army was feared. As princess, what I personally wanted was nullified. It didn't matter that I would wed someone I did not love. Nothing mattered except what my father, the king, wanted.

"Do you not think it is time you stop climbing trees to run away from your problems, cousin?" A voiced hailed me from the ground below.

I rolled my eyes. I should have known Thomas would not let me sulk in peace. We'd always been close, like siblings, but that didn't mean he didn't drive me to wanting to club him with a tree branch every now and then.

"I do not believe I asked for your counsel on the matter," I yelled down at him.

"It is a good thing, then, that I do not sit idly by and leave you to your own devices. What sort of cousin would I be if I were to let you pursue your own destructive whims? Instead, like the selfless and loving relation I am, I concern myself with what is best for you. Come down, Allete. Let us talk about this like mature adults."

"I don't want to be a mature adult. I'd rather be a petulant child and stomp my foot until someone says, *okay dear Allete, you don't have to marry that brute of a king.*"

Thomas chuckled. "How do you know he is a brute? Perhaps he is a paragon of charm and wit, not to mention dashingly handsome."

I scoffed. "No king is dashingly handsome. They are old, bossy, and uncaring of what their wife thinks."

"Oh really? Does King Albric treat your mother like he doesn't care what she thinks?" he asked, challenging my retort.

Why, oh why, did he have to talk reasonably? I hated it when he used his calm, appeasing voice, and I hated it even more when he made sense. People who thought rationally when you wanted to marinate in your misery should be automatically stomped on by a large herd of boar. "No, he doesn't most of the time," I admitted. "But you know other kings are often that way."

My father was somewhat of a forward thinker when it came to women and their intellect. He was wise enough to know that his own wife had such intelligence in abundance and that he would be a fool not to take advantage of it. Not to say he was completely reformed of his antiquated way of thinking, which was proven by his quest to marry me off to our most powerful ally without even batting an eye. Yet he did seem a tad distraught when telling me that, in a month's time, I would be leaving the only home I'd ever known, travel to a land I'd never seen, and marry a man I'd never met. However, being upset by something and standing against hundreds of years of tradition to make your daughter happy are two different things.

"Besides," Thomas yelled from below, "you should be more worried whether this *brute* of a king will even have you. If you showed up on my doorstep looking for holy matrimony, you'd be on the first skiff back to England. I would think your noble father must be playing some kind of joke on me. Surely, King Cathal can find plenty of grubby, tree-climbing children in his own country to marry. Do you really think he wants you?"

I growled at him. "Thomas, you shut your mouth."

"Happily," he said as he beamed up at me, "as soon as you come down."

I shook my head, and then, thinking he might not be able to see me very well, I spoke up. "I will come down when my father decides not to pass his oldest daughter off like she is the prized cow."

"You would actually be a heifer, dear Allete, since you are, *I hope*, still a maiden."

"I…,you…how dare you? Thomas, if you do not hold your tongue, I am going to sew your lips shut." It was a mean thing to say—I knew it—but I could not keep the words from spilling out. I just wanted to be alone to wallow in my pity and disappointment. Was that too much to ask?

He must have read my mind, because he finally relented.

"Fine, I will leave you be—for now—but if you do not come down from there in the next hour, I will send Clay after you."

"Don't you dare." I growled. Clay was the captain of the guard and the bane of my existence. Most of my life, he'd been assigned to protect me and he took his job very seriously. Not only did he prevail in his duty, but he sucked the fun out of everything until life was simply a shriveled-up husk. Thomas knew if anything would get me out of the tree, it would be the captain.

He began to whistle as he walked toward the castle, and I wanted to throw a rock at him. He knew how much I hated when he whistled— it was his way of signifying that he'd won some battle between us. This time, unfortunately, he had. I knew I would eventually have to come down to face my sentencing. Okay, so it was a marriage, not a sentencing, but it felt as though they were one in the same—like I would be walking to the gallows and the wedding was the noose to be wrapped around my neck. Perhaps I was being a tad dramatic, but better to be dramatic in private and then poised and mature in public. I wouldn't lose my dignity over this, but I knew it was going to break something inside of me. The part of me that longed to be wild and free, to roam new lands and meet new people, would be snuffed out, and there was nothing I could do about it. I was stuck, a product of my circumstances, with no way to change my lot in life.

LATER THAT EVENING, AFTER I had finally decided to put on my big-girl bloomers, I sat in the warm water of the bathtub in my chambers. The scents of freesia and bath oils wafted on the steam around me, causing me to relax and my eyelids to droop. I didn't want to think about what changes would come in a month's time. I didn't want to think about my duties or the expectations placed upon me. I just wanted to sit in peaceful silence.

"I can't believe they're making you marry that old king." My youngest sister, Dayna, came storming in to my room.

"Why do the gods hate me so," I grumbled as I reached for a towel. Usually, I would have Lidia, my handmaiden attend to me, but I'd sent her to bed, not wanting to see the pity in her eyes.

"What are you going on about?" I asked Dayna as I climbed out of the warm tub. Water dripped down my body and the air hit my wet skin, causing me to shiver. My youngest sister, who happened to be the tallest of the four of us and the most inquisitive, snatched up the towel from my hands and began drying me off. For many, the action would have been awkward, but Dayna was the type of person who always needed to be doing something. She couldn't talk unless her hands or feet were also moving, so I moved obediently as she motioned for me to step out of the tub and then lifted my arms. Her movements were quick and efficient, and all the while she barely took a breath.

"Father is expecting you to marry the king of Tara! I mean, he's ghastly, old, and he's already been married three times. I mean...bloody hell,"

"Language," I said, interrupting. Dayna waved me off, as if my pending nuptials were much more important than a loose tongue.

"Everyone says his wives died of natural causes, but how can we be sure? For all we know, he's been strangling them in their sleep."

"That's a pleasant thought," I muttered as she wrapped the towel around me and then grabbed another to begin working on my hair.

"Perhaps he's poisoned them so their deaths appeared to be natural," Dayna continued, as if I hadn't said a word. "There's something not right about it. A man, a king no less, should not have so many wives just die like that."

"Now you are the expert on the lifespan of queens?" I teased.

She narrowed her eyes at me. "Why are you taking this so easily? Why aren't you pitching a fit?"

"I didn't take it easily." I admitted. "Honestly, I'm a right mess, but there's nothing I can do to change it, love. Father said I am to marry the king of Tara, so I will be marrying the king of Tara."

Dayna groaned as she took my hand and tugged me over to the chair that sat in front of the vanity. She motioned for me to sit and then grabbed the hair brush from the counter, her fingers nimble and quick as she worked through the tangles. I'd always loved to have my hair brushed and braided. It was relaxing and could easily lull me to sleep.

After I'd endured her seemingly endless theories on how the first three wives of the king of Tara had died, Dayna let out a breath, finally resigned. "There's no hope, is there?"

I looked at her through the mirror as she finished tying off the plait into which she'd woven my hair. "I assure you, little sister, if there were anything I could do to get out of such an arrangement, I would do it in a heartbeat. I don't want to marry someone I do not love, but I am the oldest. Such is my lot in life."

"Your lot in life is about as pleasant as a mouthful of chicken shite."

I laughed. "Where do you hear such things? Mother would have fit."

She grinned back at me. "The cook's daughters have wicked tongues."

I longed for the day when I, too, could run about unfettered, playing with the other children who lived in the castle, most of whom belonged to the staff. Dayna was sixteen, still young enough that Mother and Father ignored her flightiness, but at twenty, I was expected to behave in a more mature manner. I showed just how mature I could be when I hoisted myself, dress and all, up into that tree today. I grinned, wondering how my future husband would handle finding me up in a tree after our first little argument.

"What are you grinning about?" Dayna asked.

I turned to look at her. She was sitting cross-legged on my bed, the brush disregarded to the side as she picked at the lace on her night gown.

"I have a feeling Father didn't give the dear old king of Tara an accurate picture of his future bride's true personality. If he had, I can assure you he would not have offered such a high-bride token."

Dayna smiled. "Very true. You might want to learn to sleep with one eye open, Sister. If his other wives did indeed die of natural causes, you might be his first murder victim."

"Promise to avenge me if I turn up dead," I said with a wink as I stood and stretched my arms above my head. My muscles were still tight, filled with tension from the day. Perhaps a good night's sleep would put things into perspective and tomorrow my circumstances wouldn't seem so awful. Perhaps, but probably not.

"I'm tired, runt," I told her as I shooed her off the bed.

"Runt?" She scoffed. "I'm six inches taller than you."

"Yes, but you are the baby, and, therefore, the runt. Now, off to bed with you. You are going to need your energy tomorrow if you are to nag Father to death for selling off your oldest sister for a bit of power."

Dayna took much delight in tormenting our father, maybe a tad too much. She hugged me. "I love you," she told me before hurrying out of the room.

Dayna had the softest heart of the four of us. She wore her emotions on her sleeve for all to see. I worried that one day her heart would be injured beyond repair because she bore it so openly.

I climbed into bed, relishing the feel of the cool sheets against my skin. As I pulled the drapes closed around the bed, blocking out the light from the lamps I allowed to remain lit, I pushed away the worries that plagued me. Laying back in the bed and sinking down into the soft, goose-feather mattress, I closed my eyes and thought of the many adventures I longed to embark on. I wanted to travel—to see far away parts of the world—past the borders of England, Tara, and Caledonia. I didn't want to be cooped up behind some great wall, expected to wear stiff dresses and entertain at court forever. Rather, I wanted to breathe fresh air and meet new people. And so, as I drifted off to sleep, I let my mind create a world in which I wasn't the princess of a powerful kingdom and I wasn't expected to marry a man twice my age. I built a world where anything was possible—where I could do and be anything I wanted.

The next few weeks passed in a flurry of busyness. The entire household was in an uproar as they prepared for the massive number of guests they would be receiving. Mother was in a tizzy, ensuring there was enough food, drinks, and beds. The castle had no shortage of rooms—with three stories, four wings jutting out like the four points of the compass, and well over forty rooms, including a library, study, ball room, dining hall, three sitting rooms, male and female bathing suites, and staff quarters, there was plenty of space. I personally thought our castle was a bit much. I'd always gotten lost in it when I was exploring as a little girl, and still did from time to time.

Myself, Dayna, and my other sister, Lizzy, took quiet pleasure in watching our mum flit about, looking as though she were doing some bizarre dance and the staff around her were her unwitting ensemble. We often found ourselves sitting in the center-most chamber, which housed doors on all sides, so we could watch from the best vantage point when we weren't being pressed into service ourselves. Father had the infuriating captain follow me around like a faithful mutt, making sure I couldn't run off again. At one point, I had Lidia distract him just so I could have use the ladies' privy in privacy. Perhaps he thought I'd figure out some way to climb out a window and scale down the side of the castle wall. But, if I got desperate enough, I might figure out a way to do just that.

"How many times do you think Mother will tell the cook that the king of Tara cannot eat potatoes because they do not agree with him?"

"At least another dozen." Lizzy chuckled. "The better question is how many more times will the cook listen before she makes an entire menu based on potatoes just to irritate Mother?"

Silvia, or Cook, as they called her, was not known for her patience, but she was the best cook in the kingdom and, therefore, got away with quite a bit. Father and Mother, and everyone else for that matter, knew better than to annoy her or they'd be eating boiled cabbage stew for a month.

"I wonder what happens when King Cathal eats potatoes?" I inquired.

"Maybe his face swells up like a huge squash and he cannot breathe," Lizzy, who tended to be the bloodthirsty one of the group, offered.

"Does everything have to end in death with you?" Dayna asked her.

Lizzy shrugged. "Like any of us would be sad if the old king kicked the bucket. It would make for an entertaining evening, and we would get our sister back."

I stifled my laugh. We may have been the ladies of the court and kingdom, but ladylike we were not.

"I do not want the poor man to die because of some potato mishap," I quickly said, knowing I would feel dreadful if Lizzy's words came to pass. "I do not want to marry him, but nor do I want him dead. I just wish he and Father could find another way to make an alliance."

"Do not hold your breath, dear Sister," Lizzy said with a sigh. "Kings are not known for their creative thinking."

Per our mother's insistence, each of my sisters and

Quinn Loftis

I were working on various projects that apparently were important for a well-rounded young woman to know. I was doing needle work, Lizzy was reading, and Dayna was penning a letter to an aunt we hadn't seen in ages, but to whom Mother felt it important to keep in touch. We were sitting in the main lounge where we typically accepted guests. It had the best vantage point for watching the general chaos that had become our home. Growing bored with the needlework I'd been meticulously pouring over for the past month, I set it down and stood to stretch. The captain, who'd been standing in the far-right corner of the room, pushed away from the wall, ever alert. I ground my teeth together as I attempted to keep the sharp remark growing in my mind to myself. It wouldn't do to have the eldest princess telling the captain of the guard to take his nose and put it somewhere that never saw the light of day. "I need fresh air," I told my sisters. "With all the staff hustling about, it is beginning to feel stuffy in here."

Dayna set down her pen, pushed the letter to the side, and put the paperweight on top, no doubt to keep it from getting blown off in all the hustle. She stood up eagerly, her eyes dancing with mischief. She was so much like me, always ready for an adventure. Lizzy shook her head. She'd always preferred being indoors, claiming she and dirt did not coexist well and it would not be wise to test the strains of the relationship. Yes, she really did say that.

"I don't want to have to wash up again after smelling like dirt," Lizzy huffed. "And I'm tired. I have not been sleeping well." She looked up at me, and I could see the pity in her eyes.

"Don't lose sleep over me, love," I told her as I placed a hand on her shoulder. "I will be all right. It will all work out."

"How can you be so bloody positive?" Lizzy yelled. I did

not correct her foul language. It would not have helped, anyway.

Normally one to react first and think later, I'd flown into a tizzy when Father had dropped the news on me. But once I'd had time to ponder the issue, I came to terms with it, though it was a very tenuous peace. "Believe me, I was not so positive yesterday," I replied. "But, a nice hot soak, sleep, and the realization that there is nothing I can do to change my circumstances, has put things in perspective. I can either make the best of it, or I can grumble and be miserable, and I do not want to live a life of grumbling."

Leaving Lizzie behind, Dayna followed me through the castle corridors, my ever-present shadow, Clay, was close behind her. The tall stone walls loomed over us as though they were passing judgment on all that was taking place. The castle had always seemed cold to me. I had spent my entire life there, yet it had felt less like a home and more like a temporary holding cell—I was simply passing through until I found my true place in life.

We dodged bustling maids and sidestepped Mother, who did not seem to notice us, as we made our way to the back exit through the kitchen. Cook was muttering into a large pot as we passed and, judging by the red flush on her face and the unnatural way she was whipping her spoon around, it was evident she was in no mood to talk. We kept our heads down, held our breath, and slipped through the kitchen as quickly as we could. Once outside, I stopped and closed my eyes, tilting my face toward the sun and letting its warmth seep into my skin. Autumn was fast approaching, pushing away the heat of summer away. I loved the fall—the cooler temperatures, the changing colors of the foliage, and the warm hearths being lit in the castle. It was a time of preparation for the winter, and I always felt as though the earth was holding its breath, waiting to see what force winter would bring.

"Want to go to the stable?" Dayna asked, bouncing on the balls of her feet. Mother said she was the same way in the womb, constantly kicking and moving, which drove her crazy. I did not think much had changed.

"Fresh air sounds delightful. I remember the stable boy saying a foal was to be born soon. We can see if it has made an appearance yet."

We walked on in silence, both lost in our own thoughts, even though I tried to leave my thoughts behind and just live in the moment. The castle yard, though busy, did not echo the hustle and bustle going on inside the castle walls. Banners were being hung from the ramparts. Mother had been sure to have some specially made in honor of the king of Tara to mix in with our standard adornments, but the colors clashed horribly. Ours were a deep hunter green and black while Tara's were canary yellow and white. Our crest held a lion in its center while Tara's showcased a bird. I wondered if the inharmonious hues were symbolic of the union that was to come. Would our marriage clash like the crests of our kingdoms? Would the lion devour the bird or would the bird peck out the lion's eyes? The ridiculous thought had me snorting out a laugh.

"What?" Dayna asked.

I shook my head. "My odd sense of humor is running wild with my imagination."

"It is a good thing you have a sense of humor; it may be your only saving grace."

"Captain," I called out over my shoulder. "Do you think it a terrible omen that our crests are so different from Tara's and the colors so ill matched?"

"My lady," the Captain's voice rumbled, "I do not believe in superstitions. We are represented by a lion and Tara a bird. Nothing more.

"That's a rather boring outlook. But I shall not have you flogged for it," I teased him, knowing he hated it.

"You're a right snot." Dayna laughed.

I shrugged. When it came to Clay, who often snuffed out my fun, then yes, I was a right snot. Was it too much to ask for my guard, who was nearly my constant companion, to have a bit more creative thinking? After all, the world was a drab enough place without his morose attitude.

We walked leisurely, as if we had not a care in the world, down to the stable on the far east of the castle grounds. The large, handsome structure housed over seventy-five horses. Above the stable were living quarters for the stable staff, which was comprised of twenty people who trained and cared for the herd. When we entered through the large sliding doors, I was surprised to find it empty of any employees. The horses were in place, but their caretakers were nowhere to be found, not even the stable master, Geoffrey.

"Where is everyone?" Dayna asked.

Before I could shrug, we heard voices coming from across the building and out the opposite sliding doors. I glanced at Dayna, who nodded as we both hiked up our skirts and took off at which we could easily fall flat on our faces. As we got closer to where the voices were coming from, we could see a crowd of people huddled around a figure on the ground. My first thought was that someone had gotten hurt while working or riding one of the horses, but that was not what we discovered.

It was not a worker who required attention, Instead, one of the large animals lay on its side. I froze mid-step, for it was not just any beast splayed on the ground. It was my father's favorite horse. His breathing was labored, the horse's abdomen rising and falling in rapid succession. Several of the trainers where kneeling over him and when one shifted I could see the royal animal healer, Tessa Benson. Although she wasn't a healer in the traditional sense, she cared for our sick or injured. As if sensing my presence, she looked up, her gaze meeting mine. The tightness in Tessa's face and her tightly drawn lips told me things did not look good.

It was then I felt it—the subtle stirring that rose in me when I was in the presence of the ill. Like a sixth sense, I could sense malady. Then, as always, I was drawn, irresistibly, as if by some unseen cord, toward the injured life-form.

It was my gift, and from what little I knew about it, the ability to heal was very rare and was seldom talked about. People feared things they couldn't explain or control. My mother had told me to hide my gift, because, as she said, *when people are scared, they do scary things*. Only my mother, father, siblings, and a select few people on the castle grounds knew of my ability. Thankfully, Tessa was one of them.

She stood briskly and spoke with the authority that came from many years in a position of responsibility. "I need everyone to get back to work. Princess Allete and Princess Dayna are here, and they can assist me now so the other horses can be tended. Off with you. Captain, if you could please make sure everyone leaves the stables." As she finished, she turned her back on the crowd and refocused her attention on the wounded animal.

The staff responded immediately and hurried back to their duties. When the path was clear, Dayna and I ran the rest of the way to Tessa and fell to our knees by the injured horse.

"He tripped." Tessa began. "He was being ridden in an unfamiliar part of the forest, and stumbled in a hole. The rider returned with him on-foot, the horse limping the whole way back on what I am certain is a broken leg. I just hope the long walk back did not do permanent damage. Even if it heals correctly, he could still become lame, unlikely to bear a rider or saddle due to the weight."

"Hellfire," I swore under my breath. My father would be devastated. Horses were unique animals. They formed a deep bond with their owner—both fulfilling a need for the other. Somewhere along the way, my father and Poke formed a friendship. My father would be as mournful as if he'd lost a human friend if he lost Poke.

Tessa moved to the side just a bit but stayed next to me. Now shoulder-to-shoulder, she placed her hands on the injured animal, appearing to anyone who might pass that she was tending to the horse.

"Dayna, grab that roll of gauze so we can wrap his leg." I barked to my sister. When she had done so, I pulled Dayna closer so that she hovered over Poke, further obscuring the view of the horse from anyone who happened to be in the area. Once everyone was in position, I placed my hands on the injured leg, bowed my head, and closed my eyes, as I began chanting.

I spoke as softly as I could but still said the words out loud. "I come to help not to intrude. Let my spirit heal; let it soothe. Relax your defenses, I take not your will. I only want to mend. Now, peace, be still."

I did not know where the words came from or if they were even needed, but when I attempted to heal, it was like I had to coax their spirit—their soul—open to let me in. Usually, at first, the spirit perceived me as a threat and would refuse my healing power until I made it known I was only trying to help. Most curious to me, however, was that the words were never the same. With every healing, I always said something different, and I had to say it audibly. I learned this when I'd attempted to heal a bird just outside my open window one day. I did not want to speak for fear someone in the castle courtyard below would overhear me. I thought the words, but nothing happened. I did this several times before I finally, in frustration, said the words in a whisper. Suddenly, I healed the bird.

After that incident, I began researching my abilities, trying to determine why speaking the words was necessary. I was surprised to find several books suggested that there was an innate power in the spoken word, touting many examples of great leaders shaping the destinies of their people through only speech. I read that Moses spoke with authority to free his people and caused incredible plagues. It was also noted that the decrees of great kings and pharaohs were always read aloud because the spoken word penetrated deeper in the minds of the people. It was as if the words were floating in the air and the crowds reached out and plucked them from the air, storing them away. Yet even after gathering all this information, I knew nothing of my gift. I only did what came naturally to me.

Once I felt my power flow into the injured horse, I opened my eyes and lifted my hands from his leg. Poke immediately tried to get up, as sign he no longer felt any pain, but we quickly soothed him so Tessa could wrap the leg as if it were still injured.

"I will take this off in a couple days. As far as everyone else is concerned, Poke has a mild sprain," Tessa said as we all stood up, coaxing Poke to rise slowly with us.

"Thank you," I told her.

She shook her head. "You are the one with the gift, Princess. We should be thanking you, but instead we must hide your incredible ability because *they* are so afraid." She sounded disgusted.

I knew she was talking about my parents. They loved me, of that I had no doubt, but they could not accept what I was able to do. It scared them, so I kept it to myself. My father had ordered me only to use my gift in the direst of situations, but I could not just leave someone, human or animal, in need if I could heal them.

I patted Tessa's shoulder. "They cannot stop me, and for now that is enough."

She started to lead Poke back into the barn but then turned to us, her eyes tilted down and her forehead wrinkled in worry. "I am sorry that you will be leaving us, especially under these circumstances. You should not be forced into this position."

I did not have a reply, so I bowed my head once to show her I appreciated her words. After Tessa was out of sight, I turned to look at my sister. "Are you all right?"

Dayna nodded. "But I am dreading telling Father about this." She motioned toward the castle.

I did not know if it was necessary for us to tell him what really happened. Word would get back to him, of course—the castle staff could gossip with the best of them—but he would hear it was a sprain. He need not know I was involved. "Let us leave it to the gossiping hierarchy to deliver the information to him. Poke is fine, so there is no reason to trouble Father when there are already so many other things going on."

She nodded. "So, where to now?"

I looked toward the forest. It called to me, whispering of the adventures I'd once had in its tall trees and hidden depths. My tree was just on the edge of the forest, and though I spent a lot of time there, I also spent days wandering through the shaded woods, enjoying all the mysteries nature held. It had been a while since I had visited, and now I wanted nothing more than to run through the forest— just me, my sister, and the huge trees around us.

I glanced at Dayna from the corner of my eye and raised an eyebrow at her. Captain Clay was still distracted with making sure Poke was taken care of, which meant we had a short window to make a break for it.

She took a step back. "That look always means trouble, Allete."

I chuckled. "What is life without a little trouble? Race you to the woods." I took off before the words were completely out of my mouth. Hiking up my dress and stretching out my stride, I smiled as the wind whipped through my hair and the sound of Dayna's screech caught up with me.

"You cheat!" she yelled. She was gaining on me.

"Finding a creative way to win is not cheating," I yelled back.

We finally reached the tree line and burst into the forest, the shade immediately collecting us in its arms. It was as though we'd entered another realm.

I was breathing hard, as was Dayna once she had caught up to me. I looked at her and grinned. "You, my dear sister, are getting faster."

She nudged me with her shoulder. "Maybe you are just getting slower. One of these days, I will leave you in my dust."

"Well, until that day, you can continue to be in awe of my abilities."

This made her laugh. "You've always got to have the last word."

I started walking, knowing that she would follow. "I wish we were in another world," I told her. "I wish we were able to step out of our dimension and into another—a world full of fantastic beings and unimaginable adventures."

"Lizzy would say books held other worlds," Dayna said pointedly.

I laughed. "Then I want to be sucked right into the pages of those books, the cover shut so tightly that I cannot escape."

# CHAPTER Three

WAKE EARLY IF YOU WANT ANOTHER MAN'S LIFE OR LAND. NO
LAMB FOR THE LAZY WOLF. NO BATTLES WON IN BED.

~ THE HAVAMAL, BOOK OF VIKING WISDOM

I HATED THE SOUND of retching, but it was a common sound on any vessel, large or small, in the open ocean. The long ship carried us well, but the trip was hardly a smooth one. I walked down the middle of the massive deck, trying to ignore any man who made a break for the side to empty the contents of their stomach overboard, which wasn't easy. There was a time I had been one of those lads, but not anymore. I had been on the boat enough times that my body had acclimated to the constant rocking and tossing quickly. I now seemed to instinctively shift and sway in rhythm with the ship as it rocked

"Torben, do you know how much farther we have on this blasted beast?" Brant called out to me. The huge man strained at the oars, but not nearly as much as those around him. Brant was so strong that he had to temper his vigor when it came to rowing, otherwise the boat would turn in a wide circle. Lately, I had taken to putting two men opposite him. This seemed to almost even out the power on both sides of the boat.

I had been asked that very question every few hours

by what seemed like every warrior on the ship. Each time my answer had been the same. "No man can predict the mood swings of the ocean. We will arrive when she wants us to."

"Well I hope we get there soon. I much prefer the haft of a hammer in my hands to these oars!"

"You complain like a child, Brant." I responded. "Should I have left you at home and brought Eric's newborn babe instead?"

The splash of the ship's oars drowned out his muttered reply, but I distinctly heard the words *dragon's arse* as he turned back toward the front of the ship. All the men grumbled, of course, but rarely loud enough for me to hear them. I cared not if they despised my answer, only that they obeyed orders. My job was to make them into mighty soldiers, ensure they were the strongest warriors possible, and then lead them into battle. I was not trying to win their favor. I was trying to keep them alive.

Three skeids had set out just over two fortnights ago, each containing sixty men. Magnus commanded at the helm of the lead boat, its prow intricately carved into the shape of a giant sea monster. I could hear him bellowing across the water, imploring his men to row faster. I had to coax my own shipmates to keep up, though I would have preferred to let the sail, bearing the image of the mighty grey wolf of clan Hakon, do most of the work, yet I followed Magnus' lead.

Our boats were light and strong, the muscle and sinew of our warriors and the winds of the gods driving the hulls across the open water. The head of a snarling dire wolf graced the prow of my skeid, and I prayed my men would fight like our patron symbol—as a pack, together ferocious and unrelenting.

The third boat, its prow adorned with the head of a

dragon, was commanded by the jarl's lieutenant, Halvard. He was a man loyal to the clan and had seen his share of battles. I knew he too would be reluctant to push his men to their breaking-point to keep up with Magnus' merciless pace.

On the evening of our thirtieth day at sea, our king finally called to halt. Groaning as they dropped their oars, the warriors practically collapsed into the bottom of the boat, each massaging their aching muscles as the darkness of the ocean seemed to swallow up any bit of light. I prayed to the sea giant, Aegir, that our voyage would soon be complete and that we would land on the beaches of England before my men lost their will to fight.

Morning dawned brightly the following day and I woke to the sound of snapping of sails as mighty gusts of wind propelled our ship forward, its bow cleaving the waves as if it were fighting its own endless battle with the sea. I hopped up, feeling more refreshed than I had since we began our journey, and clambered toward the back of the boat and took the handle of the side rudder. Eric, a loyal soldier who had been manning the rudder throughout the night, grunted his thanks and fell on a pile of furs like a contented cat, happy to enjoy some rest as the rest of the men began finding their place among the oars. The early morning sun warmed our backs, all grumblings from the previous day lost on the strong winds.

Even though I had only sailed to England once, I knew we were nearing our destination. Skeld, the clan's cartographer who had travelled the world more than any of us, had signaled that we should reach our destination in a day or two. Soon, I would call the men to attention and begin our battle preparations. We had practiced our landing and subsequent advancement multiple times, but I wanted the plan fresh in their mind when our boots hit dry ground. There was no way to tell what would be waiting for us, and our success depended upon the element of surprise.

As I went over the plans again, Brant ambled to the back of the boat, plopping his huge form down upon the platform next to me. I expected one of his typical remarks, but none came. He just stared out across the horizon pensively.

"Something on your mind, *vinr*?" I asked after a few minutes of silence.

"You name me Friend, eh? Likewise, do I call you, Torben? How long have we known each other?"

"All our lives. You know this. What troubles you?" I stared at him, wondering what brought on the melancholy plaguing my normally boisterous friend. After several more silent moments, he finally spoke again.

"My sleep troubles me."

I chuckled. "How much sleep did you expect to get while being tossed about in a long boat?"

"Not that." The huge man growled. "I have no trouble *falling* asleep. It is what happens afterward that has me troubled. Dreams...or *a* dream, I should say. The same one visits me over and over, like a faithful dog that comes when it's called. Except, I am not summoning the dream. It has haunted me every night of our voyage. I fall into my bed and hope it does not come, but it always does."

I grunted. "And what is this dream about?"

"You."

"Me?" I ask, feigning nervousness. "Perhaps I shouldn't have said called you friend. I take that back." I looked at him out of the corner of my eye and took an exaggerated step back from him.

"By the gods, man, be serious! I have something to say to you before the fighting starts and I want you to hear it.

Now will you listen?" He barked.

Realizing my friend was indeed serious, I nodded. "Go on."

Brant took in a deep breath and continued. "In the dream, I am hiking through the forest, tracking a wild boar after having wounded it with an arrow. I notice a raven flying above me, but I pay it no mind and continue my pursuit. Moments pass, and then I notice two ravens flying above me, then a third. They swoop down, cawing and pecking at me. I curse them and swing my axe, driving them off momentarily, still intent on finding the boar. The next thing I know, the number of birds has doubled, and then tripled. I try to drive them off but there are just too many. I begin to run, thinking that I can outdistance them, but they chase, continuing to peck and claw at my flesh. I run even faster, a blind panic taking over me. I cannot see where I am going through their wings, nor can I hear over their incessant cawing. Stumbling, I fall forward onto my belly. Then, as if someone had snuffed out a candle, all is silent. The birds are gone. I look up and see you standing with your back to me in full battle armor, carrying your sword and shield. You are staring at a large stone chair, as if you are thinking about whether you should sit in it. Turning to me, you seem confused until you recognize me. You take a step toward me, possibly to help me, when a huge brown bear, larger than I have ever seen, emerges from the thick underbrush and charges right at you. You turn just in time to bring your shield up between your body and the bear's slashing claws as you both tumble to the ground. Before I can move to help, the ravens return, but this time, they ignore me and descend upon you and the bear. I scream, trying to move, but I am pinned to the ground. From within the tangle of birds, I hear your screams, and then...then I wake up."

I did not know what to make of Brant's story. Unsure of what to do, I simply stared at him while trying to find words to offer. Finally, though my mouth felt impossibly dry, I spoke. "And you have had this same dream every night we have been at sea."

"Every night, hersir."

"And you feel this dream has some hidden meaning?"

"The gods often speak to mortals through dreams, do they not?" he asked me in return.

"I know not." I responded honestly. "They have never spoken to me."

"You never believe anything you cannot see with your own eyes, Torben. The man who was raised by the Oracle still refuses to believe in the workings of the gods."

"Oh, I believe in the gods, Brant—never doubt that. I just have trouble believing they speak to us. Would you leave paradise to meddle with foolish mortals?"

"Have you not seen your mother's prophesies come true?" He countered.

"Aye, I have, but I've seen them remain only visions. How can I know what is true from the delusions of an old woman?"

"You cannot, and that is probably the point of the whole thing," Brant responded, "but I would wager a cart-full of new longswords that this dream *does* mean something."

"Okay, self-appointed Oracle," I said pointedly. "What does it mean?"

"It means you, my commander, are in danger."

"Me? You were the one being chased by ravens."

"But they let me go in the end. They only wanted to propel me to you so I could see what would happen. Don't you see? It is the bear, you fool—the bear signifies danger, not the ravens."

I made a noise somewhere between a grunt and a

sigh. It was not that I didn't believe in signs and omens. Living with a real prophetess, I had seen too many false prophets of the gods over the years. These charlatans seemed drawn to her, as if seeking validation. But there was something more that troubled me. While Brant had recounted his dream, my mother's words had kept coming back to me. *A young warrior will take his rightful place as leader of his people.* Somewhere, deep down, I knew her words and his vision were connected. I wanted to ignore it, but I could not. Brant and my mother's warnings rang true. Upheaval was coming to the clan, and I could only hope I was not the source of that upheaval.

"And what is this danger?" I finally asked. But before Brant could respond, a loud bellow rang out across the water.

"Land ho!" A deep voice cried.

We both turned to see Magnus, leaning out over the prow of his own longboat and gripping the railing. His long, shaggy, beard and hair flew wildly in every direction. He bellowed again. "Land ho!" It was only then I noticed the large bear-skin cloak he wore, flapping behind him in the ocean breeze.

# CHAPTER Four

"SOMETHING INSIDE ME IS RESTLESS. I DON'T KNOW HOW TO
DESCRIBE THE FEELING, EXCEPT TO SAY THAT IT FEELS LIKE A
TYPHOON RAGES IN MY STOMACH LIKE SOME MIGHTY STORM
BREWING ON THE HORIZON, SURE TO BRING DRAMATIC CHANGE
TO MY LIFE. I CAN FEEL IT, COMING STEADILY TOWARD ME ON
THE WIND. AT FIRST, I THOUGHT IT RELATED TO MY PENDING
NUPTIALS, BUT NOW I FEEL IT IS BIGGER THAN THAT, MORE
SIGNIFICANT. I FEEL THE NEED TO BE READY, BUT I DON'T
KNOW WHAT TO BE READY FOR."

~DIARY OF PRINCESS ALLETE AUVRAY

ONLY A MONTH REMAINED until my very soul would be
sucked from my body, leaving only an empty shell.
Today was simply the beginning of the end. The King of
Tara would arrive today. His arrival would bring my doom.
Dramatics aside, the consequences of the coming month
were going to be dire. Deep down, I knew it was not the
courting month or the ceremony that I dreaded but what
would come after I feared most. I daydreamed about
having an out-of-body experience during my wedding
night so I could escape being mentally present for the
consummation of our union. Just thinking about the
pompous king touching me—undressing me—made me
want to scrub myself with lye soap until the first layer of

my skin was completely rubbed away.

It was nearing dawn as I sat at my window, wallowing in my self-pity. Sleep eluded me no matter how tired I was. My stomach felt as if I had swallowed a gallon of curdled milk which threatened to come up my throat and out of mouth at any moment. I had been strong the prior three days, holding my chin high, keeping my shoulders back, and plastering a fake smile on my face, but underneath, I was an utter mess.

The sun was just beginning to peak over the horizon, the rays reaching up and spreading out as though they were long arms, stretching after a good night's rest. I wished I could join in nature's enthusiasm as light rolled over the hills, through the forest, and into the streets of the kingdom. It was as though the earth was calling out. *Good morning, rise, and wake with me. It is a new day.* Yes, a new day had come… but not a good day, at least for me anyway.

I heard the stirrings of people beyond my door as the castle began to come to life, the staff bustling and scurrying about as the time for the king of Tara to arrive fast-approached. A light knock sounded at my door, pulling my attention from the morning sun. I sighed, resigning myself to the fact that no matter how I wished I could freeze time to prevent the inevitable, I couldn't. My fate was sealed.

"My lady." A soft voice said as the door was inched open and Lidia peered around. "Are you ready to dress?"

I motioned for her to come in as I stood. "I do not suppose I could say no?"

She smiled. "You could, but I have a feeling his Majesty would not appreciate presenting his eldest daughter to the king of Tara in her undergarments."

"You are wise beyond your years, lovely Lidia," I said wistfully. She giggled as she headed for my wardrobe to pick out the dress for the day.

I splashed my face with warm water from the wash basin and looked at myself in the mirror. As I blotted the water from my skin, I noted emptiness in my eyes and hated myself for letting my joy be robbed from my life.

I let Lidia help me dress and fix my hair. The things she could do were amazing—true works of art—but today, she opted for a simple braid that flowed down my back, a ribbon that matched my dress woven in.

When she was finished, Lidia went about tidying the room—making the bed, picking up the dirty clothes, and dumping the dirty water from the basin. I knew when I returned that evening, there would be clean water along with a clean towel to dry with. Lidia was a wonderful handmaiden. I was reluctant to ask her to come to Tara with me; I couldn't decide if I could ask it of her. It would be a huge boon to have her with me, but for her to leave the only home she had ever known—to leave her family and friends—would be a huge sacrifice. I could force her to come, of course, but I would never do that. I knew what it meant to be forced to live a life you did not want. However, if I was going to ask her, I needed to do it soon.

I stepped out of my room to the usual sight of Clay waiting to accompany me. I had no energy for taunting him. And I was pretty sure he was still peeved at me for leaving him at the stable when I'd healed Poke.

As I walked down the castle corridors, I awed at the transformation the dreary stone structure had undergone. My mother had outdone herself. Banners heralded our family crest proudly as they hung throughout the halls. Four long strips of fabric had been woven together—two were our colors and two were Tara's. It was fastened along the wall, rising and falling like rolling hills. At every dip, a huge bouquet of flowers, also the two kingdoms' colors, was attached to the fabric. This continued along every corridor, on every wall throughout the castle. Every oil lamp was also adorned with flowers and a bow. The harmonization of the colors still left something to be desired, but against the grey stone of the walls, there was something striking about the green, black, yellow, and white joining in a kaleidoscope of disjointed adornment.

Once the shock of the splendor had settled, I continued my trek to snag some of Sylvia's bacon. Even though I could've had breakfast brought to my room, I preferred to get it myself, mostly so I had an excuse to see Sylvia, and today I really needed her matter-of-fact air and tell-it-like-it-is ways. She would not blow smoke up my petticoat or tell me what I wanted to hear. Sylvia would tell me what she thought, regardless of how it might make me feel.

I passed through the main dining hall through a swinging door that lead to a small hallway. The hallway opened into a large kitchen where no less than ten cooks moved with practiced ease around each other. It looked like a synchronized dance. The clanking of pots, swishing of spoons, and sizzling of food was their music and Sylvia their choreographer. The head cook called out orders, pointed directions, and worked just as hard as the staff she pushed.

"Bacon, eggs, and toast, Allie?" Sylvia asked without even turning around to see I was there. She was the only person who shortened my name to Allie, but I liked the endearment.

"You know the way to my heart, Sylvia." I grinned and took my spot on the empty stool and out of the way. I only waited a few minutes before she set a plate in my lap with a towel underneath it to keep from burning me or getting anything on my dress. I nearly drooled at the mouthwatering food; its tantalizing aromas rising to fill my nose.

"Why, hello there," I said to the food. "Fancy meeting you here."

"You are talking to your food, Allete," Dayna said from behind me. "I think you have officially cracked."

"Why, dear Sister, whatever do you mean?" I said in a mock-haughty voice. "What pressure could possibly crack one such as I?"

"I do not know, but that intolerable voice just proved my point." Dayna eyed my plate. "Going to share?"

"Did you meet a grizzly bear in full court-dress this morning ready to attend my wedding?" I asked just before taking a bite of bacon. I moaned as the rich flavor filled my mouth, and I wondered if Sylvia would want to go with me to Tara—not that Father would ever let her leave.

"Sounds like you're practicing the sounds you will be making on your wedding night," Thomas said as he slipped in through the side door that led to the chicken coupes.

Dayna snorted as she attempted to cover her laughter. I did not find it quite as amusing.

"And how, exactly, do you know what sounds are made on a wedding night, Thomas? Have you been a scoundrel and taken the virtue of maidens who fell for your handsome face?" I asked him and then followed it with a bite of eggs. I easily ignored any other comments my cousin or sister made, my focus keen on my meal, which had begun to feel a bit like a *last* meal.

"Are you planning on eating like that in front of your future husband this evening at the reception feast?" Thomas laughed as he nodded his head to my now-empty plate. Perhaps I did eat a little like a pig at a feeding trough, but Sylvia's food could do that to a person.

"Thomas, is there a reason you are disturbing my morning with your ridiculous comments and tiring questions?" I asked as I glared up at him.

He walked over and patted my head in the patronizing manner he knew I hated. "I just wanted to spend some time with my dearest cousin while she is still innocent and unjaded by the pressures and responsibilities of a queen."

While his statement was meant to tease, I could hear the sincerity in his words. He was going to miss me, and I would miss him just as fiercely.

I stood up and took my plate to the wash basin, but one of the cooks snatched it out of my hand before I could even begin to wash it. Turning to Thomas and Dayna, I put on my best I-can-do-this smile. "How about the fearsome trio take one last ride together?"

Thomas glanced over to Captain Clay. "I'll take it from here. When we return, you can resume your guard."

Clay gave a slight bow to Thomas, but shot me a look that said I had better behave.

We had been riding for a little over two hours when we heard the trumpets announcing the arrival of the Tara's king and his entourage. I pulled my horse to a halt, looking back at the palace I'd called home for eighteen years. My chest tightened as the reality of my situation began to set in—in a month's time. I was leaving for good. Even though I'd always hoped to leave—that was not in question—this was not the way I'd imagined. I wanted to leave without a king for a husband in tow.

"Should we go back?" Dayna asked, sounding as if she thought this was the worst idea ever.

"Why?" Thomas asked. "It is not like he is going anywhere. You have a month to endure his wooing. He will still be there when we are finished with our ride."

"Father is going to be a right pissed boar," Dayna said with too much delight.

"Language." I snapped at her. "If you do not clean up

your mouth, how will a young man ever want to kiss it?"

"I will not change my ways just to suit a man. He can take me as I am—dirty mouth and all—or he can find a wench in a tavern willing to do his bidding for some change."

I shook my head as I pinched the bridge of my nose. "And Father thinks I am the unruly one? Do not speak of such women. You have no idea the hardships they face or what has led them to such a life."

Dayna's shoulders drooped under my scolding. It was not my intention to upset her, but she needed to learn to be considerate of others before she unleashed that loose tongue of hers.

"You are right. I do not know such things," she said and then perked up. "You are going to make a wise and compassionate queen, sister mine. I only wish it was of our kingdom and not that pig of a king's kingdom."

Thomas chuckled. "I still do not see why you both assume he is an ugly beast. Just because he is older doesn't mean he isn't fit, charming, and handsome."

"Are you just saying that to bolster my spirits?" I asked him, raising one of my eyebrows, as if that small action would cause the truth to spring from his lips.

He stared back at me for several seconds and, for a moment, a thoughtful look passed over his features, but it was gone just as quickly. He nodded his head. "You're right. He is most likely a disgusting creature with a personality to match."

"Never mind. I liked it better when you lied to me." I jested.

"No, you do not," Thomas said, suddenly serious. "You like a person who is straightforward and does not attempt to placate you. Its one of the many things I will miss about you."

I quickly turned my head away from him, feigning that something in the trees had caught my attention as I fought back tears. Why does doing the right thing hurt so badly? *Just cinch up your petticoat and do what you need to do.*

"Are we going to finish this ride?" Dayna asked, a distinct challenge lacing her words.

I turned to look at my youngest sister and narrowed my eyes. "King be damned! Not even the gods shall stop us."

Dayna sucked in a breath with a huge grin plastered on her face. "Language, Allete."

After giving my horse a quick squeeze and pat on the flank, the beast took off, bolting past my shocked sister and dumbfounded cousin. I refrained from looking back to see if they had recovered—I was too busy absorbing what little freedom I had left. The wind whipped the hair that had escaped my braid and my eyes began to water as I pushed my horse faster. Perhaps with every step farther away from the castle she took, I felt my chances of outrunning my fate were growing. Somehow, I thought, every furlong galloped was leading me closer and closer to freedom.

Only later would I realize what a foolish thought that was. No matter how fast I ran, I could not escape my fate.

# CHAPTER Five

"I DO NOT KNOW WHAT LIES AHEAD OF ME. I DO NOT KNOW
WHAT THE OUTCOME OF THIS BATTLE SHALL BE. ALL I CAN DO
IS HOPE THAT WE END UP ON THE SIDE OF GOOD."

~ TORBEN

I STOOD, WATCHING AS each of the long ships came ashore and the warriors scurried like ants onto the land. The relief on their faces mirrored my own, but it would be short-lived. Magnus was already setting up a tent for his temporary dwelling, which meant he intended to do just as he'd said. We would stay in England a full month to spy on the king, looking for weaknesses in his court and placing our own men inside the castle by relieving the king's guards of their duties, or more accurately, killing the king's men to take their uniforms.

I wondered how long we could pull the charade off before someone found out and the tides turned. Magnus had many flaws, but one would be his downfall—Magnus believed his intelligence was superior to all others. He could not fathom his foe strategically besting him. I, however, was under no such illusion. There would be loss on both sides, and whether we would be successful was yet to be seen.

Brant walked over and stood next to me, his large

arms folded across his chest. His eyes were filled with alert intensity. "Is this a mistake, Torben?"

I clenched my fists at my sides, and I felt as though the weight of the world had been lowered onto my shoulders. "No," I began, "this is not just *a* mistake. This is the first of many."

Suddenly, a loud horn was blown and all eyes were on our leader. Two more notes and all the warriors were headed for the spot where Magnus stood.

"Why is he blowing that damn horn?" Brant muttered under his breath as we began to walk toward the gathered men. "He is going to bring all of England down upon us."

"He does not care if they know we're here." I explained. "He is daring them to make a move." Brant started to say something but I held up a hand to stop him. "A few of his sympathizers are close by," I said as a couple warriors positioned themselves close to us. Brant nodded and pressed his lips closed.

"Torben!" Magnus bellowed.

I pushed through the crowd until I was standing next to my jarl.

Magnus held up his hand to silence his army. "We will spend the better part of a month here." He projected his voice to carry over the troops. "Torben will be choosing small contingents of men to go in and gain access to the palace as well as information."

"What is the goal?" Halvard asked.

Jarl Magnus narrowed his eyes. "The *goal* is to show them how weak they are and that their weakness makes them unfit to live, but before we make any moves, I'm sending in a spy to assess the situation, and then we will go from there. Everyone begin setting up camp. Stay alert—we might have to defend the beach, and I will not lose before this has even begun.

My men and I didn't bother setting up our own camp, considering we would be staying in the palace if things went as planned. Instead, we helped the others unload the ships and set up defensive stations with spiked blockades in case the English came in on horses. We checked with the archers and made sure the bows were in working order and that there were plenty of arrows. Several hours later, we hear a shout as Magnus' spy came running over the hill and down to the beach. He was holding something in his hand, but was too far away to tell what it was.

I motioned for my men to follow and we headed for the jarl's tent. When we arrived, it was already surrounded by most of the men.

"What have you found out?" Magnus asked the spy.

"The other king has indeed arrived, and he only brought a small contingency of guards, not an entire army. However, I wonder, my lord, if we might need to pick another kingdom to raid."

"What are you talking about?" Magnus snapped.

"The people are poor. I overheard some villagers talking and they've been relentlessly raided by another Viking clan for months. They've practically cleaned King Albric out, which is why Albric has agreed to the marriage of his daughter to the king of Tara."

"If they have no funds, they are weak, making easy to defeat," Magnus said.

I frowned. Did he not just hear what the spy said? There were no riches to be had here. Why on earth would he still want to raid the English? His madness was becoming more and more apparent, and it was going to get us all killed. The spy continued to tell Magnus what he'd learned, but I'd heard enough. I moved quietly away from the group and headed back to where we'd left our things.

"It seems we have no reason to be here," Rush spoke up

as all six of my men joined me by our packs and weapons. I began gathering my weapons and went through my pack, throwing out anything I felt was unnecessary. The others followed suit.

"We are here for a reason," I said. "Regardless of the jarl's plans, we have our own. The Oracle has spoken, and I am here to fulfill her prophecy. But no one," I paused, looking each of them in the eye, "no one is to know about it. This is a private mission. Understood?"

Each of them nodded their heads and gave their word to take the secret to their graves. I didn't feel the need to elaborate on what the Oracle had told me, and nobody asked. I glanced back over toward Magnus' tent and saw he was still occupied. "Wait here for me," I told Brant. "I need to speak with my mother before we take our leave."

I didn't have to look long to find Hilda. She was bossing around some warriors who were setting up her tent. She looked to be in good health for being on a ship so long. She was strong, my mother, and it was a good thing, too.

"Are you just going to stand there watching or are you going to help?" She asked me without bothering to look at me.

I chuckled as I picked up a large trunk that probably held her clothes and possibly a few hidden weapons. "It didn't appear as though you needed my help."

"I raised better than to have you stand and watch others work," she told me.

"Yes, Mother, you did. And see," I motioned to the trunk in my arms, "I am proving you right."

She pointed, telling me where to place the trunk, and once it was in its temporary home, she turned to the others. "Thank you for your assistance; I can take it from here." She waited until the men had gone before speaking again. "Why are you still here? You need to be in the castle."

"My closest men and I were just about to begin our trek, but I wanted to check in with you before we departed. Are you well?" I asked.

"Aside from being stuck on a boat with that crazy oaf of a jarl, I'm fine."

"You've brought weapons with you?"

She clucked her tongue at me. "Do you take me for a fool or a child? Of course, I brought weapons. I will be fine, unless you fail to woo your princess—then none of us will be fine. Do not just snatch her up, Torben. She is meant to be yours; you only need to be available for her and fate will take over."

She made it sound so easy, yet I knew it would not be that simple. There would be obstacles to overcome, like infiltrating the castle without getting caught.

"Deal with things one thing at a time, Torben. Once you get in the castle, you can forge ahead with a more laid-out plan. Don't try to have it all figured out before you know what the situation is."

"I will do what I must to ensure that our clan survives," I told her. "You just make sure that idiot of a jarl we have doesn't put you in any more harm than he already has by bringing you on his fool's errand."

"You don't need to worry about me. I've been taking care of myself for quite a while now. Now, off with you." She pushed me in the direction from which I'd come from. "And do not fail."

"Thank you for your encouragement, Mother," I said dryly.

"It's not my job to encourage you, Son. It's my job to kick you in your arse when you need it. Now go get my future daughter-in-law and keep her safe."

I left, chuckling at my mother's words. The woman had a wicked, sharp tongue, but I would do as she asked.

I would somehow convince the princess to come with me. I would do whatever it took to save my clan. What I didn't know, was that I would soon want to save her and her people, too.

# CHAPTER
## Six

She Viking Ca...

"I NEVER REALIZED THE CURSE OF BEAUTY. UNDOUBTEDLY, I'M
NOT THE FAIREST IN ALL OF BRITANNIA, BUT I HAVE CAUGHT
THE EYES OF CERTAIN MEN, MOST OF THEM POWERFUL ALLIES
OF MY FATHER. FOR THE MOST PART, I'VE AVOIDED THEIR
ADVANCES. BUT AFTER MEETING MY FUTURE HUSBAND, I
WOULD GIVE ANYTHING TO BE AS UGLY AS AN OLD WRINKLED
HAG."

~DIARY OF PRINCESS ALLETE AUVRAY

"AT LEAST HE DOES not resemble the back-end of a boar,"
Dayna whispered.

I shot my sister a quick nod of agreement then covertly
turned to peer at my future husband, who was conversing
with my father. After our morning ride, my sister and I had
found a hiding spot behind some large drapes just to the
left of the room now occupied by our guests. It afforded us
the surreptitious ability to listen and watch the two kings
interact. Thomas had taken his leave, but not before he
informed me what he thought about our childish behavior.
I did not care if I was being childish. I was not yet ready to
meet King Cathal.

"He's not ugly," I murmured back, "but his
handsomeness is marred by that tight-lipped frown. He
looks cruel."

I had been surprised to learn my future husband was not nearly as old as I thought he was. If I had to guess, I would put him at eight and thirty, or, at the very oldest, two and forty. His hair was dark and short, and he had deep green eyes, a hawkish nose, and thin lips that seemed frozen in a perpetual scowl. Standing at a little over six feet, King Cathal was lean but obviously muscular. Yes, he was handsome, but the cold, detached look in his eyes ruined any favor I might have felt for him.

"Do you think it hurts to hold his face like that?" Dayna asked.

I bit my bottom lip to keep from laughing. "Perhaps he was just born that way."

"Tis a shame to be so handsome and yet such a pompous ass."

"Hush." I chastised. "That pompous ass could have your head if he felt your offense warranted it."

"Father would not allow it, Allete." Dayna assured me. "I am his favorite."

I made a motion with my hand to quiet her so we could hear what our father was saying to the king of Tara.

"She has to know by now that I have arrived," King Cathal said, his words clipped.

"Allete tends to have her own mind about things. I am sure she will join us when she is ready," Father replied, attempting to placate our irritated guest.

"And who allows such independent thinking?" Cathal challenged. "A woman should know her place." His pointed look was aimed at the queen, who stood quietly next to King Albric.

I was sure my mother was going to smack the rude man, but a subtle touch to her wrist from my father held her in place.

"I understand your frustration, Cathal, but please

be considerate of Allete's situation. She is to be courted by a man she has never met and is expected to leave in a month's time and travel to a place that is not her home, where she has no friends—no family. She deserves time to adjust." King Albric, ever the diplomat, attempted to ease the king of Tara's temper, but judging by Cathal's pinched lips, his efforts were wasted.

"Could you at least send for her," King Cathal asked in a more civil tone, "Please?" He added, albeit a bit begrudgingly.

I gently tugged Dayna's sleeve, indicating it was time for us to go. Like mice being hunted by a cat, we scurried from our hiding place and snuck to my bedchamber. We had barely made it inside when there was a knock at the door.

"Enter," I said, attempting to keep from sounding breathless.

Lidia entered, the look on her face one of trepidation.

"The king requests your presence," my handmaiden said softly.

I smiled at the girl. "Chin up, Lidia. All is well."

Lidia let out a huff, her manners momentarily forgotten. "You have not met the man. He is positively awful." Her hand flew to her mouth and her eyes widened. "Forgive my frankness."

Dayna laughed. "Allete would never punish you, especially not when you've told the truth." She lowered her voice conspiratorially. "We already saw him—we spied on them." Dayna winked, completely unrepentant.

Lidia lowered her hand and made an *O* shape with her mouth.

I straightened my dress and pulled my shoulders back. "Might as well face the music. I doubt he is going to turn around and sail back home without me."

"We could make him *go away*," Dayna offered. "I am sure we could afford an assassin."

Lidia gasped, and I shot my sister a warning look. "Bite your tongue. The walls have ears. Words like that would make it impossible for Father to protect you."

Dayna shrugged. *Petulant child.* I worried my sister's mouth would get her in more trouble than she thought possible. Our father's crown could only protect her so much.

I made a motion for Lidia to lead the way. The atmosphere turned somber, as if we were headed to a funeral instead of an introduction to my future husband. Imagining how we must have looked made my mouth twitch upward just a smidge.

As we approached the sitting room, I could feel tension rolling in not so subtle waves. I took a deep breath, and then I walked past my sister and Lidia. As I entered the room, my eyes met my father's first. My heart broke at the look of regret I found there. I gave him a small smile, hoping to assure him I would be fine. I understood my duty to the kingdom and stood ready and willing to do it. At least that's what I told myself. The truth was much more complicated.

"King Cathal," my father said loudly, stepping forward and reaching for my hand, "this is my daughter, Princess Allete."

I turned to the king and curtsied, though I really wanted to stomp on his foot—behavior that was oh so befitting of a future queen.

"My Lord," I said as I rose and looked up at him. It took everything in me not to take a step back at the look of lust and longing in his eyes. I had never been in a relationship, or even fancied a man, but I was no stranger to the attention Cathal was giving me. It made my skin crawl, feeling as though I was covered in a thousand ants.

He reached for my hand, and, after the briefest hesitation, I complied. When his large hand closed around mine, I felt like an animal caught in a hunter's trap and I struggled to suppress the violent urge to riot against my restraints. He leaned down and placed a kiss on the back of my hand, lingering a little too long. When he rose, I attempted to pull my hand away, but he only tightened his grasp.

"You are more beautiful than I expected," he said, his deep voice sending a chill down my spine.

"Thank you," I responded, earning a toothy smile in return.

"I wonder if you would join me for a walk before the banquet?" Cathal requested.

I looked at my father, hoping he could see the pleading in my eyes to refuse the king's request. I knew it would be an insult to refuse, but I could not help but hope.

"I can't think of anyone better to show you around the castle, King Cathal," my father replied in my stead, "with a chaperone, of course."

Cathal looked irritated at the caveat, but there was no way King Albric would allow me to be alone with any man before I wed, regardless of his status.

"Of course," Cathal said.

"Lidia," King Albric called, knowing she would not be far from me. The young girl hurried in, followed by Dayna. "You and Dayna please accompany King Cathal and Allete on a walk of the grounds."

Lidia curtsied and came to stand behind me. Dayna quickly joined her, not bothering to introduce herself to the king.

Cathal took my hand and tucked it into the crook of his arm, effectively drawing me closer to him. Our shoulders brushed, and I wanted to gag from the proximity. I let him lead me from the room, wishing an opening in the floor would suddenly swallow me whole.

"You seem nervous." Cathal pointed out.

*Really? Because I feel so incredibly comfortable.*

"I apologize, my Lord. I admit, the idea of becoming the queen of a kingdom I am not familiar with and marrying a man I do not know is a bit daunting."

"Surely you were prepared for such a fate from an early age."

"I was, but preparation and experience are vastly different from each other."

He seemed to consider my words before he spoke. "I suppose, but you will have to learn to adapt. Being a queen is not easy. My people will look to you as an example. You must not show weakness."

*Pompous ass.* Who was he to tell me how to behave? He would be my husband, but that did not make him my master. "I'm sure I am up to the task," I said through gritted teeth.

I felt his stare as he looked down at me. He continued to lead me down the hall until we reached the large front doors of the palace. "Have I offended you?" Cathal asked.

"Forgive my brusqueness, King Cathal." I managed to respond in a cordial voice. "I did not sleep well and find myself in a foul mood."

"I like a woman who has a little fight in her, Allete. Breaking you in will be much more interesting."

He had spoken so softly that I knew my sister and Lidia could not have heard him. I clenched my free hand into a fist and slowly counted to ten. Otherwise, I would have smacked the smug look off his face. I had no response to his comment, at least not one that wouldn't jeopardize the prospect of my upcoming nuptials and, thereby, the

Quinn Loftis

fate of our entire kingdom.

"Where are the gardens?" he asked after we had stepped outside in silence.

I pointed to the left. "Just around the corner."

Cathal turned in that direction, his large strides difficult to for me to keep up with. He did not seem to notice.

"Do you have gardens on your palace grounds?" I asked him, attempting to engage in conversation.

"Of course." He snapped. "A man should take pride in the land he owns. Having pride in something requires making it shine. Speaking of," he said as he looked down at me again, his gaze wandering over my form. "We will have to do something about your clothing—it is much too plain for a queen of Tara. I expect you to look like the prize you are."

Dayna's gasp indicated she heard his words. I glanced over my shoulder at my sister, giving the younger girl a warning glare. The last thing I needed was for my sister to anger the king.

When we reached the gardens, he paused, scrutinizing them as his eyes roamed over the area. "Tis a bit small, isn't it?"

"What the grounds lack in size, they more than make up for in beauty," I offered, working to keep my voice soft and my tone light.

"I am not taking you as my bride so I can hear your opinion on the appropriateness of castle grounds."

I could not hold my tongue any longer, consequences be damned. "Pray tell, my Lord, what *do* you need from me?"

His lips quirked in a smile, though there was no warmth in it. "I need you to warm my bed and bear my heirs." The hunger in his eyes as he looked over me awakened an intense need to take a scalding bath with several bars of soap. "You have perfect birthing hips and breasts that should be more than adequate for nourishing my children."

Dayna was not the only one to gasp that time.

"Sir, such comments are not appropriate." I desperately wanted to fold my arms across my chest to keep him from looking at me.

"I am a king, and I am your husband—"

"Beg your pardon, My Lord, but you are not yet my husband."

He tightened his lips into a straight line. I could tell he wanted to snap at me but was trying remain composed. "There is time for you to learn your place," he said, and it almost seemed as though he was reassuring himself.

I continued to walk with him in silence, only bothering to nod my head when he asked me questions, or giving him curt, one-word answers. By the time we returned to the palace, I was ready to put a quarrel into the man I was destined to marry.

"Shall I accompany you to your room and help you ready yourself for this evening?"

Dayna stepped forward, unable to hold her tongue any longer. "Your highness," she said in a syrupy tone, "that will not be necessary. Lidia and I have spent half our lives preparing my sister for royal events. We are certainly capable of the task."

Cathal did not look happy with the offer but did not press the issue.

"Given the state of her, some might disagree," he said in a clipped tone, "but your backward ways will have to do for now." He leaned down to me and pressed his lips against my cheek, and I fought the urge to gag. I was screaming inside, and now I would have to scrub my face until the first layer of skin peeled away.

As soon as he stepped back, I turned on my heel and hurried away, with Lidia and Dayna only a step behind me. I was so very thankful for their presence, and I dreaded the moment I would have to be alone with the king.

We reached my room, and I slammed the door shut and locked it the instant we all clambered inside.

"That insufferable pig!" Dayna growled. "How dare he treat you in such an awful manner? Who the hell does he think he is?"

"He is the king of his nation." I pointed out. "Who is there to stop him?"

"You cannot marry him, Allete." Dayna pleaded. "Tell Father how awful King Cathal is; he could not possibly expect you to marry such a person."

I walked to the window and looked out over the kingdom I called home. I still yearned for adventure but not with Cathal. Certainly, a life with him would be miserable. I was beginning to believe it was a mercy that his previous wives died rather than having endured a life with him. Still, it was odd that a king so young had already been married three times, and each of those wives had met their untimely demise. Regardless, Father could not stop the wedding now. Agreements had been made, plans laid, and treaties signed. It would be seen as an act of war to withdraw the transaction. I would not be the reason our country went to war.

"I could not ask such a thing of him."

"So, you are just going to marry him?" Dayna challenged. "What will you do when he loses his temper with you and lets his hand fly? He will not put up with any amount of argument or opinion. What will you do then?"

I knew what my sister said was true. Cathal was the kind of man who believed it was okay to strike a woman to keep her in her place.

"If I want to keep peace for our father and our kingdom, I have to marry him."

"Then you are not going with him alone," Dayna declared. "I will go with you."

"And I," Lidia added.

"I cannot ask that of either of you," I said, shaking my head, even though my heart swelled with love for the two women in front of me.

"You, dear Sister, are not asking," Dayna said. "We are telling you—there is no way you are going to live with that abomination of a man without us."

Lidia nodded her head, her lips set in a tight line—the face of determination.

"Out of the question." I continued. "I, at least, will be the queen, affording me at least some protection. You two will have even less, especially you, Lidia. There is no predicting what could happen to you."

"But we know what will happen to you." Dayna countered. "And we will not allow it. I am going. I don't care if I must sneak aboard his ship or if I have to seduce one of his guards and convince him to bring me along."

I gasped. "You wouldn't."

"You know she would." Lidia interjected. "And I will go with her. She is your sister and, if I may be so bold, you are like a sister to me—one of the only friends I've ever had. I've lived my entire life, not just in your family's service, but in *your* service. I shan't stop now."

I sighed, knowing further argument was pointless. Lidia was right about Dayna. When the girl had her mind set on something, all the armies of Hell couldn't dissuade her. "I suppose I need to get dressed for this evening," I said after a long pause.

"About that," Dayna said, heading toward the wardrobe.

"I have a particular dress in mind that would be perfect for the occasion—the one Mother bought for you last year."

Lidia frowned. "That thing is awful... no offense," she added, looking at the ground.

"Yes, well, Mother did not think so. It was in fashion, at the time," Dayna said.

I crossed my arms in front of my chest and cocked an eyebrow at my sister. "What are you up to?"

"I just do not see any reason for you to go through great lengths to look your best for him like you care what he thinks. Maybe if he finds you unattractive, he will change his mind."

I wished that were the case, but I had seen the determination in King Cathal's eyes. He saw me as a challenge, and he wanted nothing more than to break me. *Do your best, wretched king.* Whatever he did, I refused to break. It was not a part of who I was.

"I doubt it will work, but I certainly have no desire to encourage his advances." I rubbed my hands together. "Ladies... do your worst."

Lidia and Dayna both jumped into their work with excitement. It made me laugh to see how eager they were to make me as unattractive as possible. Lidia began by coercing my hair into a ghastly number of braids. She then coiled each one on top of my head so it looked as though I had tiny birds' nests all over my head. I was almost embarrassed to be seen by the court, but I did not really care what they thought of me. Because of my magic, they had refused to accept me. What did it matter if they disapproved of me being less than beautiful?

"If this was not for a worthy cause, Sister, I would be embarrassed to be seen with you," Dayna admitted. "Although, your face is still much too pretty. Maybe we should overdo the rouge and powder."

"Good idea," Lidia responded.

"Dayna, I don't want to look like a rosy-cheeked specter," I argued.

"You will be considered less if we cannot dissuade Cathal," she countered. "Have at it, Lidia."

There was a knock at the door. Before I could respond, Dayna hurried to answer it. She pulled the door open a crack, peered through, and the opened the door fully, allowing Lizzy to enter.

Her eyes were so wide it was comical as she looked me over. "What have you two done to her?" Lizzy asked as she began to circle me.

"Have you met her future husband?" Dayna asked.

Lizzy shook her head. "I have been out all morning tending to the sick in the village."

Now it was my turn to look at her with surprise. "Since when do you nurse the ill?"

Lizzy shrugged. "I decided I should take more of an interest in helping others."

"And you decided this just about the same time our guests arrived? Why?" Dayna asked.

"Because we have so much and they have so little. And having another kingdom come in showing off all their wealth just made it more apparent that I should be helping."

"I think that is very noble of you," I said as I smiled at my younger sister, but I could not help but wonder if there was an ulterior motive for Lizzy's actions.

"Yes, yes." Lizzy waved my comment off. "Now, explain to me why you look like you are attempting to win the ugliest princess contest."

"Dayna and Lidia are attempting to put Cathal off his pursuit of me. They think if they make me unattractive, he will not want me."

Lizzy frowned. "Word around the palace is that he is exceedingly handsome."

"Handsome or not, he is the biggest horse's ass I have ever had the displeasure of meeting," Dayna said, clenching her jaw so tightly it looked as though it might break.

"Allete, is this true?" Lizzy questioned.

I nodded. "She speaks the truth, I'm afraid. Cathal was awful. He desires nothing more than a brood mare to break and bear his offspring, which he made perfectly clear."

Lizzy's expression reflected the horror I felt. Dayna recounted the events of our morning walk around the grounds with my future husband. Lizzy's face burned brighter and brighter with anger as Dayna continued.

"You have to tell Father." Lizzy pleaded.

"That is what I told her." Dayna agreed.

I shook her head, once again explaining why that could not happen. "I will not cause him guilt over what cannot be changed. If Father backs out of the arrangement now, his actions would be a declaration of war, which our coffers cannot afford."

"How can you sacrifice your happiness for us?" Lizzy asked. "Allete, your life will be one of anguish if you marry this fool."

"Duty above all else." Lidia interrupted. "She is so much like Father."

My heart clenched painfully in my chest as I considered all I would be giving up by marrying Cathal. I would never see beyond the Tara castle walls, I would never fall in love, and I would probably never truly be happy again. Shaking off the fear and disgust, I pulled on the strength instilled in me by my royal parents.

"I will do what is necessary. Now," I pulled my shoulders

back and lifted me chin, "we have a banquet to attend and my future husband to embarrass. Let us take joy where we can."

Dayna laughed and clapped her hands like an excited child. "I cannot wait to see his face when he lays eyes on you."

Lizzy shook her head and pinched the bridge of her nose. "Tis sure to be an interesting evening. Lead the way, dear Allete. Lidia, please sing a funeral ballad. Our sister is walking straight into the arms of the devil, himself."

"Always a ray of sunshine, Lizzy." Dayna huffed. "I am sure your presence among the sick lifted their spirits immeasurably."

I coughed to cover my laugh. If nothing else, the night promised to be entertaining. My sisters would make sure of it.

# CHAPTER Seven

"WHY IS POWER SO CORROSIVE? I AM LEARNING THAT WEAK
MEN SEEM TO DESIRE POWER MORE THAN OTHERS. WEAK MEN
ARE NEVER SATISFIED, BECAUSE THEY LACK THE STRENGTH TO
DENY THEMSELVES WHAT IS NOT THEIRS TO BEGIN WITH. MAY
THE GODS GIVE ME STRENGTH TO QUASH MY OWN WEAKNESS."

~TORBEN

"IS OUR JARL GOING mad?" Brant asked as we walked
through the cover of trees toward the English palace.
Six of my closest warriors surrounded us, soldiers I knew I
could trust without question.

I had been expecting such a question, having seen
the mania that seemed to dance in Magnus' eyes as he
explained his month-long plan to infiltrate the English
kingdom. To the surprise of us all, the jarl had made it
clear that he wanted his spoils to include more than just
English gold—if there was even any left. He wanted to
bring the monarchy to its knees. Magnus was sure of the
inevitable success of his plan, convinced that if we could
infiltrate the ranks of the guards, we could cause the
Britons to implode upon themselves. Perhaps with enough
men, such a dangerous plan might be plausible, but it was
not only the English army with which we had to contend.
The king of Tara had arrived in Britannia ahead of us and

would remain for some time, courting his future queen. While the state of Magnus' sanity was debatable, but his intellect was sound. He had picked precisely this time to invade due to the presence of the second king. Two kings meant twice as much treasure, not to mention the bride-price that would be exchanged.

Even if Magnus' invasion was a fool's errand, the jarl still had too many loyal soldiers. My own soldiers and I would not be able to overthrow Magnus if dissent erupted within the clan. It was better to bide my time and wait for the others to grasp the danger into which their jarl was leading them. I only hoped they did not come to the realization too late.

"He is power hungry," I told my lieutenant, my voice low as we drew closer to the palace walls.

"He will ruin us." Amund joined in. "How can the others not see that?"

"They are blinded by their own greed," Kjell said in the gravelly voice familiar to those who knew him.

"Why are we doing this, Torben?" Amund asked.

"Because, at the moment, we have no other choice."

"Has the Oracle seen anything that would benefit us?" Brant asked.

I was tempted to tell them of the prophecy, but something stayed my tongue. I did not know if I was being protective of the female my mother claimed would be mine, or if I was afraid of altering the outcome. So, I shook my head and left it at that.

As we crested a small hill, I got a sinking feeling in my gut. There was something evil prowling inside the castle walls. I didn't know how I knew, other than that I could feel an ominous presence. Even though I did not yet know the English princess, my instincts screamed to get her out of that dark place. I was still without any idea on how to persuade her to leave with me willingly, and I did not like the idea of abducting her, but kidnapping might be my only option.

I signaled for the men to follow me, and moved swiftly to the wall, not wanting to be seen by the guards patrolling above. Once our backs were pressed firmly against the stone, we began walking, our steps completely silent. The only thing threatening to betray our presence were the muted shadows of our forms following us on the ground.

I rounded a corner of the castle wall and my hopes were confirmed. An arched opening rested at the bottom of the structure—the main drainage system for the entire castle. While the walls of most palaces held a similar apparatus for removing castle waste, some had figured out ways to create drains that did not weaken the structure of the wall. Such an undertaking was expensive, and only the richest kingdoms upgraded to the stronger design.

We hurried forward and pushed against the iron grate. The stone overhanging the arch shielded us from above, and even though I suspected that no one would see us in the shadows of the crevice, I didn't want to linger. A small trickle of water flowed past our feet, eventually spilling into the castle's moat. There, it would enter a drainage ditch that would most likely take it to a nearby river. Pushing aside all thought of what might be drained through the mote, I focused on finding the hinges I hoped were on the sides of the grate.

"Are there hinges on that side?" I whisper-yelled to Brant, who stood across from me on the other side of the drain.

He nodded, and I scuttled across the water to stand next to him. There were five large metal tubes housing large pins that held the grate in place. We needed only to force the heavy grate upward high enough to pop it loose.

"It will take all of us to lift it," I said as I motioned for the five other men to join Brant and I at the grate. We each grabbed onto the metal bars and lowered our legs for leverage.

"On three," I told them. "One, two, three." All at once, we pushed up, using our arms and shoulders to lift. It did not budge.

"Again," I said once I had let them rest. I counted, and we strained once more against the iron, grunting as silently as we could. Again, the grate refused to move.

"It's no use," Brant said. "The hinges have rusted. Who knows how long it has been since this accursed grate has been opened, if ever. Let me go to work with Eve, and it'll soon be loosed." Brant fingered the quarter-stone sledge that hung from his belt. The warrior named all his hammers after women. I'd asked him about this once, and he replied that the only thing that could break a man quicker than a hammer blow was a woman. Because of the covert nature of this mission, we'd all left our battle weapons back at the camp, which is why he wasn't lugging his huge war hammer, Bertha. Each of us carried only a dagger with us, save Brant, who, of course, had no use for "maiden pokers," so he carried his small hammer, Eve.

"Way too loud." I grunted. "Do you want to bring the whole of the king's guard down upon us?"

"Let them come," he said with the growl of a wolf.

"We need a distraction." Rush suggested.

"Any ideas?" Amund asked the five other men.

"Fire?" Delvin asked.

"Why are you always looking for reasons to burn stuff down?" Rush asked with a sly smirk.

Delvin shrugged. "I like fires. Fires are pretty and warm, just the way I like my women."

"They also burn you," Amund pointed out, "which is

also just like your women."

"As intellectually stimulating as this conversation is, I personally don't want to spend all night in the castle muck talking about Delvin's love life," I said while glancing up to make sure we had not been spotted by any English soldiers. "Now, listen up."

My men moved in so our heads were close together as we huddled around each other.

"Delvin, do you have your flint and steel?" I asked him.

"Always," he answered with the kind of grin that concerned me every time I saw it. Brant thought the man had an unhealthy fascination with flames, and while this was probably true, every clan needed a match man.

"You, Rush, and Kjell head for the trees. I want you far enough away that the fire will not spread to the palace grounds, but close enough to be of concern to them. While the palace staff busies themselves with putting it out, the rest of us will work on the hinges." I looked at Brant, who was giving me his own fearsome grin. If Delvin was fascinated with fire, Brant was keen on blunt-force destruction.

I gave a silent command for Delvin and the others to move out, and I watched them slink through the drainage ditch until it joined the moat. They then lowered themselves into the water and swam across, emerging on the other side. By that point, I could barely catch a glimpse of them as they took cover in the tall grass and slunk toward the trees, soundless as a pack of wolves tracking their prey.

"I'm not sure if they will sound an alarm at this time of night, so we wait until we see movement toward the fire," I said to the others. Brant had a tight grip on Eve, waiting for my signal.

A quarter of an hour later, smoke was rising high into the air, and the rumblings of concerned citizens began. As soon as the first soldiers carrying buckets of water emerged from the gates, Brant shot me a grin.

"Feel like hitting something?" I asked him.

"Always." He chuckled.

The sound of Brant's hammer on steel echoed like a high-pitched cannon in the confined space. I constantly looked toward the top of the battlements, sure someone would hear the loud banging and find us attempting to break through the grate. So far, the gods had been with us. Everyone was too concerned with putting out the blaze to worry about us. Ten minutes of agonizing bashing later, which felt like ten hours as I stood watch, Delvin, Rush, and Kjell popped up a few feet from me, each of them smiling from ear-to-ear.

"That was fun," Delvin said a little breathlessly.

Amund shook his head. "And you wonder why no woman can stand to be with you for longer than a week."

"Hey, they just can't handle the heat," replied Delvin.

I rolled my eyes and patted Brant on the shoulder, who was still grunting and pounding on the iron bars. "Easy, big guy. I just want the grate hinges loosened, not the entire castle to come down on top of us.

"Hopefully, they are ready," Siv, the quiet one of the bunch, said as he stepped to the middle of the grate and gripped the bars.

Each of us moved to surround the grate, Brant and myself closest to the hinges on either side. "On three," I said once again. "One, two, three." Our grunts and groans were finally rewarded as the large pins lifted from the hinges. The grate was as heavy as the dead weight of a bear and just as awkward to carry. "Lean it against the wall." I grunted. We set the heavy grate aside and, one-by-one, climbed through the opening of the drain.

The cramped space felt much like I imagined an

underground tomb would feel, and I had no desire to dawdle. "Let's slide it back into place, but prop it against the hinges so it looks as though it hasn't been tampered with."

Even pushing the grate across the muck was no easy task, having to pull the large grate back into place from inside the opening using only the strength of our upper bodies. Luckily, everyone outside the drain was still too focused on the fire to notice the struggle going on in the crevice of the castle wall. As soon as the grate was again resting near the hinges, we turned and let our eyes adjust to the dark tunnel ahead. "Delvin..." I started to say.

"Already ahead of you, Commander," he said as I turned to see him working on a small torch. Once the torch was glowing, we could see about ten paces in front of and behind us, and we slowly began our journey into the belly of the castle grounds.

"Amund," I called out. "Keep count of our steps." Knowing the approximate distance of our escape route could help us know whether to hide or to flee, should an emergency arise.

We continued relative silence, only commenting occasionally in hushed tones. I assumed the others were, like me, trying to ignore the smells were breathing into our lungs.

After what felt like an eternity, I began to hear hurried footsteps and muffled voices. Soon, we reached a ladder built into the stone, which extended up to a grate on the sewer roof. As quietly as I could, I ascended the ladder and peered out into the moonlit darkness. The fresh air could not have been more welcome. I pressed my face against the grate, straining to get a good look at my surroundings. With my visibility limited, I could see only the night sky above me and a few paces of cobblestones in each direction. We would need be careful exiting the drain. Our task would have been much easier had we been able to procure guard's uniforms before entering the grounds, but no such opportunity had presented itself. Now, we had to emerge inside the castle gates covered in waste from the knee down, and three of us dripping wet.

I waited until I could hear no one close by. Then, I reached up and carefully pushed the grate up and away, wincing as it ground nosily across the stone floor of the courtyard until the opening was wide enough for us to get through. I motioned down to the others to follow, and I clambered out of the hole, quickly ducking behind an empty cart against the wall. I didn't have to tell the others to make themselves scarce—we would all find a place to hide.

One by one, my men propelled themselves out of the drain, each waiting to surface until there were no voices or footsteps. A few times, I heard signals given in our private battle language, meaning either *halt* or *go now*.

Finally, Siv, the last man, appeared and replaced the grate before sneaking off to find his own hiding place. We all rested for a few minutes, watching each other in the darkness. Eventually, when I felt the coast was clear, I give a hand signal for my soldiers to follow me. I rose and began to walk down a narrow alley, knowing that each of my warrior would covertly follow at their own pace. Then, a voice stopped me in my tracks.

"Oy. There is a fire outside the gates. We need all able-bodies. Where are you going?"

I turned and shrugged, narrowing my eyes and cocking my head to the side as if I hadn't heard him.

"Don't play dumb with me." He barked, marching quickly toward me. Five figures sprang into the alley behind the soldier, who was so intent on dressing me down that he didn't even hear my men lining up behind him. As he neared, the man's eyes widened as he took in my appearance. I imagined I was quite a sight. We looked nothing like their people. The soldier was clean-cut and clean-shaven, not traits that would have describe any of my warriors. I then realized we were all going to have to cut our hair and shave our beards if we were going to have any hope of blending in with the English. Long hair and beards were a sign of strength in my clan. The thought of cutting either stirred my ire. Damn Magnus and his need for power,

"Who..." the soldier began, but I cut him off as I slid my hand around his throat.

"I am sorry about this," I said in a low growl. I did not want to kill him, but I had no other choice. To save my clan, according to the prophecy, I had to take this foreign bride. Magnus ordered me to infiltrate the castle and, for now, I must obey him. Our mission would have been doomed to failure if I left the poor man alive. I twisted my hand, breaking his neck instantly, and found a small amount of comfort in knowing his death had been quick.

"Siv, he looks to be about your size," I said. "Move quickly." We stripped the soldier of his clothes and Siv began putting them on. The others then pulled the body behind some barrels of mead that lined the alley. My mind was a mix of duty and guilt. I knew of the tough decisions a clan leader must make, which is why I had never sought the post for myself. The responsibility of such decisions was the curse of holding power, and mistakes affected not only the leader, but those who depended upon him.

"Ready?" Brant's voice came from behind me. I turned to behold Siv, who, other than his hair, now looked somewhat like an English soldier.

"We have to cut our hair." I told them gruffly.

"I hope you know what you are doing." Brant grumbled.

"I'm keeping us alive," I said, my blood suddenly hot with anger. The burden of the prophecy and the weight from the heinous act I had just committed suddenly settled heavily upon me. Killing men in battle, men who would kill me if they got the chance, was entirely different from what I had just done. Even though it was done under Magnus' orders, I had committed murder.

Brant held up his hands and lowered his head. "You have always put the clan first. We trust your judgment, hersir."

My jaw clenched as I looked at each man who had pledged his loyalty to me. "I am doing the best I can with the information the Oracle has given me. When the time is right, I will share it with you, but that time has not come." They each nodded.

"Now, we need to find a quiet place out of the way so we can observe the guards. We need five more uniforms." We let Siv take the lead as he would draw the least attention.

We walked farther into the grounds, keeping our eyes lowered so no one could later identify us. A few minutes later, we found ourselves in a dingy alley crammed with small, dilapidated shops. One caught my attention because its door was resting wide open, which would be unusual, for this time of night. The interior was cloaked in darkness and I could see nothing of the inside. A painted sign, reading *Myra's Mixes*, hung on a rusty chain above the door. Seeing the place sent a jolt through my belly. I couldn't explain why, but I felt something pulling me toward the small store, as if I was meant to go inside. There was a subtle, pulsing energy flowing out of the place. A person who had never encountered magic would not have recognized the faint traces, but I had been raised by the Oracle. Where some would feel a cold chill or the shudder of deja vu, I felt magic.

I moved toward the door, knowing my men would follow without question, and when I inside the small hut-like room, I felt something pushing at my mind. Picturing a wall in my head, I looked over my shoulder at the warriors. "Shield your minds. There is something more at work here." All of them had, at some point in their lives, spent time with my mother, and she was adamant that I and those closest to me learn to protect ourselves from dark power. It did not feel as though whatever presence attempting to see into my mind was dark, but I still did not like the idea of anything helping itself to my memories.

As we crept farther into the shop, my eyes began to adjust to the dimness, the only light coming from the moonlight filtering in from the open door behind us. Suddenly, a small elderly woman stepped from behind a shelf directly to my right, and I stopped in my tracks. With whispered grunting and cursing, the men behind me stumbled into my back, challenging me to stay upright before the woman.

"Torben, commander of the Hakon clan, king to be, I have been waiting for you," the old woman said in an ominous voice.

"This cannot be good," Brant mumbled.

# CHAPTER Eight

"GROWING UP, IT IS FUN FOR A LITTLE GIRL TO DREAM OF WHAT
HER LIFE WILL LOOK LIKE WHEN SHE IS FINALLY REACHES
ADULTHOOD. OF COURSE, SHE PICTURES HAVING THE PERFECT
WEDDING, A HANDSOME MAN WHO ADORES HER, AND A
HAPPILY EVER AFTER SURROUNDED BY LOVELY CHILDREN. NO
ONE TELLS THE LITTLE GIRL THAT THE LIKELIHOOD OF THESE
DREAMS COMING TRUE IS ABOUT THE SAME AS THAT OF HER
IMAGINARY FRIEND COMING TO LIFE DURING ONE OF THEIR
TEA PARTIES."

~ALLETE AUVRAYS DIARY

MY HEART WAS POUNDING so loudly I was sure everyone
around me could hear it. I had never been thankful
for a wildfire before, but the blaze outside the castle walls
kept everyone from staring at me as I leaned as far away
from Cathal as possible while he struggled to whisper in
my ear. I wasn't sure who had started the fire, but I would
gladly shake their hand and thank them if I could.

Thomas sat across the table and three seats to my left.
He caught my eye and wiggled his eyebrows suggestively.
I really wanted to throw a chicken leg at him, but I was
pretty sure Cathal might turn me over his knee and spank
me in front of everyone if I did, or at the very least, scold
me verbally. *Pompous ass.* I might never say it aloud, but I

decided then I would call him P.A. to myself every time I thought of him. It was a petty and vindictive sentiment, sure, but I had to take pleasure where I could find it.

When the king of Tara finally turned to talk to someone on his left, I picked up my fork while looking at my cousin and pretended to stab myself in the eye. Dayna, who was sitting to Thomas' left, must have seen me, because she snorted and sip she'd just taken spewed from her nose and mouth, sending Thomas into an uncontrollable belly-laugh. My mother stared wit at her youngest daughter, eyes wide, and my father looked at me with a knowing grin on his face. I didn't know if he saw my gesture, but he probably guessed who had caused the commotion.

"Excuse me," Dayna said, patting her mouth dry. "I saw a fly in my drink as I was taking a sip and it startled me."

At her comment, almost everyone in the room picked up their glasses and looked down into them. Thomas was still laughing, and I was so very tempted to throw a dinner roll at him. Perhaps everyone would be too preoccupied with the possibility of ingesting an insect to notice a flying baked good.

My father cleared his throat, immediately drawing everyone's attention, and Thomas shot me one last wink before he, too, turned to look at my father.

"Distinguished guests," my father began. As he stood, he took my mother's hand and pulled her up to stand beside him. She looked like she wanted to be there about as much as she wanted to be struck by lightning. "Please allow me to introduce our guest of honor, the noble king of Tara and my future son-in-law, King Cathal. Soon, he will wed my eldest daughter, Allete. Their marriage will not only be a happy and blessed union for the young couple, but for both kingdoms. Our subjects will soon benefit from increased trade and security, as we now have such a strong and trusted ally close by. Thank you both." He looked at me and my gut clenched. "Marring a stranger is no small sacrifice. We recognize the cost, and we honor you."

I swallowed the urge to vomit what little I had eaten all over the table—or better yet, in Cathal's lap. This was my father's way of apologizing to me. I wasn't sure he fully understood how detestable the king of Tara was, but he saw enough to know that my marriage would not be a joyous one.

Cathal gave my father a slight nod and then stood as well. I could feel everyone staring at me as I fixed my gaze on the uneaten chicken on my plate. Perhaps I was hoping that if I avoided their inquisitive looks long enough, everyone would lose interest in me, but among all the glances and stares, I felt one that made the hair on the back of my neck stand up—*his*. Cathal cleared his throat, and when that failed to illicit a response from me, he placed his cool hand on my shoulder. I could no longer ignore him without causing a scene, so I gathered myself and swallowed down the bile.

I stood slowly, plastering on my best smile. Judging by the looks on the diners' faces, I had not succeeded in appearing courtly, but may have looked a bit demented. I saw Clay take a step away from the wall where he'd been standing guard and discreetly motioned with my hand for him to stay put. Dayna stared up at me as she bit her lip, and I knew she was trying desperately not to laugh. My eyes moved over the table, taking in the faces of the courtiers, most of whom I barely knew. Some were faithful friends of our family, lords and dukes concerned about our kingdom and hopeful this new alliance would yield prosperity for our people. Others were simply there to engage in gossip and partake of the king's free wine.

I was so distracted by my thoughts, I did not hear

Cathal speaking next to me. In fact, I did not even acknowledge him until I felt his cool hand move to my neck. I whipped my head around so fast that I nearly lost my balance due to the weight of the braids Lidia had piled on top of my head. Cathal steadied me with that damn hand on my neck and stared down at me with what must have seemed like adoration. What they did not see was the hint of violence dancing just beyond his ever-present, royal facade. He was angry—no, infuriated but I smiled sweetly at him and watched the rage in him grow. His firm grip was a reminder that he was a man, much larger than me, and he saw me as nothing more than an object to own and use whenever he pleased.

"As I was saying," Cathal continued smoothly, "my bride is even more beautiful than I could have imagined. I assure you all, it is no hardship to be yoked to a lovely vision such as Allete."

*Did he nearly choke on the word, beautiful?* I wondered.

"Thank you for offering me and my people a warm welcome. I look forward to getting to know your kingdom, its people, and my bride-to-be."

The guests responded with gentle clapping and beaming smiles. I even heard sighs coming from some of the ladies, young and old. I nearly rolled my eyes but stopped myself when I caught Cathal's brooding stare. He leaned near me as we sat down, as if he was stealing a quick moment to whisper something loving in my ear. Oh, how surprised our onlookers would be to know his words conveyed quite the opposite sentiment.

"I have no idea why you showed up looking like trussed-up harlot, but mark my words, you will never again embarrass me in this. From now on, you will wear *only* the wardrobe I brought for you."

I pulled back to look up at him. Nothing in his

expression revealed the disgust carried in his tone of voice. I was so close to spitting in his eyes that I had to force myself to swallow down the saliva pooling in my mouth, as if my body had anticipated my desire. Taking a deep breath, I slightly bowed my head. "As you wish."

The dinner was agonizingly slow. So slow, that I found myself staring at the staff, willing them to move faster. But no matter how hard I glared at them, their pace did not increase. For a moment, I wished I could trade my gift of healing so I could silently influence the minds of others. How wonderful it would be to make them skip the remaining courses and bring us our desserts

When the final course was served an hour later, I could not bring myself to eat it, even though it was my favorite. Cook must have felt pity for me and prepared peach pie.

"Do you not like the pie, my sweet?" Cathal asked me loud enough for the entire table to take notice.

"It is her favorite." Dayna offered. I shot her a glare but she just smiled.

"I foolishly overindulged and now have no room for Cook's delicious treat." I did not understand why I felt the need to explain myself to him.

"But you did not eat very much tonight," Cathal said as he took another bite of his own pie. "It would not do for you to get too thin. I prefer my wife to have a bit of girth to her."

That was the final straw—I was not about to sit at the table with my family and two courts from two kingdoms and allow him discuss my girth. I stood abruptly. "Please forgive me, my Lord," I looked at Cathal, and then I turned to my father. "Father, I must retire. I suddenly feel unwell."

My mother, bless her soul, stood and walked to me. She wrapped an arm around my shoulders and began to lead me from the room. "I will take care of our daughter, my love," she called over her shoulder to my father. Clay followed at a discreet distance. For once, I was thankful for his presence. He would know I didn't want Cathal following me.

I heard Dayna and Lizzy making excuses to take their leave and then their hurried footsteps behind us. When we were a good distance from the dining hall, I let out the breath I had been holding.

"He is positively dreadful," Mother said with unveiled disgust thick in her voice.

I held my finger to my lips, reminding her there were always ears listening. She nodded, and we continued the rest of the way in silence.

We reached my bedchamber in record time. As the door closed behind my sisters, I could not help but feel that escaping to my room had become a bit of a habit in the brief time Cathal had been in our kingdom.

My mother turned to look at me and I hated the distress I saw in her eyes. "I am so sorry. If I had known he was such an awful man, I would have fought your father on this matter."

"I do not blame you, or Father, for that matter," I said, hoping she could hear the sincerity in my voice. "I will figure out a way to make the best of it."

"I still vote we hire an assassin," Dayna said.

"What?" Mother gasped.

I shook my head and patted her shoulder. "Do not mind her. Dayna says things before thinking of the repercussions."

"That is not true, Sister. I know the consequences of hiring an assassin—death. Specifically, the death of that awful excuse for a man."

Lizzy snickered.

"Do not encourage her." I warned my middle sister.

"Dayna, you must not say such things," Mother chastised.

"If heard by the wrong person, those words could get you hanged."

Dayna did not look concerned in the least.

My mother eyed me critically before chuckling. "That really is a terrible dress. I picked that out?"

"You were going through a phase." I grinned. "And it proved to be useful after all."

"I must admit, if you were attempting to turn him off, you might have come close by attending the banquet in such a state. But, Allete, your beauty still shines through."

"You have to say that—you're my mother."

"That does not make it any less true," she replied.

"So, are we to continue with trying to make you as unattractive as possible during the courtship?" Lizzy asked.

"That would have been the plan, but Cathal chastised me at dinner and told me I am only to wear the clothes he has brought for me."

"Where are they?" my mother asked.

Dayna was already making her way to my wardrobe. When she pulled the doors open, we all gasped. It was full of lavish dresses—all in the latest style—which I was not fond of.

Lizzy pulled one out and tugged at the bodice. "Where is the rest of the front?"

Dayna snapped. "That *prick*."

My mother rounded on her. "Where did you learn such language?"

She shrugged. "Cook."

Mother shook her head, but was once again distracted by the dress Lizzy was holding.

"It is the popular style in France," I said. "The tight bodice is cut especially low so it can effectively push up a woman's... assets."

"Just say *breasts*—they push up your breasts so a man

can have a conversation with them instead of your face," Dayna huffed. "I'm sure this was designed by a man. It is ridiculous."

"I cannot believe he wants me to parade around so exposed," I muttered, almost to myself.

"I can," Lizzy said as she put the dress back. "To him, you are like a prize mare. He wants to prance you around so everyone can gawk over you as, if he had something to do with how you turned out."

I walked to my bed and flung myself on it, shutting my eyes as I felt like the walls closing in around me. I could not escape my fate, and it just kept getting worse.

"Do not fret, sister mine," Dayna said, patting my arm. "I have another idea. So, he wants you to look beautiful—fine. If we cannot make you ugly, we will just make you stink."

My eye popped open. "What?" My voice came out in a squawk. Around anyone else, I would have been embarrassed at the suggestion.

"No man wants to cozy up to a smelly woman." Dayna pointed out. "If we make you stink, he will not want to be around you. It is genius."

"What if *I* do not want to stink?"

"That does seem a little extreme." My mother agreed.

"Picture this, dear Allete," Dayna said as she raised her hand and gestured like she was revealing something. "Cathal's arms are wrapped around you in a tight embrace. His mouth is near your neck, his snake-like tongue flashing out to taste the forbidden fruit. His warm breath caresses your skin and his hands roam lower—,"

My stomach roiled. "Stop!" I practically yelled, interrupting any further perverse imaginings. "Make me stink."

"Thought you would see it my way."

# CHAPTER nine

"MAGIC. THERE ARE THOSE WHO TREMBLE BEFORE IT, AFRAID
OF WHAT THEY CANNOT CONTROL. SOME WIELD IT RUTHLESSLY
WHILE OTHERS USE IT FOR GOOD—DOING WHAT THEY CAN
TO HELP THOSE AROUND THEM, EVEN IF IT GOES UNNOTICED.
MAGIC CANNOT BE CONTAINED, IT CANNOT BE EXTINGUISHED,
AND IT CANNOT BE EXPLAINED. WE CAN EITHER ACCEPT IT,
LEARNING FROM THOSE WHO ARE GIFTED, OR WE CAN LET IT
DESTROY US."

~ TORBEN

I FOLLOWED THE CROOKED and bent old woman, who had
introduced herself as Myra, farther into the store. My
men stayed close, Brant cussing under his breath the
whole way.

"Relax," I said as I glanced back at him.

"Sure, Torben, I'll relax," the nervous giant responded.
"Nothing to be concerned about here. There isn't anything
creepy about an ancient crone who looks as if she could
turn us all into frogs, and who, by the way, knew your name
even though she has never met you. Nothing terrifying
about that *at all*."

I understood his reservations, but I did not feel any
evil emanating from the woman. She had some form of
magic—that much was obvious—but that did not mean

she posed a threat. Brant's unease aside, Myra held information I needed to know.

When we reached the back of the store, she walked through a parted curtain. I paused when I felt Brant's hand on my shoulder, but before I could speak to him, Myra's face appeared at the opening. She looked past me to my second in command.

"I mean you no harm, big one, but it would be better if no one overheard us. It would not benefit you if any passing soldiers spotted you chatting with me," she told him.

After a brief hesitation, he patted my shoulder, a signal of surrender, and we all followed Myra into the room. Judging by the bed, small table and chairs, and a tiny counter used for preparing food, we had entered her living space. She motioned for Brant and me to take seats as she sat opposite us. There were only four chairs; the rest of my men would have to stand. I was a little worried we would crush the small chairs beneath us. They did not exactly seem designed to handle men of our stature.

"They are sturdier than they look," Myra said with a small smile, having noticed my observation.

Brant and I sat, and the room seemed to shrink several sizes. Right away, I noticed a small shelf, which housed many well-worn magical items: a bowl, tiles that were probably scrying dice, a looking glass, and set of tattered tarot cards.

"You are a witch." I blurted out without thinking of how my men would react, and react they did. As they reached for their swords, the ringing of pulled steel reverberated in the small space. "Hold!" I growled. To my surprise, Myra did not so much as flinch. She simply watched us through keen grey eyes, a knowing smirk on her face.

"Put your weapons away." My words were stern as

my lips tightened. The muscles in my body coiled tightly. I was ready to react quickly, but to what, I had no idea. Though I still did not feel any danger, the circumstances had changed. We were not dealing with a person who possessed magical powers; we were dealing with a person who knew how to *wield* that magic. The variation was not mere semantics. It was the difference between a torch and a bonfire. Both should be respected, but one was much more dangerous.

In fact, according to my mother, there were more people who possessed magical powers and did not know it than those who practiced magic. Those who housed powers but were unaware generally ignored the strange events that often occurred around them. Myra was no such person—she was well-versed in her magical abilities.

With audible mutterings, my men obeyed my command and sheathed their swords. Her hands were clasped, resting in her lap. Her shoulders slumped forward a little, as though she had been carrying heavy bags in both hands for a long time. Her eyes roved, taking in everything about me and my warriors. Regardless how ancient and fragile she appeared, Myra was a formidable force.

"I've been called many things over the years: sorceress, enchantress, and, yes, even witch," she said after a few moments. "While I find such labels ill-fitting for who I really am, I suppose they adequately answer what others really want to know—can I use magic? Yes, I can."

"Surely the Britons do not condone your use of magic?" I asked.

"I don't go around calling fire down from the sky, now, do I? To everyone else, I'm but a peddler of healing plants. If, after imbibing my tinctures, some find they have been miraculously healed, well... I make sure to give all credit to Mother Earth, who provides us with these wonderful herbs. Sure, there are some who have suspected over the years, but I have always managed to assuage any suspicions. Most just think me a crackpot or a charlatan. Either is fine with me."

"So, this kingdom is unkind to those who wield sacred powers?" Amund asked.

"That is putting it mildly. They fear anything they cannot explain. People who are scared make rash decisions." Myra explained.

I understood what she meant. My people were among the few who openly accepted those with gifts and sought to harness their power rather than shun them... or worse.

"How do you know who I am?" I asked, finally addressing the reason I was sitting in the witch's home.

"I have seen you, Torben, many times from afar. Over the past year, I have been unable to scry without your face appearing in my bowl. I was not sure when you were coming, but I knew you would be here. Your coming is the mark of a major change in the future of this kingdom as well as that of your own Hakon clan."

A chill ran down my spine when I heard her say the name of my clan when I had not mentioned it. I did not doubt she had seen what she claimed, especially after hearing my mother's premonition. "What did you see?"

"Two futures continually appear to me." Myra began. "One is a future filled with war and cruelty, where Britain is conquered by King Cathal of Tara. King Albric believes the union of his eldest daughter and the king of Tara is of equal benefit to both kingdoms, but he is mistaken. Cathal plans to overtake the kingdom and add it to his empire, making Albric's people subjects of Tara. Any who resist will be killed or enslaved."

"That's encouraging." Brant grumbled.

"And the other future?" I asked.

"You are to take Allete as your bride, and your union will eventually lead to a peaceful alliance with King Albric. Clan Hakon will prosper with the gift your bride brings to your people. You and Albric will align to defeat Cathal. Although there will be many casualties, you will be victorious."

"Magnus would never let that happen." Amund interrupted. "He's never had much use for allies."

"Your own chieftain must fall for this future to come to pass," she responded, eyeing me warily as she spoke.

As I listened to her, I debated whether I should tell her about my mother and her prophecy.

"I already know about Hilda the Oracle."

My eyes widened. Once again, the witch had managed to surprise me. "What do you know of her?" My soldiers did not know my mother was also a healer, but I needed to know if Myra was aware.

The witch hesitated before speaking. "I know of you mother's gifts, but they are is not common knowledge."

I nodded my thanks.

"Yet understand that the future is never certain. Regardless of what your mother or I have seen, there is always a chance something else could happen. People are unpredictable. A single act, however seemingly insignificant, can change the course of history," Myra said.

"I appreciate the information," I said sincerely—it was reassuring to hear from another seer that my actions were not misguided.

"I have one more thing to offer," she said, "which has a bit more practical value." Myra stood and walked to a shelf filled with small vials of powder, liquids, and all manner of unrecognizable substances. On the end of the shelf, an ancient well-worn book rested, its crumbling pages hanging on by the slightest of threads. She laid it on the table between us.

"If you will allow it, I would like to cast a spell over each one of you. This spell will make you appear as a Briton to everyone but your own people, allowing you to blend in— you don't exactly look like the other men around here.

I heard grumblings from the men standing behind me, but Myra continued, undaunted.

"The spell will also subtly influence the minds of those you encounter. You will be familiar to them, causing them to trust you when they might otherwise question your words or actions. To your own people, if you whisper the word *reveal*, the spell will lift from their eyes and they will see you clearly beneath the magic. My recommendation to you," she said, pointing at me, "would be to get on the guard detail assigned to Allete. That way, you can be close to her. You," she continued, pointing at Brant, "should go with Torben. The rest of you need to spread out among Albric and Cathal's guards, allowing you to gather information on Cathal's people and perhaps ferret out any plans he has."

"Of course," I answered. We appreciate your help very much, Myra."

"There is one more thing you should know—another thing I have seen. A time will come when you will be required to offer your own life for Allete's. At that time, the spell will break."

I was shocked at her words. At no point had my mother mentioned that the princess' life would be in danger.

"I'm confused." I stared at Myra with a puzzled expression on my face. "How will I take the princess as my wife if I am to die for her?" The old woman smirked.

"I never said you would die, only that you would offer your life for hers, but be wary. As I mentioned before, nothing is certain."

Myra then closed her eyes and flipped through the pages of the ancient book while we sat watching.

"This is mad," Kjell whispered.

"Agreed," I said in return, "but it might be the only chance we have to succeed." I heard the reluctant agreement from the others and thanked the gods my men trusted me.

"Quiet now," Myra told them as she walked toward me. She placed her hands on my head and closed her eyes, speaking in a language unfamiliar to me. Warmth radiated from her hands and flowed over me like cascading water. It was not an unpleasant feeling, but it was strange. I felt my hair shorten, leaving my neck bare and the rest of me feeling naked. I looked down at my clothes, and I no longer wore my warrior garments, but was instead dressed in the uniform of an English guard. After she was done with me, she moved to Brant, repeating the process. This continued until she had touched the heads of each of my men and cast her magic over them. When she was finished, she handed us a looking glass so we could get accustomed to our new appearances. I could not help but chuckle at how different we each looked.

"I miss my hair already," Brant muttered.

"You will live," I told him.

"Or maybe you will not," Rush offered with a rueful smile.

"You must never return to see me while you remain in this form. I don't get visits from castle guards. If anyone saw you coming or going, it would arouse suspicion."

"Are you in danger?" I felt it was my duty to make sure she was safe, just like I would want my mother protected from those who would hurt her because of her abilities.

"I can take care of myself," she answered with a small smile. It was silly of me to think a witch of her power couldn't protect herself.

She motioned for us to follow her and opened a door at the back of her store. "Make haste to the castle and take your necessary places. What follows is a chess match—the pieces must be in the right place for the enemy king to be taken."

"Thank you for your help," I said.

She patted my shoulder affectionately, and then she motioned for us to go. I hurried out with my warriors trailing behind me. We moved with purpose, attempting to blend in with the other guards walking nearby. When we reached the entrance to the inner castle grounds, we were stopped by the gatekeeper.

"Your assignment?" He called down from his post.

"Two of us have been added to the guard detail of the princess. The other five are reporting to receive their orders," I yelled back. I was holding my breath, waiting to see if Myra's spell would prove effective.

"Open the gate," he finally said.

A collective sigh whooshed out from us all as we watched the gates slowly open. One hurdle crossed. Now we must convince both kings' guards that we belonged.

"What do we do if someone denies our claim?" Kjell whispered.

I set my lips in a grim line and answered. "We stick to our story no matter what. The more confident we act, the less they will question us."

"This is going to be fun," Amund said.

Brant snorted. "We seriously need to discuss your ideas of fun, Amund. You are beginning to worry me."

"You are just now worrying about him?" Delvin asked.

"I tend to be unobservant until it is absolutely necessary."

"You say unobservant where others might say

dimwitted." I teased.

"Do not fret, general," Brant said coolly. "I will retaliate."

"Please refrain until after we have live through the ordeal," I said dryly. "Now, shut your traps and pay attention."

"I cannot wait to see you panting at the princess' feet." Brant chuckled.

"What makes you think she will not be panting at *my* feet?" I asked, forgetting I had just told him to be silent.

"Because she has breasts and you do not." The other men attempted to cover their laughter with coughs. My thoughts were racing with everything we had learned. I needed to get my mind back to reality. The lives of my men, and my clan, were depending on it.

# CHAPTER Ten

"IT IS OFFICIAL. I AM MARRYING A DEMON. SURE, HE MAY LOOK LIKE A MAN. HE MAY WALK AND TALK LIKE A MAN, BUT A MAN HE IS NOT. HE IS THE SPAWN OF SOME EVIL CREATURE, SENT TO EARTH TO TORMENT ME. THAT IS THE ONLY LOGICAL CONCLUSION THAT CAN BE DRAWN. NO MAN WOULD TREAT HIS FUTURE WIFE AND HER FAMILY THE WAY CATHAL HAS TREATED US."

~DIARY OF PRINCESS ALLETE AUVRAY

As I stared up at the ceiling in my bedchambers, my eyes refused to become heavy. I had finally convinced my mother and sister to retire to their own rooms, assuring them that I was not going to throw myself from my window to escape my fate, though I was sorely tempted. I was more concerned about my mother's mental state much more than my own. She was much more upset at Cathal's behavior than I had originally anticipated. I hoped she would not do anything rash.

Trepidation about the following day kept me from my rest. I would be expected to spend most of my day in the company of my future husband and I would rather clean out the chamber pots in every room in the castle than be with Cathal. I chuckled silently as I imagined the shocked faces of the castle court if they saw me carrying chamber pots in the dress Cathal expected me to wear.

"Ugh!" I groaned. "Why could he not just be a kind old man looking for companionship in his old age?" I asked the quiet room. I wouldn't have romance, of course, but at least I wouldn't be disrespected—or worse—fear for my safety. I suppose I could wish that my circumstances were different until I was blue in the face, but that would not change anything.

After another hour of tossing and turning, I finally drifted off into a restless sleep. Dreams of a dragon with the head of Cathal tormented my mind, leaving me feeling shaky and overwhelmed. No matter how many times I told myself it was just a dream, the fear in my belly would not diminish.

When my eyes snapped open the following morning, I felt as though a heard of wild boar had done a jig in my head. The pain was nauseating. I climbed out of bed, grabbed my robe, and wrapped it tightly around me. There was a knock at my door and my stomach dropped. I was not ready to face Cathal. I walked slowly toward the door and jumped when a second, and louder knock, rang out.

I took a deep breath as I grasped the handle and pulled the door open. I came face to face with a broad chest clothed by a palace guard uniform. For once, it wasn't Captain Clay. That thought flew out the window when I tilted my head back, and still farther back, as I looked up at the person who owned the impressive chest. My eyes widened as I saw the stern silver eyes staring down at me. He was breathtaking. There really was no other way to describe the fierce looking man before me. He was not pretty. He was too masculine for pretty. He was striking. His unwavering stare and large, solid frame was incredibly intimidating and yet I was not afraid of him. Something in his gaze was...protective of me. I knew that he would never hurt me.

"Princess." The man finally spoke and his deep voice caused chill bumps to rise all over my arms.

"Who are you?" I asked, once I had finally found the good sense to close my mouth and quit drooling like an adolescent staring at her first crush.

"Forgive me for bothering you, your highness," the guard rumbled. "Brant," he motioned to the even larger mountain standing behind him, who I had yet to even notice, "and I have been assigned to your guard detail."

"Uh-huh," I said slowly. My eyes narrowed as I glanced at the one called Brant and then back at the vision in front of me that had spoken. "And who exactly are you?"

His lips twitched as if he was amused by my scrutiny. He bowed his head slightly. "I am Torben."

"Torben," I repeated as if he was speaking another language. What was wrong with me? A handsome face and mesmerizing voice seemed to be enough to turn me into a brainless ninny. But really, what kind of name was Torben? I don't think I'd ever heard it before. It certainly did not sound native.

"Yes, Torben. I know my name is unique. I'm not sure how my mother came up with it. I've asked her plenty of times, but she never gives me a straight answer."

"Uh-huh," I responded, once again showing my brilliant linguistic abilities. I stood there staring up at him stupidly while he stared back at me. Torben did not seem to feel awkward about the silence between us. He stood stock, still simply staring at me, as if he would not mind spending the entire day doing just that. I, on the other hand, fought the urge to shift from foot to foot under his intensity.

The other one, Brant, cleared his throat and the trance between us lifted. My brain, which I knew I still possessed somewhere in my head, suddenly reengaged. "My father did not inform me that I was getting a new guard," I said, watching closely to see if my words caused any insecurity in Torben. I knew many of the palace guards and certainly all the ones assigned to my protection. My father would have informed me if there was to be a change among the men.

"I am sure he has not had time to tell you, just yet. It may not be my place to tell you, but he was concerned that the fire that was started last eve might be more than just an accident," Torben answered calmly. "He wanted to make sure you were protected, especially with all the visitors in the castle."

Either this man was truly my new assigned guard, or he was as smooth as churned butter at lying. I couldn't tell for certain, but he didn't feel evil to me. I didn't have any supernatural ability to discern a person's intentions. However, my power has, at times in the past, warned me about danger. I didn't understand how it worked, but I guessed it was a defense mechanism to alert me when I in the process of healing someone. During those times, my attention was completely focused on my task and I was vulnerable, so knowing if danger is close at hand is important.

This *sixth sense,* as I had come to call it, had saved me in the past. Once I came upon a rabbit that had been attacked by a predator. As I knelt to check the frightened creature's wounds, I was completely unaware that a wolf was hiding close by in the foliage. Just as I placed my hands upon the rabbit to heal the scratches and bites, an overwhelming feeling of being watched came over me. I jumped up and yelled, spinning in place. The wolf, startled, matched my yelp, and bolted away, leaving the rabbit and I behind. Since that day, I've never ignored my *sixth sense* when it tells me danger is near.

"Princess, are you all right?" Torben asked me. I shook my head and refocused. His voice was musical, but that wasn't what had drawn my attention. It was the large hand that was currently resting on my shoulder. He was touching me.

"You are touching me," I said stupidly, as if the man did not know he had placed his hand on my shoulder.

A small smile tugged at his full lips. "I am," he said without apology. "I called your name several times but you did not respond."

I looked from his hand back to his face. "Oh." That was my brilliant response. I shook my head and took a step backward. I needed to put some distance between myself and this new guard. Something about him, I didn't know what, disarmed me.

"Thank you for introducing yourself, Torben. I need to ready myself for the day. If that is all, good day." I said all of that with the speed of an exuberant child and then shrugged off his hand before quickly shutting the door right in his handsome, yet confused face.

I stared at the closed door as though if I looked at it long enough I would be able to see straight through it to the man beyond. After several minutes, I slowly turned away from the door and let out a shuttering breath. I had never felt so shaken over anyone. Do not get me wrong, I had noticed handsome men in the past, but none of them caught my attention the way Torben had. Something about him captivated me, which, in turn, made me sound like a bumbling idiot. I shook my head as if I could remove the image of him from my mind and began my morning routine. It would be the first time I would have to spend the entire day with King Cathal. The thought was nauseating. Being in his presence was the equivalent of allowing chickens to peck out my eyes, only the chickens would probably be better conversationalists.

A half hour later, there was another knock at the door. Instead of walking over to it, I simply stared at it as though it was a three-headed monster preparing to devour me. My heart began to beat painfully hard in my chest and my palms grew damp. I wasn't sure whose presence I feared most on the other side of the door—Cathal or Torben.

The choice was suddenly taken out of my hands when the door opened and in walked Lidia. My handmaiden glanced out into the hall, confusion marring her brow before she closed the door and turned to face me.

"I was not aware that you were getting new guards," she said.

"I was not either," I said with a sigh. I watched as Lidia moved about the room, making the bed and straightening pillows that were already straight. "I can tell you have more to say on the matter, Lidia. By all means, speak already."

She shrugged her shoulders as if it was of no consequence. "I was just thinking that they were both quite handsome."

"You make it sound as though guards cannot be handsome."

Lidia tsked at me. "When have you ever seen a guard that looked like those two?" She motioned toward the door.

I had no argument. Torben and even Brant, I could admit, were both exceedingly handsome. "Have you ever seen them before?" I asked her.

Lidia shook her head. "I would not have forgotten either of them nor would I have failed to have mentioned it. They are new. Those two will be the talk of the castle staff."

I smiled at her. "That, my dear friend, is quite true."

Lidia, quiet though she may be, did enjoy sharing any

tidbits with me that she heard or saw outside of the castle. She was never quite as graphic as Dayna, but every bit as eager.

Just as Lidia was assisting me with removing my night clothes, the door flew open again, giving me a brief glimpse of a wide eyed Torben. I jerked my gown up over my bare shoulder and tore my eyes from his to glare at my sister.

Dayna slammed the door with just as much fervor as she had opened it.

"Have you not heard of knocking?" I snapped at her, embarrassment at Torben having seen me in such a state burning up my flesh.

"Sure, I have *heard* of knocking. But why should I have to knock to enter my own sister's room? And besides, I assumed by this hour you would already be changed and ready for the day," Dayna countered. "How was I to know that you were dragging around your room like a sickly snail?"

"Can you think of one reason why I should be jumping for joy to begin the day?"

A mischievous smile lit my sister's face. "Well, I can think of two and they are both standing just outside your room. Where has Father been hiding those two?"

"I have no idea. They were there when I awoke this morn. Now would you please *lock* the door so that no one else barges in while I am changing?"

"Yes, yes," she waved me off. "Get ready, but while you are doing so we must discuss our strategy."

"What strategy?" I asked as Lidia slid my dressing gown over my head and then held out one of Cathal's dresses for me to step into. The fabric was slick and cool. It felt good against my heated skin. But once she raised it all the way up and I slipped my arms in it, I realized how little it covered and my skin flushed even hotter. I glanced down at the overabundance of cleavage that was pressed up and out by the cut of the dress.

"The strategy we shall employ to convince King Cathal that you are not the bride for him," Dayna answered as she tapped her chin. The wheels were turning in my sister's head and I did not know if I should be thankful or scared.

"Perhaps he is not a man who likes breasts," I pointed to my own. "Since mine seem to be handing out engraved invitations, he will be repulsed and sail back to Tara without delay."

Dayna made a sound between a snort and a laugh. "Breasts are like sunshine, my dear sister. Everyone likes them."

Lidia scrunched her nose up at the offensive gown. "I cannot believe that this is the fashion in France."

"The French encourage embracing the beauty of the feminine form," Dayna said absently.

"Can they not embrace it behind closed doors?" I said as I walked over to the mirror and stared, wide eyed at the woman before me. "I am not leaving this room...not like this," I declared.

"I am a bit surprised he would allow you to be paraded around like that. Won't he be jealous? The eyes of every man in the castle will be upon you." Dayna asked, having abandoned, for the time being, her plans to derail the impending nuptials.

I stared at my image, feeling like a woman of the night. How could I hold my head up as a princess of my people while dressed like a harlot?

"No," I finally responded. "Cathal is a man who is absolutely confident in his own position. He wants other men to see me and know that they could never have me. He wants other men to be jealous of him, lording over them what they could never touch."

The three of us stared at the mirror for several moments in silence until I finally threw my hands up. "There is nothing to be done about it now." I turned from the mirror and motioned for Lidia to follow. "Could you please just do something simple with it?" I asked pointing to the mass of hair still mused from my sleep.

"I have taken it upon myself to be your escort, sister mine," Dayna informed me as she flopped down on the chair across from me.

"Do not feel that you must. I will have my guards with me."

She grinned back at me and winked. "Oh, believe me, it has not slipped my notice that you will have those two handsome beasts with you."

"Handsome beasts?" I asked while Lidia giggled.

Dayna shrugged shamelessly. "I may be only sixteen, mind you I am very close to seventeen, but that does not mean I do not know a prime stallion when I see one. Or two," she added cheekily.

I pointed my finger at her, attempting to sound as stern as possible. "Well, you just make sure you don't suddenly develop an interest in equestrianism, Dayna Auvray."

"I think interest isn't a strong enough word. I'm thinking of taking up trick riding."

I closed my eyes and rubbed my temple, attempting to keep the headache I felt coming on at bay. "Bloody hell, you will be the death of me."

# CHAPTER Eleven

"THERE HAVE BEEN VERY FEW TIMES IN MY LIFE WHEN I
HAVE HAD THE WIND KNOCKED OUT OF ME, AND IT'S NEVER
HAPPENED WHEN I WASN'T IN A FIGHT."

~ TORBEN

"THAT IS TO BE your wife?" Brant asked.

I heard my friend's words, but I was still too busy staring at the door that had just been closed in my face a second time. My brain was stuck on the exposed collar bone and shoulder of the woman who held me captive.

I felt a smack to the back of my head and whipped around with a snarl on my face. "Mind yourself, Brant."

He held up his hands. "I meant no offense, but you seemed a little distracted. I do not blame you. She is quite a lovely piece." Brant's eyes flashed with something that looked like amusement. "Not to mention, she is pure as the driven snow. A woman who has known the touch of a man would never turn that shade of red."

I felt my muscles tense at the fact that my next in command was having such thoughts regarding Allete. Pure as the driven snow was just another way of saying she had never been unclothed in front of a man. "It would behoove you to keep your thoughts far from the skin of Allete and whether she has been touched by a man," I snapped. For whatever reason, one I was not about to examine too closely, I felt very protective of the small, feisty princess.

"All teasing aside," Brant said after several minutes of silence. "She is beautiful. I hope the prophecy is correct, and she is the woman who you will have. You deserve something beautiful in this life of war we live."

"When did you become so philosophical?" I jested.

Brant shrugged his large shoulders. "I have layers."

I chuckled. "Yes, you are certainly like an onion. Peel back the layers to find something underneath, but by doing so, a stench is released that brings tears to the eyes of those around you."

"You are simply a riot," Brant said dryly. "Oh, and just to ease your mind, I have no designs on your woman. Now the lively one who just whipped past us with only a passing glance, she is intriguing." He licked his lips. "She is more to my taste."

I groaned. "We are on a mission. Please refrain from attempting to bed a host of the English women."

Brant reached out and clapped me on the shoulder. "Do not worry. I do not want to bed a host of them. Just that one." He nodded his head toward the door where the woman in question had disappeared.

"Did you notice the likeness? And the clothes? She is probably Allete's younger sister," I said, crossing my arms and giving him my best *do as I tell you* glare.

"Relax, Torben. I will not jeopardize the mission for a gown...even if it is royal and encasing such a beauty."

I rolled my eyes. "Bloody hell, when did you become such a wielder of words?" Footsteps moving quickly from the right side of the corridor caused us both straighten and slip into the roles we were playing.

Under the pretense of acting as a watchful guard, I jerked my head to the side to look at the approaching man who was striding toward us. He was tall, though still a few inches shorter than myself. I imagined the women probably classified him as handsome, though there was a cruelty that danced in his narrowed eyes. His mouth was thin and tightly stretched across his face, as though he was perpetually offended by everything around him. The man stunk of wealth and entitlement. He was the type of man who believed everyone to be beneath him, and he proved it when he opened his mouth to speak.

"Are you going to open the door, or do you need a heralding trumpet to prompt you to do your job?"

My jaw tightened, and I was sure I was going to break some teeth. "Forgive me, my lord,"

The man interrupted me. "Your Highness," he snapped.

"No, I am simply the guard," I retorted. Brant attempted to cover his laugh with a cough.

The man in front of me was seething, which only made me want to laugh.

"Not you, you idiot. I was speaking of *me*. You do not address me as 'my lord,' you address me as 'Your Highness.' I am Cathal, the king of Tara."

He paused, looking expectantly at me as though I was going to break out into applause. I simply returned his stare.

"Now, open the door," Cathal ordered.

"I cannot," I said. "The lady is still dressing. I am sure you would want to protect her reputation and virtue, seeing as how you are to wed her." I knew I was walking a fine line with the king, but it was so easy to bait the man, which might have been the only thing that kept me from punching him.

I turned, pushing my body in between his and the door, and knocked gently. As soon as the door opened, I stepped quickly inside, gently moving the woman in front of me aside and shutting the door behind me. When I looked up, I saw three sets of eyes staring at me. One set was quite appreciative, one set was clearly confused and shocked, and the third set was curious. I dismissed the appreciative and curious pair and looked at the woman who was staring at me with her mouth opening and closing, unsure of what to say. Butterflies assaulted my stomach as I took in her beautiful form, followed by a roaring dragon that threatened to consume me as I realized what she was wearing. I clenched my fist, pushing down the rage, and taking a deep breath, steadied myself.

"Forgive the intrusion, my lady, and my also impertinence, but where the hell is the rest of your dress?" I said, bowing my head slightly though my eyes never left her. "King Cathal is waiting for you, and I did not want to let him enter until I knew you were appropriate. It was a good thing I did not let him in, considering that ..." I could not even call it a dress. There was practically no top half; I would be more apt to call it a skirt with suspenders. Allete stood and stalked toward me, stopping when she was a few feet away.

"And what about you?"

"Excuse me?"

"Do you think you can come into my chambers any time you like? You are a guard, not my nursemaid. My life is yours to protect, not my honor. And what if I wasn't decent? I could have your head for storming in here." She was angry that I had called her out on the scrap of material she was pretending was a dress. But she had a point. I had no right to enter her room, of course. Perhaps I should not have acted so hastily. The idea of Cathal alone with her, however, twisted in my gut like rotten meat and spurned on my rash behavior.

"You are right, my lady. I should not have intruded, but I did not know how else to keep him from entering. I know that your father would not wish the man in your bedchamber before the wedding." I fought to keep my eyes on her face, though I was man enough to admit that they did drop to the ample bust that was threatening to make a full appearance. I wanted to throw a blanket over her so that no other would ever see her in such a state. Why in the gods would she put on something so revealing?

Allete held my gaze a moment longer but did not acknowledge my words. Instead she turned to one of the other women in the room. "Dayna, this is Torben, the new guard I was telling you about. Torben, this is my sister, Dayna. And the beauty who answered the door is Lidia, my handmaiden."

I bowed to each of them. "Ladies." It did not escape my notice that Dayna was clothed much more appropriately than her older sister.

"Please allow the king to enter," Allete commanded. She pulled her shoulders back and raised her chin slightly.

My blood boiled, and it wasn't because she had given me, a clan general, an order. Rather, I was incensed she was going to let that slime into her chambers. "Perhaps you should meet him in the dining hall after you have put on something more akin to what your lovely sister is wearing," I suggested through clenched teeth.

Her eyes snapped to mine quick as lightning. "My attire is not your concern."

"I am your guard, Your Highness. Anything involving your person is my concern."

"I think you mean anything involving my safety," she attempted to correct me. "My choice of gown does not affect my safety."

"Forgive me if I disagree. I will have to fight off every

male in the castle if you parade around looking like—"

"Be very careful how you end that sentence, Torben," she seethed.

"Every man's desire," I bit out.

"Every man?" she asked coyly, her demeanor changing without warning.

"Do you really want to play with me, Princess?" I challenged as I took a step toward her. My six and a half foot frame towered over her diminutive form. She tilted her head back to look up at me. Apprehension filled her light brown eyes, but no fear, for which I was glad. I did not want her to fear me, just follow my instructions regarded her safety. I nearly laughed to myself. It was apparent that Princess Allete was not about to turn belly up and submit.

Smothered laughter reminded me that we were not alone. Allete seemed to draw my attention so completely that everyone else faded into the background while in her presence—a dangerous weakness to have.

"Open the door," she all but growled at me.

"I will not," I refused. "He has no business being in your chambers."

"I have chaperones." She pointed to her sister and Lidia.

I snorted. "Two females. What kind of safety do they offer if he decides to take what he already thinks is his? Especially when you offer it up in such desirable wrapping."

Allete gasped at my blatant reference to the intimacy between man and wife. I could not stop the grin that lifted on my lips. She was beautiful, but especially so when she was angry. She looked like an avenging angel. All she needed was a glowing sword.

Allete stomped her foot. The laughter I had held back rolled out. "Did you just stomp your foot?"

"You have been my guard all of an hour, and already

you are worse than Clay." She stopped abruptly and narrowed her eyes on me. "Where is Clay?" She glanced around the room as if he might suddenly appear. "I was so surprised by your appearance earlier that I did not think to ask."

"Your previous guard has been reassigned. He will be a liaison to your betrothed's own men."

"Do not call him that," Allete snapped.

"Do not call him your previous guard?" My brow drew together as I watched her begin to pace.

"Not that. I meant, do not call Cathal my betrothed."

I tilted my head, trying to understand her sudden change in demeanor. "But he is your betrothed."

She was in my face faster than I would have thought possible. Her words were bitten out through clenched teeth, and the emotion that flowed with them fueled my own rage. "He is a man who made the right promises and offered the highest price to obtain me. That is not a betrothed; that is a merchant, and I am simply his merchandise."

"You do not want to marry him?" I could not stop myself from asking. The question seemed to bring Allete back from her angry rant. She straightened her dress before turning away, no doubt in the hopes that it would go unnoticed that she was attempting to pull the bodice of the dress higher.

"I do not know why we are speaking of this." Her voice was once again formal and reserved. "Please let Cathal know I will meet him in the dining hall."

I continued to stare at her, knowing she could feel my eyes boring into her.

Finally, she turned around, holding her head high. She wore her responsibility like a heavy cloak and it showed in the weariness etched on her face. "If you are still standing there instead of doing my bidding because of the dress, then rest assured I will not be wearing it. Now please leave so that I may change."

I turned to go, making sure to keep the smile to myself. As I reached the door I heard her say, "I am not changing for you. I am changing to preserve my dignity. You were simply the vessel that was used to help me see that."

"Whatever you need to tell yourself, Princess," I said as I looked over my shoulder and winked at her. I saw her reach for a hair brush and pull her arm back to throw it. I quickly stepped out and heard a thunk against the door only made me want to laugh more.

The grin was quickly wiped from my face as I nearly bumped into Cathal.

"Well?" he growled. "Why the hell were you in there so long?"

"We were discussing the logistics of her safety today as you both move about the grounds," I answered smoothly. "She asked me to inform you that she will meet you in the dining hall momentarily."

I glanced over the king's shoulder to see Brant nearly doubled over in silent laughter. When Cathal turned abruptly, my second-in-command straightened faster than a flying arrow and wiped the humor from his face. We watched as Cathal practically shook with anger at having been rebuffed by Allete.

"I don't take orders from you," he growled, attempting to take a step around me and push through the door.

"Stop," I said simply. I did not move, and I did not raise my voice, but the king froze in his tracks. "I am not ordering you. But you will honor the queen's wishes."

He turned and stared at me; I could practically hear his teeth grinding together. I could see the man weighing his options. He was incensed that neither I nor Allete were bending to his wishes. At the same time, it was clear that he didn't want to cause an altercation with Allete's guard while trying to force his way into her bedroom. I held his gaze without blinking, ready to react in an instant if I needed to. Without taking my eyes off Cathal, I could feel Brant tensing himself to act as well. After several long moments, he took a step backward.

"Albric will hear of this," he spat, turning on his heel and stomping loudly away.

"That is a dangerous one," Brant muttered.

I nodded. "He is the type of man who is always just on the edge of violence. Instead of trying to avoid it, he is eagerly waiting for an opportunity to partake in a fight, but only when he knows he has the upper hand." I knew his type, and it made me sick to think of Allete married to a man like that.

The door opened behind me, and I stepped to the side, turning to face the ladies emerging. My eyes immediately sought out Allete. I nearly sighed when I saw she had changed into a dress with a bodice that came up over her collar bone. The more skin that was covered, the happier I would be.

Her eyes met mine briefly, and her skin took on the lovely flush I was beginning to thoroughly enjoy. Dayna grabbed her sister's hand and pulled her forward. I did not miss the wink she shot Brant. I made a cutting motion across my neck. He knew exactly what I meant. Pursue her and die. But it would not be by my hand. I imagine King Albric would not be too keen on his youngest daughter becoming entangled with a guard. And he would probably be even angrier if the guard turned out to be a Viking warrior in disguise.

We took our spots on either side of the women, keeping in step with them. My eyes repeatedly landed on Allete, but

I continued to scan everything around us. After the short amount of time I had spent with her, I knew she would be perfect for my clan because of the fire that burned within her. I was no longer protecting just the Princess of England; I was protecting my future bride. I conveniently ignored the fact that she was currently betrothed to another and that I was going to have to endure their fruitless courtship. Instead, I focused on the future encounters and banter that I would share with Allete, thanks to my proximity to her as her guard. It had been a while since I'd truly enjoyed something. Getting under the princess's skin was something I enjoyed.

She was nothing like I imagined. The spoiled image I had built up in my head was the furthest thing from who she truly was. I could tell that she was a good person, and my heart broke when I remembered how she had described her situation with Cathal—a young, innocent girl willing to marry a stranger because her father had said she must. She held herself regally, but in no way did she appear to be looking down on those around her. Allete was a girl on the verge of becoming an incredible woman, and if she married Cathal, he would tear her down, piece by beautiful piece.

By the gods, I was not about to let that happen. Even if she were not meant to be mine, I could not let a woman be wed to that poor excuse for a man.

"I am glad to see you could finally join us." Cathal's voice, both his words and the vehemence in which he said them, grabbed my attention.

"Do forgive me, my lord," Allete said sweetly. "I did not sleep well last night, which caused me some lethargy this morn."

When Allete reached the chair where she was to sit, Cathal did not stand to help her with the chair. Allete simply stood there, smiling at everyone.

*Cheeky female*, I thought.

I stepped forward and pulled the chair back so she could step around it and then pushed it forward as she sat down. She glanced back at me, surprise filling her eyes.

"Thank you," she said.

I bowed. "My lady."

The next words out of Cathal's mouth made it perfectly clear that I was going to have to remind myself all day long of all the reasons I could not kill the King of Tara.

The king leaned over to Allete in the pretense of whispering, but speaking in a normal voice. "I thought I instructed you to wear the dresses I brought you. I prefer to be able to enjoy the sight of the body that will soon belong to me."

She looked up into his eyes and blinked innocently. "This is one of the dresses you brought me. But it is still hard to let go of my things, so I had it altered a bit."

It was then I noticed the dress was the same one she had been wearing when I had been in her room. She had simply added some fabric to the top of it. I chuckled and shook my head slightly. Yes, she was perfect for Clan Hakon. She was perfect for me.

# CHAPTER Twelve

"I HAVE NEVER BEEN BOTH SO UTTERLY FRUSTRATED BY A
HUMAN BEING, YET SO ATTRACTED TO HIM AT THE SAME TIME.
AFTER SPENDING ONLY HALF AN HOUR WITH TORBEN, MY NEW
MYSTERIOUS GUARD, ALREADY HE IS ALL I CAN THINK ABOUT.
WELL, I WILL HAVE TO NIP THAT IN THE BUD QUICKLY. EVEN
IF IT WERE POSSIBLE TO BE WITH SOMEONE OF HIS STATION,
WHICH IT IS NOT, HE WOULD DRIVE ME TO JUMP OFF A CLIFF
WITHIN HOURS OF BEGINNING OUR COURTSHIP."

~DIARY OF PRINCESS ALLETE AUVRAY

WHILE STARING OUT AT the bright flowers and rich foliage, I contemplated all the ways I could kill myself in the garden as I stood next to Cathal. This place had always been a sight that inspired joy and happiness, but all I could think about was whether we had any plants containing deadly thorns. That was something I needed to speak to the gardener about. Surely, having a supply of deadly plants on hand would be quite useful. Not only for the poisoning of a high-ranking dignitary, but, perhaps more importantly, for use by forlorn princesses who need to put themselves out of their misery.

"What sorts of plants do you have in *your* gardens?" I found myself asking the king.

Cathal looked down at me as if I were a child who

had just asked an ignorant question. But he answered nonetheless. "I prefer exotic, unusual plants."

My brow rose. "Really?" I turned my body slightly so I was facing him. "What kind, exactly?"

"Flowers from all over the world. Vines the size of a man's leg, flowers as bright as the sun, and a few deadly bushes, of course."

"Deadly?"

He chuckled, and it was not a happy sound. It sent chills down my back.

"As I said, I like unusual plants."

"Are those the plants you used to kill your previous wives?" Dayna's voice carried from several feet away.

My jaw clenched as I turned toward my sister. I was too afraid to look at Cathal's reaction. I shot daggers at Torben and Brant, as if it was their fault that Dayna could not keep her mouth closed at the proper times.

"You are one of Allete's sisters?" Cathal asked casually.

"I am. We have actually already met."

"Well, I am sure you understand why I would have forgotten you. Standing next to your stunning sister would cause anyone to become insignificant."

My head whipped around so fast that I nearly lost my balance. A warm hand caught my elbow helping me right myself, and I knew it was Torben. He did not move back again but lingered only a few feet from me.

"I do not like you saying such things to my sister, my lord," I said as respectfully as I could at that moment.

"Then your sister should learn her place and keep her mouth shut." The cold, calculating look in his eyes caused me to take a step back.

"I think it is time for lunch," I said, choosing to ignore his harsh comment. I turned to go but was stopped by Cathal's rough hand on my arm as he jerked me back to stand beside him.

"You are my betrothed; you will walk with me. Your pet guard dog can give us some space."

My body was stiff as a rod as I walked beside him. His hand remained on my arm, and it took every ounce of self-control I possessed not to jerk it from him. I did not want him touching me. I did not even want to breathe the same air as the vile man beside me. I was beginning to believe that perhaps he had not killed his wives after all. Maybe they had taken their own lives.

A WEEK HAD PASSED since my first full day spent with Cathal, and each day he had grown more and more aggressive. There had been several times during this week that I noticed Brant holding Torben back when Cathal had grabbed me roughly or snapped at me. The way Torben watched me, the way his barely contained anger stayed just on the surface, was peculiar. He was not like any guard I had ever had. Sure, they had protected me, but none of them looked at me the way Torben did. He watched me as if my life was the only thing that mattered to him. I had to continually remind myself that I could not be with him. Even if I were not already betrothed to Cathal, my father would never allow me to marry a guard.

By the eighth night of the courtship, I felt I could bear Cathal no longer. My body was shaking with rage by the time he left me at my chambers after the evening meal. Surprisingly, he had behaved himself at dinner, no doubt putting on an act for my parents. But as soon as we were out of their presence, the demon was back.

His words echoed in my mind as I closed the door.

"Until I break you, and I will break you, I will have to

settle for enjoying your beauty and form. If you are not willing to respond to my words, then you will respond to my touch."

He grabbed my arms, and when Torben and Brant went to intercept him, two of Cathal's own men stepped from the shadows, cutting them off. His hold was tight, no doubt leaving bruises on my arms.

"All day I have asked you to do things, and you have repeatedly ignored me. Every time you disobey me, there will be consequences."

I thought he was going to kiss me, but instead he darted forward and bit me hard on my shoulder. I gasped and tried to step away, but his grasp was as strong as iron bindings. I could hear Torben behind me attempting to get to me, snarling and cursing at the guards who would not move. Cathal's teeth sank in deeper until I felt the trickle of blood down my arm. When he finally pulled away, his eyes were gleaming with madness.

"You are mine. I will mark you all over your luscious body until you understand that." He turned on his heel and walked away, as if he had not just gnawed on me like a dog with a bone.

His men waited until he was out of sight before they left. It was when they turned that I saw they had pulled their short swords on Torben and Brant. My eyes widened when I looked down at Torben's abdomen and saw blood seeping through his uniform. I immediately felt my magic growing inside of me—the need to heal overpowering my self-preservation.

I looked up at him and pleaded with my eyes as I spoke. "Please, do not tell anyone about this. Pretend it was a dream if you must. You." I pointed to Brant. "Make sure no one sees this."

I lifted Torben's jerkin and placed my hand over the

wound.

Torben hissed and spoke through clenched teeth. "If I was going to have a dream about you, Princess, I would not be injured, and you would have considerably less clothing on."

I pressed a little harder than necessary and took satisfaction in his grunt of pain. Then I pushed the outside world away and focused my energy on the wound. The chant rose in my mind, and I spoke it without thought.

"Wounded flesh, damaged skin,
Feel my power, let me in.
Let my light heal you,
My energy fill you.
Veins that carry life,
Rejoin the cut,
Relieve the pain and the strife."

I felt the healing power flowing into Torben, but that was not all I felt. There, just beyond the wound, was a chord—gold and thick. It seemed to be reaching for my magic, coaxing my power to itself. I felt myself wanting to respond, and I did. But the minute my light touched the chord, an overwhelming emotion assailed me. I pulled my hand away as if I had been burned. I looked up at Torben. Being so close to him only emphasized how much larger than me he was. My eyes were wide, and my mouth probably looked as though it was going to drop to the floor.

I pulled my hand from under his shirt and stepped back. My eyes never left his. After a few moments, the shock from the golden chord left me, and I looked around. It was then that I realized that neither Torben nor Brant seemed amazed about what I had done. In fact, it was almost as if they had been aware that I had such a power.

I took another step back when Torben made a move to close the distance between us. Brant placed his hand on Torben's arm.

"Let her be," the large man told his friend.

Torben's eyes bore into mine as he spoke. "That piece of vermin bit her. At least let me make sure it has stopped bleeding."

While I said nothing, I secretly wanted Torben to touch me. I wanted him to ensure that I was safe and well. I wanted him to hold me and tell me everything would be okay. I wanted him to shelter me from storm I had found myself in. And for that reason, I turned and rushed into my room, slamming the door behind me and jamming the lock into place.

I slid down to the floor, my back pressed firmly against the wood. I heard Torben speak through the door.

"Allete, you have healed me. Now I must do what I can for you. Please let me tend to your shoulder." His worried voice wrapped around me and eased a little of the fear I was feeling.

"Please." My voice cracked, and I tried again. "Please, just get Lidia. She will tend to me."

I heard his growl and then muffled words. It was no surprise to me when I heard his voice again. "I sent Brant to find her. Can I get you anything? Can I help in any way?"

An insane thought came to me, and I had to bite down on my tongue before I blurted out that he could help by killing my fiancé. *Madness*, I thought to myself. If Torben killed Cathal, and I was pretty sure he would if I only asked, then he would be hanged for murder. I would never let someone die for me. Certainly Cathal's death did not bother me in the least, but the thought of Torben dead almost caused me to retch.

I shook my head and rubbed the tears from my face.

It was okay for me to care for Torben because he cared for me. I cared for my friends among the castle staff. That was all this was. I loved Lidia, and I cared deeply for other workers that I had come to know. Torben was irritating, but it was apparent he was a man of good character, and that was why I was attracted to him. Hell, anyone looked better than Cathal at this point.

"If you will not let me in, will you at least talk to me, so that I can know you are okay?" The anguish in his voice nearly broke my heart.

"What is there to say?" I asked as I bit my lip, hoping that my tears would not be evident in the sound of my voice.

I heard Torben curse. Apparently, I could not disguise my pain as well as I had hoped.

"What is your favorite color?" he asked.

I frowned. I had just been bitten by a mad man. I had healed a stab wound. I had discovered … something, some kind of magical connection between Torben and me, and now he was asking me what my favorite color was? Perhaps I hadn't fully healed him, and he was now going into shock?

"Silver," I said instinctively, trying to pretend I wasn't elated just hearing him speak.

"What is your favorite time of day?"

I furrowed my brow as I considered his question. "Do people really have a favorite time of day?"

"I do, or at least I believe I will," he answered.

"What do you mean?"

"Morning." His deep voice rumbled. "Morning will be my favorite time of day because one day I will have a woman to wake up beside me to share the sunrise. I picture her in my mind, as I open my eyes to see her form lying beside me, her hair all a mess as the morning light streams across her face and down her body. I will run my fingertips across her cheek down to her full lips, feeling the silky skin that is mine alone. The warmth of our bodies will keep me in bed too long, but I will not care because as long as she is beside me every morning, I can face anything."

*Whoa.* I sat with my back leaned up against the door, mere feet from a man who could feel so deeply, who could treasure the gift of a good wife. Just when the tears had stopped, they began again, but I kept them quiet this time. What he had said was beautiful. It was what I wanted as well but would never have. My mind could not help but imagine the things Torben had described, putting myself in the place of the woman in his bed. What would it be like to wake up to the warmth of his large body pressed against mine? Would my heart be able to withstand the overwhelming emotions that would flow through me when he touched my lips?

"Allete?" Torben said, his voice slightly hesitant.

"I am here," I answered.

"Did I say something wrong?"

I shook my head but then remembered that he would not be able to see me. "No. That is the problem, Torben. You said everything right. That woman in your bed will be very lucky indeed."

"She might not feel that way after being stuck with me for a few decades," he chuckled. "I am a warrior first and a lover second."

"A warrior is what is needed first. A warrior is what keeps her safe, protected, and you alive so you can be a lover to her. I say, be the best warrior you can be to ensure you always return to her." I did not know where these words came from, but they felt right.

I heard some commotion outside of the door, and then my sister's voice. "Move out of my way, or I will skewer you where you stand."

That brought a smile to my face.

"We are not the enemy," Brant said gruffly. "I told you it was Cathal who hurt her."

"You are her guards, are you not? So why in bloody hell were you not guarding her?"

"Dayna." Torben's voice, calm but firm, spoke up. "Cathal had his own men here. We could not have stopped them without resorting violence. If we had killed his guards, it would have reflected poorly on your father."

"Well, you could have done something," she spat.

Deciding she had abused them enough, I stood, wiping the remaining tears from my eyes, and opened the door. The sight before me was quite comical. Dayna had a short sword in each hand. She had backed Brant up against the wall with one of the swords dangerously close to parts I was sure the poor man would not want to lose. My sister always did have a mean streak.

The other sword was held up to fend off Torben, who stood with his hands raised, trying, but failing, to make his bulky frame look nonthreatening. When their heads turned to look at me, Brant made his move. One hand grabbed Dayna's wrist and relieved her of the sword, while the other wrapped around her waist, turning her until her back was pressed to his chest. At the same time, Torben grabbed the other wrist and took that sword. Their movements were coordinated, as if they knew instinctively what the other one was thinking.

My eyes were wide, and I was sure matched Dayna's dazed look.

"What just happened?" Dayna said a little breathlessly.

"You made a fatal mistake, little warrior," Brant said gruffly, though his eyes gleamed with humor.

"You took your eyes off your opponent," Torben

explained. "You allowed yourself to be distracted. It is a deadly error to make, and one you will only make once."

My lips tilted up slightly as I watched my sister's face redden as she frowned at Torben's jest.

"Thank you for the tip," she bit out and attempted to pull away from Brant's hold. "Let me go."

"Nay, I like where you are," Brant said as he winked at me.

Dayna shot me a look that promised retaliation if I did not interfere. She had come to my defense so I decided not to let her torture continue. "Brant, please release my sister."

The large man let his hand run across her stomach to her waist where he squeezed her gently before letting her go. Dayna whipped around and glared at him. Brant was not ashamed in the least.

"My sword?" she said, holding out her hand.

"I think I should hold onto it until you learn how to use it safely."

She was about to say something more, but I grabbed her hand and pulled her back until she was standing beside me in the threshold.

"Thank you for fetching my sister," I told Brant and then looked at Torben. I had felt his eyes on me ever since he had taken my sister's sword, but I had not been able to look at him. I did not want him to see the longing that I knew would be in my eyes—longing for him and the words he had shared with me. "Thank you for..." I paused, unsure of what to say. Did I say thank you for talking to me through the door and distracting me? That seemed like a little more info than Brant and my sister needed to hear, at least until Dayna nagged the information out of me. "Just... thank you," I finally breathed out.

I pushed Dayna behind me and walked backward

into the room. As I was closing the door, Torben stepped forward, putting his hand out to stop it. "We will be out here all night. Just us. We will not be changing guards this evening."

"That is not necessary. The other guards have been trained to protect me and have always done a respectable job," I said, mentally stomping on the butterflies that were currently throwing a ball in my stomach.

"Good is not sufficient," Torben said. He narrowed his eyes at me, and his lips grew taunt across his handsome face. "After what that bastard—" He paused. "Forgive my crudeness. But after what he did, you need superior guards. Guards willing to die for you. Are any of your guards, with families of their own, really willing to die for you?"

I was taken aback by his blunt question and irritated that he thought himself to be so much better than the men who had guarded me for so long. I did not want to admit that he did have a point. Some of my guards did have families of their own. I would not want them to put their lives before my own when they had people depending on them.

"You only met me a week and a half ago. And now you are saying you are willing to die for me?" I asked as I crossed my arms across my chest and began tapping my foot. My shoulder was throbbing, but I attempted to look fierce and hide the discomfort. Apparently, I was not convincing.

"We do not need to get into this right now, Princess. You are tired and in pain." He leaned in closer, and his silver eyes seemed to be swirling as the flames of the torches on the wall were reflected in them. "For now, just trust that you will be safest in my care."

I was done arguing. There would be a time later when I would have my wits about me. Then I would be able to question him further, but not now.

"Fine. Have a good night."

Torben dropped his hand and stepped back, allowing me to close the door. My eyes held his until the door blocked my sight of him.

"Sit down," Dayna commanded as she gathered the wash basin and a cloth. She pulled a small vile from her dress pocket and set it on the vanity. "Now, I am going to clean up this bite and you are going to tell me what the bloody hell happened. And then you are going to tell me what is going on between you and Torben."

"What do you mean?" I asked, feigning puzzlement.

"Oh, come on. There are sparks between you a blind woman could see. No, wait, those aren't sparks. It is more like a blazing inferno."

"That is ridiculous," I scoffed. Inwardly, I was screaming that I needed to be better about hiding my attraction to him. I knew I glanced at him entirely too often. I thought of him way more than a betrothed woman should think about another man.

"I know you," Dayna said softly as she moved the dress from my shoulder and then let out a string of curses. "That man is mad. There is no way a sane man would do something like this."

She began cleaning the wound and poured a bit of the liquid from the vial into the puncture marks. It smelled rank and burned like fire. I flinched and gritted my teeth.

"Ouch, what is that? Are you cleaning the wound or trying to kill me?"

"Just a bit of something I picked up from an acquaintance in the market. You're not the only one with healing powers. You'll be good as new in the morning. Now, quit being a baby and spill your guts."

Just as I suspected, she continued her inquisition. "All

right, start from the top and do not dare attempt to spare me from the grizzly details. I am not a child, Allete. If you do, you get the whole bottle." She shook the putrid green vial at me.

I looked at her in the mirror as she stood behind me. "I know you are not a child. You are growing into a remarkable, albeit foul-mouthed, woman."

"You bet your arse I am." She grinned. "Now, get on with it."

And so I did. I relived every detail for her and somehow managed to keep the tears at bay. After all, I was truly beginning to wonder how long I would be alive once I returned with Cathal to his kingdom—probably just long to bear him an heir. Once he had a male child, I would no longer have any value to him, unless he decided to keep me to meet his carnal needs. If that was what was to happen, then I would take matters into my own hands, literally. I would not live as a man's slave. Death was a much better alternative, and one I would gladly embrace when the time came.

"The worse part of it wasn't what Cathal did," I said. "The worst part was Torben seeing it." My stomach clenched as I remembered the look in his eyes and the embarrassment I felt at having him witness something so vile.

"He didn't do anything?" Dayna asked.

"He wanted to, but Cathal was just waiting for a reason to have his guards stab Torben and Brant. I didn't want that."

"You have feelings for him."

I nodded. How could I deny it? She was right. There were sparks between us, and I liked him so much more than I should. "I can't be with him. Not only am I getting married, but he's a guard. No matter how I feel about him, even without Cathal in the picture, I could never marry Torben."

"It's so wrong," Dayna grumbled. "You shouldn't have to be with someone you don't love just because you're the firstborn daughter to a king."

I shrugged. "I don't want to let Father or Mother down."

"If they knew what Cathal was doing to you, they would never allow you to marry him."

"And our kingdom would fall to ruin," I reminded her. "We need what Cathal can offer."

"We need to just kill him and take his kingdom," Dayna growled.

"Bite your tongue, Dayna Auvray. That's treason."

"I don't care. That man doesn't deserve to be king of a mole hill. He needs to get a taste of his own medicine, preferably the kind that would stop his wicked heart in his chest."

I wanted to disagree with her but I couldn't, so I just kept my mouth shut. Instead, I let my thoughts drift to Torben, a man who was slowly stealing my heart. How was I going to marry Cathal when I wanted so desperately to explore what my guard and I had between us? It was a hopeless situation. I wanted to fall asleep, wake up, and realize it had all been a nightmare, or at least the parts that had Cathal in them.

# CHAPTER Thirteen

"NEVER HAVE I WANTED TO TORTURE A HUMAN BEING WITHOUT
ANY MERCY AS I DO NOW. PERHAPS I HAVE NEVER KNOWN
JUST EXACTLY WHAT I AM CAPABLE OF. BUT SOMEONE I HOLD
DEAR TO MY HEART IS IN DANGER. SHE DRIVES ME CRAZY. YET
THINKING ABOUT A LIFE WITHOUT HER LEAVES AN EMPTINESS
INSIDE ME THAT I CANNOT BEAR. I WOULD DO ANYTHING TO
PROTECT HER. IF THAT MEANS TORTURE OR MURDER ... SO BE
IT."

~TORBEN

I WAS ENVISIONING THE most painful ways I could remove
Cathal's hands from his body when I heard the screams.
Brant and I immediately moved to cover Allete. It did not
go unnoticed that Cathal simply turned in the direction of
the noise without offering any sort of shelter to the woman
he was pledged to marry.

"Northmen!" I heard someone shout. My shoulders
tensed as I looked at Brant from the corner of my eye.

At first, I feared someone had discovered one of my
men masquerading as a Briton soldier. But I dismissed
the idea quickly. Much more likely, some of Magnus' men
had been discovered. I had no reason to think that witch's
charm was no longer working, and Magnus' men were
sloppy, a reflection of their leader. I had not sent anyone

back to check in with our Jarl, because I did not want to them risk being seen by the wrong person. It would look too suspicious if a palace guard or king's soldier were seen continually sneaking off into the woods. But I had seen a few of our comrades, if that was what we should call them, dressed in peasant or merchant clothes, milling about the grounds.

"Do you not think you should go and see what the commotion is about?" Cathal asked me. He was straightening his cuffs, and his lips were tight, making his simple question sound like a command.

I did not particularly like taking commands, especially from men like Cathal who preyed on the weak and vulnerable. And there was no way I was going to leave Allete alone with Cathal and his men.

"The princess is our charge," I said, looking him straight in the eye, something kings did not appreciate from those of lower rank. "We are not to leave her for any reason."

The pompous ass waved my words off. "That was before she had my men and me to look after her. You are no longer needed here."

Brant bumped me. It was subtle, as though he had tripped a little as he turned. That small bump spoke volumes. In essence, he was telling me shut the hell up. But he, of anyone, should have known that I did not take orders from men like Cathal. I was the commander of the warriors of the Hakon clan. I had proven myself in battle over and over. Therefore, during any battle, I was the final word. But now I knew something bigger than myself and my men was at stake. I had Allete to consider.

I turned to Allete and attempted to soften my voice. "Princess, would you like us to investigate the disturbance?"

"I—"

"You do not need to ask her." Cathal cut her off.

His face was as red as a ripe tomato, and I thought at any moment steam would be coming out of his ears.

"I am her husband, and I will answer for her."

I was about to correct him but Allete beat me to it.

"Excuse me," she snapped at Cathal. She had turned her body so that she was facing him directly. Her back was as straight as a Viking short sword, and her eyes were that of a hawk eyeing its prey. She was beautiful.

"You speak out of turn, *my lord*. I am no man's wife. Not yet. I am the princess of England, and I have the power to give orders to my own guardsmen."

Then she turned those fierce eyes on me. I struggled to keep from smiling at her, but that would only enrage Cathal more. So instead I remained motionless, holding her gaze, silently willing her to understand my intentions. I needn't have worried. I wasn't yet sure if she cared that I was the one guarding her, but it was obvious she did not want to be alone with Cathal.

"My father gave you orders to protect me. You cannot do that if you are not with me. So my little female brain deduces that you must stay here to obey *your* king's command."

Cathal was glaring at Allete. She simply turned and returned his stare. She was not about to back down. I was proud of her; she had the heart of a warrior. I was also worried for her. Her betrothed did not handle confrontation well. He would not let the slight go, even if he was momentarily bested.

Cathal stepped closer to her and wrapped his hand around her arm. His grip was tight and his manner possessive. He jerked her forward, and Brant and I moved to follow them. When he saw our intent, he turned to stare daggers at us. The contempt in his gaze would have made a lesser man tremble. But it simply made me more eager to have his neck at the end of my sword.

"Proper etiquette dictates that chaperones remain sixteen yards behind their charges, unseen and unheard. You will abide by *your* king's rules."

I wanted to refuse. But as soon as Cathal had turned away, Allete brought her arm behind her back and rocked her finger back and forth as if she were reprimanding a child. She did not want me to interfere. My jaw clenched as I stood still, watching them get farther and farther away.

"Dammit," I bit out. "How can I protect her if she is that far away?" I slung my hand out in the direction Allete and Cathal were walking.

Brant chuckled lightly. "Would you carry her instead?" he whispered.

I growled in response.

Brant nudged me. "That is far enough. We can proceed."

My body was tense and my movements rigid as I watched Cathal wrap an arm around Allete's waist and pull her into his body.

"Don't forget hanging him from the back of a skeid," Brant said conversationally.

"What?" I was momentarily taken aback.

"The skeid. One of my personal favorites. I can see you are thinking of ways to dismember the man. Hanging a scoundrel from the back of the skeid with his torso above water and letting the fish do their work. That has always been one of my personal favorites. I don't want you to forget it," Brant said, humor coloring his voice.

"Good point," I responded. "Victims stay conscious during most of that one. All the better to hear his screams ..."

For the next hour, we walked behind the couple as

they meandered around the castle grounds. Apparently, Magnus' man had been captured or had escaped. We heard no further commotion coming from anywhere in the castle. When the pair came to a shady grove, Cathal held up his hand, motioning us to stop. I watched as he leaned into Allete, his lips touching her ear as he spoke. His eyes were on me the entire time he whispered to her. I could tell he was issuing a blatant challenge to me. That was not a wise move.

When he stepped back, Allete turned and began walking toward us. Her face was pinched, and she was wringing her hands in front of her. My attention was drawn to movement behind her, and I saw Cathal's men suddenly walk away toward the castle. Allete stopped about three feet from us. Her eyes seemed to bounce around, landing everywhere but our faces.

"I..." Her lips trembled slightly, but then she took a deep breath and lifted her chin. She clasped her hands together in front of her, halting their fidgeting. "Cathal is sending for Beatrice. She can chaperone us while we sit and have our noon meal. You both may go take your breaks as well. We will be here in view of people, and we will have a chaperone."

"Allete," I said using the voice that I used on my men when I wanted them to give me their immediate attention. "Look at me." When she stopped looking around but still did not raise her eyes to mine I added, "Now." She was so nervous that she did not even notice I had used her name instead of addressing her as my superior.

Her head shot up as irritation replaced the timidity she had previously been expressing, which was exactly what I wanted to happen.

"What?" she snapped back.

"Are you ordering us to leave? Is that what you really

want, or is Cathal making you?"

"Of course, he is not making me. I have my own mind."

"I know that you do. And I see no sense in this action. Which means he must be threatening you somehow," I said, leaning forward slightly so I could see her pupils. The eyes revealed so much about a person, sometimes more than words.

"I would not belittle myself in such a way. Not to protect myself from harm." Her voice fluctuated a small amount when she said the word "myself". She was trying to communicate something.

She turned, looking back at Cathal, and then spoke. "Please take your leave. Beatrice has arrived, and Cathal's men have brought the food."

Before I could argue, she turned and walked away. Her steps were slow and measured, almost as if she was walking to the gallows to be hung. It ripped my heart to pieces to be unable to protect her. I had to stand by like a damn spectator while the woman destined to be mine was verbally and physically abused.

When Allete reached Cathal, she glanced over shoulder. Seeing us still standing there, she motioned for us to leave, her face betraying no emotion. She was blank, as if a colorful canvas had been ripped away and a fresh one put in its place. I knew that if Allete married Cathal, her blank canvas would be replaced with muted grays and deep blacks. The colorful young lady I was coming to know would be gone forever.

"We must go now," said Brant. "That girl with Allete seems intelligent. He will not try anything with a witness around, and we must not disobey orders. Do you want to give Cathal an excuse to have us replaced? Because disobedience would certainly be sufficient grounds."

My soul was screaming at me to go after her. I just did

not know how to do that without getting myself beheaded. Reluctantly, I grunted my agreement.

Brant began walking, and I followed, but my boots felt as if they had a mind of their own, struggling with every step to turn and rush back to her. I felt a great weight pressing on my shoulders as well, impending my movement even more. But Brant was not having it. He placed his hand on my back, practically shoving me along beside him.

"Don't make this any worse on yourself. Besides, this will give us a chance to check and see how the other men are doing," Brant suggested.

He was right. It was the perfect time to make sure my men were safe, or at least as safe as they could be. Regardless of my feelings for Allete, I could not forget the mission. With those thoughts in mind, I could move of my own accord. I still did not like leaving her, but there was only so far I could push before Cathal decided to petition King Albric to replace me or have me seriously punished for insubordination. The latter would not surprise me.

"I wonder if there is a way to get in contact with my mother," I said. Not only did I want to make sure my mother was safe, but I also needed reassurance. Was the prophecy still the same? Or had Cathal's presence altered it somehow? The prophecy had not mentioned my queen was already betrothed.

An hour later, Brant and I had discreetly checked on our comrades. They were each watchful, doing mundane guard duties as they awaited my further instructions. None had any information as to the shouted reports of Northmen we had heard earlier. Once I had given each man encouragement and further orders to remain in place, we walked back to where we had left Allete. Surely their noon meal was over by now. I just hoped that Cathal hadn't led Allete away from their picnic spot. I would likely panic if I did not see that she was safe, and that wouldn't help anyone. A hiss caught my attention. I glanced in the direction of the noise and saw a form hidden behind a wagon full of bags of wheat.

I patted Brant's arm and motioned him to follow me. As soon as I was close enough, a hand reached out and grabbed my arm, jerking me forward. I started to protest until saw who it was.

"Oracle," I said bowing low.

"Tsk, tsk, none of that. Give me a hug, boy. I have been worried. None of the other soldiers had news of your wellbeing."

I wrapped my arms around my mother's small form and breathed in her familiar scent. I was relieved to see that she was safe.

She pushed away and reached for Brant. He leaned around me to give her a hug as well.

"Now then," she began, her eyes were dancing with joy. "You have met her." It was not a question.

"Have you seen something?" I asked, wanting to know the answer but fearful that it would not be something I wanted to hear.

"You have met your match, Torben." My mother looked entirely too pleased with herself.

"She's what any man would want in a woman," I responded. "Feisty, strong, vulnerable, infuriating, and bold. If Cathal gets her, he will destroy her and steal away any semblance of who she is now." My heart beat painfully in my chest, and my hands were clenched into tight fists. I was hanging onto my control, but it was quickly slipping away.

My mother placed a hand on my arm. "I still see her as your bride. But the path to that future will not be an easy one, I'm afraid." Suddenly my mother's eyes lost focus, and she grew very still. We were in the presence of the Oracle. When she began to speak, I closed my eyes, attempting to add images to her words.

"Death, pain, lies, betrayal, love, joy and life all stand between you and your union with Allete. It will be your perseverance, integrity, determination, need, and love that will lead you to your destiny. Nothing great and beautiful and right happens without struggle. It is the growth in the journey that gives meaning to the ultimate outcome. You must be strong, Torben, future king of your people. You must not falter, and you must not give up on your destiny. If you do, your beloved will be surrounded in darkness, instead of your light. She will be punished with pain, instead of touched out of love and desire. Should you fail, your beloved will be stripped bare until she is just an empty shell. Only then will her captor grant her death."

Her words hit me like a cannon ball. The breath was knocked from my lungs, and had not Brant grabbed me beneath my arms, I would have landed on my knees. I hung my head down as the words, *should I fail*, beat against my head.

"There is hope, son," my mother said, her voice returning to normal. "She is not gone. She is still here, and she still has your protection." She lifted my head and stared into my eyes. "You are one of the strongest men I have ever known. I do not just mean physically. When you make a decision, there is nothing that can stand between you and what you want. Do you want Allete? Do you want to be the one who provides for her, protects her, and fights with and for her? Do you want to love her?"

There was no hesitation when I spoke. "With everything inside of me."

"Then *you* have to be the one that makes it so. You. Others will help you, and you will need their help.

Ultimately, you will be their commander, and you will be the one to lead them to victory."

I felt the iron will that my mother spoke of rise like a phoenix from the ashes inside of me. As usual, my mother was right. I was relentless when I set my sights on something, and now I had. Not something, but someone— someone to inspire me to be relentless.

"Go now," my mother said, pushing us back the way we had come. "Protect her with your life. She is not just what saves our people. She is what saves you as well."

I had no idea what she meant, and I knew she would not explain it to me, so I did not bother asking. Instead I gave her forehead a quick kiss and then marched back in the direction of the castle—in the direction of Allete. And I beseeched every god I knew that she was unharmed.

# CHAPTER Fourteen

"I HAVE BEEN TOLD MANY TIMES THAT TRIAL IS WHAT MAKES US STRONGER. FACING ADVERSITY BUILDS CHARACTER. THAT NO GREAT LEADER CAN LEARN TO BE GREAT WITHOUT GOING THROUGH GREAT CHALLENGES. I AM BEGINNING TO THINK THAT BEING GREAT IS A TAD OVER RATED."

~DIARY OF PRINCESS ALLETE AUVRAY

WATCHING TORBEN AND BRANT walk away was one of the scariest things I had ever had to do. But I had no choice. When Cathal had threatened me with lashes if I did not do what he wanted, he saw in my eyes that physical harm wasn't going to be enough to control me. But then he threatened who I love most—Dayna. The things he had said he would do to her caused bile rise in my throat. There was nothing I would not do to keep my sisters, both of them, safe.

As soon as my guards were out of view, Cathal pulled me farther into the grove of trees while Beatrice followed. She was a beautiful young woman. Probably not much older than me. When we were sufficiently masked from prying eyes, Cathal jerked me, unnecessarily, to a stop. He looked at Beatrice, and she practically withered under his glare.

"You will watch for any interruptions. You will not

speak a word of what you hear or see. If you do, that worthless husband of yours will find out all about the times you asked me into your bed. How do you think he would feel about our affair? What about your children? How would they view their mother if they knew you were so easily led from your own marriage bed?"

Beatrice's lip trembled as she nodded her understanding.

Cathal sneered at the terrified woman and then spit at her feet. "Weak. Pathetic. I do not know why I ever wanted you."

When she turned to face me, her eyes met mine. I tried so hard to convey that I did not blame her. I would not hold her silence against her. She wiped the tears away and then turned to face outward, obeying Cathal's instructions. Not because she did not have a choice, but because the choices before her were both soul ripping ones to make. Beatrice did not make the choice she thought she could live with. She made the choice that would keep those she loved alive

My attention was drawn away from Beatrice when I felt Cathal's breath on my neck. I would rather a thousand crawl all over me than have him breathing on me. I shivered, and he chuckled.

"You aren't as stoic as you pretend, are you, lover?" he whispered against my ear.

"This is completely inappropriate, my lord." I knew it would not work. Cathal cared about the appropriateness of his actions about as much as he cared about women in general.

His hand wrapped around my throat, and he began backing me up until I was pressed against a tree. The bark bit in to my back painfully. He pushed harder when he noticed my slight flinch at the pain. Cathal pressed his body closer until he was touching me from thigh to chest.

As he held my throat with one hand, he gripped my waist with the other, digging in with his fingers. I had yet to fight back at this point. I knew that it would only make things worse, and I decided that I could live with anything he did, unless he tried to take my innocence. But if he began attempting to remove clothing, the claws were coming out.

He began kissing my neck while he whispered to me. "You will not make a noise. You will not refuse me. You will give yourself to me freely, or I swear to you the things I will do to your sister will give you nightmares for the rest of your pathetic life. And if that is not enough to make you behave, then I will behead your guard, the one that cannot keep his eyes off you. But I would not kill him until he had watched me take your body over and over again." The kissing continued long after the threats had ended. He never kissed me on the lips, only my neck, collar bone and across the tops of my breasts. His hands did not caress me, but he pushed his body against mine in a repulsive rhythm, which I imagined looked like an undulating snake climbing a tree.

I gasped when he bit into my flesh again, though not nearly as hard as he had the first time. This time he not only bit, but he also sucked on my skin until it felt as if he was going to rip it off. He was marking me. He was ensuring that when I looked in the mirror I would see the evidence of what he had done to me.

I do not know how long he stood there, molesting me with his mouth and body. But some time later, I saw them walk out from the shadows of the trees. Beatrice did not see them because they crept quietly up from behind her vantage point. I tried not to stiffen, to alert Cathal that there was something amiss. But the emotions I felt when I saw Torben made this almost impossible.

Torben was shaking. He was a volcano on the verge of

erupting and destroying everything in his path. I shook my head slightly while mouthing, 'no' to them. I pleaded with my eyes for them to obey me. He was so headstrong that I feared he would ignore my desperate request.

Instead of leaving, like I had hoped he would do, Torben stood there with Brant's hand on his shoulder holding him back. His eyes held mine, and I could not look away. I wanted so badly to close my eyes and pretend that none of it was happening. I knew it was not my fault, but it was still embarrassing to have Torben, whom I was coming to care so deeply for, watch as this monster defiled me. It was bad enough that *I* had to endure it. I did not want Torben having this memory of me.

His eyes took on a glassy sheen. After a moment, I realized that he had unshed tears in his beautiful silver eyes. Tears for me. My chest tightened as I forced myself not to react. I was on the verge of crying, but I did not want to give Cathal the satisfaction of seeing tears that he did not deserve. As I continued to stare back at Torben, I contemplated why he would cry for me. A guard who had only known me a couple of weeks was shaking with rage and holding back tears for me. He cared. Torben cared for me, and not just as a friend. My brow drew together, and my lips trembled as I absorbed this new knowledge, and he could see in my eyes that I knew. I did not know if the man loved me, but there was certainly something there— something that could, perhaps, grow into love one day.

As I stared back at him, unable to look away because of the tears he would dare shed for me, I realized that what I felt for him could easily turn into love as well. What had I done to earn such a cruel fate? To be given away like a prize horse and then to find an honorable man with whom I knew, given enough time, I could fall in love. How was I to endure such agony? How could I marry Cathal, go to his kingdom, and be touched by him against my will, knowing Torben was out there in the world? I would have rather had my life end than be tethered to a man such as Cathal. He was a vile, despicable man with a twisted soul and an evil heart. But how could I get out of marrying him, short of death?

I was pulled out of my own mind when Cathal finally stepped back. His mouth was curved into a perverse smile, and his eyes danced with madness. I fought the tremor that wanted to travel through my body. I didn't want him to have the satisfaction of any response from me. I kept my face blank and emotionless as I stared back at him.

He released my throat and ran a finger down my neck. "You will do everything I ask from this point forward. If you do not, those you love will be the ones who bear my wrath."

For a moment, I was worried he would turn and spot Torben and Brant. To my relief, however, he walked past me in the opposite direction of my guards.

"I will see you at dinner," he called over his shoulder without looking back. Cathal snapped his fingers, and Beatrice jumped before scurrying after him.

Less than a minute later, Torben was standing in front of me. His eyes practically glowed with rage, and his hands trembled as he lifted them to my face. His touch was incredibly gentle, despite the size and roughness of his hands. He lifted my chin and ran a finger down my neck and across my collar bone. His mouth tightened into a straight line, and his breathing quickened the longer he stared at me. His anger was nearly palpable.

"Why?" he said in a quiet growl. "Why would you not let me come to you?"

"It would have been your word against the word of a king, Torben. Who do you think would be believed? And even if my father didn't believe Cathal, he would not be able to punish him. It would start a war. Cathal is more powerful, has more money, and a larger army at his disposal. He would demand your death, and my father wouldn't be able to save you. I wouldn't be able to save you." My voice trembled as I imagined Torben with a noose around his strong neck. No. I would not let that happen. No matter what I had to endure. I would not let anyone I care for be hurt by the evil king.

"My fate is my own choice. Not yours," he told me. "I decide what risks to take. That responsibility should not fall on your shoulders, Princess."

I nearly collapsed under the emotion behind his words. This was not just a guard doing his duty. This was a man needing to protect something precious to him. As he leaned his forehead against mine and took a deep breath, inhaling my scent, I closed my eyes and allowed myself a minute to find comfort in his touch. I needed to compose myself before anyone else saw me. Especially Dayna. She would know in a heartbeat that something was amiss.

"I have to release you before someone sees me touching you in such a manner. Would that I could take you captive and leave this place. I need to protect you, Allete. The things Cathal is capable of make me sick. Thinking about you being the object of his attention makes me completely capable of cold-blooded murder."

I gasped as I heard the absolute certainty in his voice. He would kill for me without reservation. Torben would kill Cathal and probably not feel an ounce of regret. Perhaps such a thing should frighten me. Instead, it made me feel protected.

When he stepped away, I suddenly felt very alone and exposed. His stout frame had sheltered me from the scary things in the world. But he wasn't mine. I couldn't hide behind him from my fate. I would have to face it head on and deal with the consequences on my own.

I raised my chin and straightened my dress. "Would you please accompany me back to my chambers and then send for Lidia?"

Torben bowed his head slightly. "As you wish, my lady."

My steps were quick, though I attempted to project an outward appearance of calm. I had no idea if I was succeeding in my endeavor, but I'd be damned if I cowered like a wilted flower in my own home. Cathal may have scared me, but he had not broken me—not yet anyway.

As we reached my chambers, Torben stepped in front of me and opened the door. He went inside before me and walked around the room, glancing behind the changing screen and checking under the bed. He walked quickly across to the bathing chamber and peered in before coming back out and then checking the wardrobe.

"It looks to be clear," he said as his eyes met mine. "We will be just outside. Brant will fetch your hand maiden."

Both men were out the door before I could respond to his brisk words. The door closed gently behind them. I walked around the room myself, wringing my hands in front of me and trying hard not to claw at my skin to remove the memory of Cathal's touch. My stomach clenched at the memory of his mouth, and I had to run to make it to the washbasin in the bathing chamber to keep from vomiting on the floor. I heaved and heaved, but nothing came up. I hadn't eaten since breakfast so my stomach was empty. I took a dry cloth and dipped it into the pitcher of water and pressed it to my face and neck, helping to cool the heat of my skin.

"Sister mine, where are you?" Dayna's voice came from the main room. The fact that I hadn't heard the door open or close gave testament to what a mess I was.

I set the cloth down and walked out into the room.

The gasp from my sister was enough to know that I looked as bad as I felt.

"What the bloody hell happened to you?" Dayna breathed as she hurried to my side. She lifted her hand and ran a finger across my neck. No doubt Cathal had left bruises from his mouth and fingers. He'd marked me like I was his property.

"Cathal happened," I finally managed to say. I was determined to not fall apart in front of her, knowing it would only add to her worry. Before Dayna could respond, the door opened, and Lizzy rushed in. Her mouth dropped open as her eyes went unnaturally wide.

"Your guard said you needed me," she said. The initial shock dissipated as she hurried over to me. "Did that *king* do this?" Lizzy asked.

I really didn't want to talk about it. I felt dirty. My skin crawled, and I wanted so desperately to climb out of it. I wanted the memory of his mouth and hands on me gone. At that point, I was willing to give up all my memories just to get the man out of my mind. I wasn't even married to him yet and already he was making me utterly miserable.

"I know you want us to leave you be," Dayna said, her perceptive eyes narrowing on me. "But let us help get you cleaned up and into your night clothes."

"And we'll bring you some food so you won't have to go down to dinner," offered Lizzy.

"And some of Father's whiskey," said Dayna.

I nearly smiled. Leave it to my youngest sister to bring whiskey in as the savior. "Whiskey doesn't fix everything," I teased.

She shrugged. "Maybe, but it sure as hell calms the nerves. Makes things seem a bit less dire, if only for a little while."

Lizzy was nodding as if what Dayna was saying was the

most logical explanation ever.

"Fine, let's get this all done. I just want to climb in bed and forget today ever happened."

My sisters spent the next half hour sponge-bathing me, braiding my hair, and rubbing me down with the lotion that I usually only reserved for special occasions. Several times I simply closed my eyes and let myself take comfort in their ministrations. I didn't like feeling helpless. I didn't like feeling as though I was completely out of control of my own life. Pushing it all aside for the brief time that it took my sisters to pamper me, feed me, and then tuck me into bed had been exactly what I needed. In that moment, I was so very thankful for Dayna's pushiness and Lizzy's quiet presence.

By the time they left me, I was completely relaxed. I wanted it to last. I wanted to be able to keep the memories of his touch at bay at least until morning. Unfortunately, my mind had other plans. Gradually, his words refilled my mind, and his face sneered at me again as he held me captive against the rough bark of the tree. I should have fought. I should have screamed, or done something to gain the attention of anyone who might have been close by. But I hadn't. I had stood there like a whipped dog and let that man violate me. Where the hell had my courage gone? When had I become a doormat for him to walk on?

My spirit felt crushed as I considered all the things I should have done rather than enduring his vile behavior. The tears pooled in my eyes, and my gut clenched violently under the pain that was threatening to crush me. He'd threatened my sisters, my family, those I loved. I hadn't wanted to take a chance that he was bluffing. I wouldn't be able to live with myself if something happened to any of them, especially if it was because of something I'd done or refused to do. I shook my head. *I was given no choice*, I told myself. I'd had to do what he told me to in order to protect those who were precious to me. No matter how disgusted I was, I wouldn't have changed what I'd done. I wouldn't take a risk with the lives of my friends and family.

Regardless, it still hurt, dammit. I felt completely filthy. I felt that, even if by some miracle I could escape my pending marriage with Cathal, I would probably never be able to let another man touch me. Would I ever feel worthy of a man's touch or would I always feel unclean? I wasn't sure.

"Why?" I groaned into the pillow as I tucked my knees close to my chest. "Why, why, why!" The tears fell fast with every word, and my breathing became ragged as my lungs tightened, refusing any intake of air. My body shook relentlessly as my emotions lashed out. I couldn't control them. My mind was incapable of forming rational thoughts. I sat up quickly, consciously forcing large gulps of air into my lungs. I felt as though I was I was suffocating. I felt anew his hand around my throat, the tightening of his fingers threatening to crush my windpipe. His body pressed up against mine, keeping me from being able to move even an inch. And then I felt his mouth. His slithering tongue running along my throat, his lips latching onto my skin, and sucking painfully. I gagged as bile rose from my stomach threatening to project from my mouth. Even as I attempted to hold in the vomit, I tore at my nightgown. The fabric felt as if it was full of nettles, scratching my skin.

I wondered dimly if the pain and fear would fade, or would I always feel as I did in that moment? The tears continued to flow as huge sobs broke through my chest and the sorrow I felt from the things Cathal had taken from me overwhelmed me.

I STOOD OUTSIDE OF Allete's door, my jaw clenched as I attempted to maintain control of my temper. I wanted nothing more than to go to Cathal's room and slit his throat, but only after I had tortured him slowly. How could a man be so dishonorable? How wicked did his heart have to be to treat a woman in such a vile manner?

There was no doubt in my mind now, Allete could not be allowed to marry that monster. She would never be alone with him again. I didn't know how I could accomplish such a feat without getting arrested, but I knew that Allete must be protected. If I wasn't already aware of the prophesy—if I didn't know how important our union would be—I would gladly kill Cathal now and accept my fate with my head held high. Who knows how many women I would save from his evil if his life was snuffed from the earth? Would anyone really miss him? I had a feeling the people of his country would rejoice, rather than mourn. He was not the type of leader that inspired any form of loyalty. His people only followed him out of fear. They didn't respect him or trust him.

"Are you trying to figure out a way to kill him without getting caught?" Brant asked quietly from beside him.

"How'd you know?"

"Because I'm trying to figure out the same thing. That man cannot live, Torben."

I let out a resigned sigh. Brant was right. Even if we stopped Allete from marrying him, someone else would bear his wrath. Another innocent soul would suffer as a prisoner to his sick mind. Could we really leave him alive to torture someone else?

"No, he cannot," I agreed.

"We agree the king of Tara will die."

I nodded. "We are of one accord," I answered formally.

Our words were not empty. Though our declaration,

Brant and I had bound ourselves and our fate to one another in the accomplishment of a shared purpose. By our agreement, we had pledged together to kill Cathal, creating a binding oath that neither of us would abandon until our purpose was fulfilled.

We were silent after our declaration. With the decision made, all I could think about was the woman in the room behind me. Her sisters had left an hour ago. It worried me that being alone was not the best thing for Allete, but Dayna had assured me that Allete was going to be okay—she just needed time to process things. They knew their sister better than I did, though I hoped one day that would no longer be true. Regardless, I felt leaving anyone alone after such an assault could be dangerous.

As if my very thoughts had called out to her, I heard a desperate cry and the sound of something hitting the floor, hard. I turned to the door and grabbed the handle. "Do not let anyone come in this room for any reason," I said to Brant, knowing my comrade would die to keep my orders from being disobeyed.

I pushed the door closed behind me and stood still for a moment, letting my eyes adjust to the darkness. The only light in the room was a weak flickering flame from a small lamp resting on a table near Allete's bed. My eyes roamed over the bed, looking for the lump that would indicate Allete's body was safely tucked in. The bed was empty. I felt my heart begin to race as my eyes jumped to every corner of the room. I'd just started in the direction of the bathing room when I heard her desperate pleas.

"Please make it stop," her small voice sobbed.

Her voice came from the other side of the bed and I hurried over, only to freeze as I stared down at the beautiful princess who'd stolen my heart. I dropped to my knees and inched closer to her, my hands out in a placating gesture.

My beautiful Allete was completely naked, the night gown she'd worn was ripped into shreds, and she was clawing at her neck, rubbing it raw.

"Princess," I said softly, hoping I didn't startle her. It appeared she didn't recognize her surroundings. Her mind was not here with me, that was clear. She was back against that tree with Cathal's hand around her throat, experiencing again his desecration of her body. She was in shock. I knew something like this might happen, but I didn't realize it would be so bad.

"Princess," I said again, slightly louder, as I moved closer. I gently placed my hand on her head and patted down her hair, attempting to soothe her. "Allete, love, please look at me."

She froze, the only sound was the ragged breathing that was coming from her chest. I didn't want to move. I felt like the slightest motion might cause her to lose all control. But I couldn't just leave her sitting on the cold floor. Though I would willingly wait there with her for an eternity, I knew that she needed to be cleaned up, dressed, and put safely back into her bed. Mentally kicking myself, I finally spoke again.

"Allete, could you please look at me?"

It took her so long to respond that I didn't think she'd heard me. But then her head turned slowly, and her eyes met mine.

I groaned. "Oh, precious one." My heart crumbled in my chest as I looked into the eyes of my broken princess. "I'm sorry. I'm so sorry that I wasn't there to protect you."

Silent tears slid down her face, and the fact that she still didn't attempt to hide her nakedness told me she still wasn't all there. Part of her was still lost.

"I can still feel him," she whispered after several quiet minutes. "I can't get the feel of him off me." She scratched at her neck. With her head turned, I could see the damage she'd done to herself. Her soft skin was a bloody mess. She'd scratched until her beautiful flesh was raw and angry looking. Her arms too were covered with scrapes, as was the skin just above her breasts. She looked as though several angry cats had attacked her all at once. Her braided hair was coming loose, and her skin bore bruises in addition to the scratches. Those must have been the bruises left from Cathal's rough treatment of her precious body. My blood boiled as I looked at her damaged flesh.

"Allete, will you let me help you? Do you want me to get your sisters?"

Her eyes widened at my question. "No," she shook her head quickly. "Not my sisters. No. I don't want them to see this." She looked down at herself and covered her mouth to keep the sob inside. "Look what I've done," she whispered. She was horrified and even disgusted with herself.

I wasn't about to let that stand. "Princess, look at me." She didn't, so I used the voice I used when commanding my men. "Now."

Her eyes snapped to mine, wide with fear and anguish.

"Let me help you."

"But..." She started to argue, but I took one of her small hands in mine and shook my head at her.

"You will let me care for you. It is my honor, and you must let me do this. Understand?"

After several heartbeats, she finally shrugged. "It's not like I could possibly humiliate myself any more. I'm sitting in the floor, naked, scratched all to hell."

I stood up and snatched the sheet from her bed and draped it over her, covering her beautiful body. Then I helped her stand. Her legs were weak and shaky. I wasn't about to let her fall, so I swept her easily up into my arms. She didn't even make a sound. I carried her to the other side of the bed and set her down gently. "Will you be okay if I let you go?"

Her head shot up and the fear that gripped her was evident on her face. "Don't leave. Please."

I gently ran a finger across her jaw. "I wouldn't dare. You're stuck with me, Princess. I'm just going to start a fire," I motioned to the fireplace on the far wall. "I need to heat up some water for you." As if she was trying to convince herself that I was telling the truth, she simply stared into my eyes. Finally, she gave a single nod and released my arm.

I moved quickly and efficiently to get a fire started and then set a metal pitcher full of water down into the hot coals. I glanced at my charge and saw that she was playing with a piece of hair that had fallen forward. This gave me an idea, an appropriate action to kill the time while we waited for the water to heat. I walked over to her vanity and opened a drawer. A small hand mirror and brush sat neatly inside. I took the brush and walked over to her. I gently moved her forward and climbed into the bed behind her. She offered no resistance. I pulled Allete back toward me so she was sitting in between my legs. I pulled out the ties that held her hair in place and gently untwined the braid. The dark strands of hair ran through my fingers, feeling like a cascade of silk. For some reason, being allowed to touch her hair, to care for her in such a way, felt even more intimate to me than a kiss.

"Is this all right?" I asked her, not wanting to take liberties she wasn't willing to give.

She sighed and let her head fall back. "It feels wonderful," she answered a tad breathlessly. At least she wasn't crying anymore. Her sobs had broken my heart.

"Your hair is beautiful. Just like the rest of you."

She let out a un-lady like snort. "Yes, I'm sure I'm

quite a sight to behold right now."

"You are always a sight to behold, Allete. You light up a room when you walk into it. The fire in your eyes can dance with mirth, or cut down a person quicker than a sword. You hold yourself with confidence, yet there is no judgment in your eyes when you look at others. And you're humble despite these things." I didn't want to make her uncomfortable, but after having been treated the way Cathal had treated her, I felt it was important for her to know she was a woman of worth.

"I'm not really sure what to say to that," she admitted.

"You don't have to say anything, Princess. Just accept it as truth."

# CHAPTER Fifteen

"WE ARE BORN INTO THIS WORLD TO PARENTS WHO ARE FULL OF HOPE. THEY WANT TO SEE US SUCCEED AT ANYTHING AND EVERYTHING. THEY WANT US SAFE, HEALTHY, AND HAPPY. BUT NO MATTER HOW STRONGLY THEY MAY WANT A THING, DESIRE IS NOT ENOUGH TO MAKE IT SO. EACH OF US MUST DECIDE FOR OURSELVES WHAT WE WANT IN THIS LIFE. WE HAVE TO CHOOSE TO PURSUE OUR HAPPINESS, NOT JUST HOPE THAT WHAT OUR MOTHERS AND FATHERS WANT FOR US WILL SUDDENLY HAPPEN."

~TORBEN.

TORBEN—MY PERSONAL GUARDSMAN—WHO I now knew was so much more than that, was brushing my hair while I wore nothing but a sheet. It sounded terrible when I thought about it. And it would certainly look terrible to an outsider. But the gesture was completely innocent on both of our parts. Regardless, I would never be able to admit that it had happened to anyone. I was sure my mother would faint where she stood if she happened upon us, and my sister Dayna would start singing a halleluiah chorus.

I myself was about to curl up in a ball and purr like a well-loved kitten. After having had Cathal's repugnant hands and mouth on me, Torben's hands were like a cleansing rain, washing away the filth of the memories that were attempting to overwhelm me. I had been sinking into the pit of my mind, sure that nothing would ever be the same again. Then he had come. Torben had come and rescued me, pulling me from the mire of my thoughts.

"What are you thinking about?" Torben asked as he stood and retrieved the pitcher he'd left heating in the fires' embers. He poured the steaming water into a small wash basin and picked up a hand towel that was resting on the table beside my bed.

"I am thinking about how my mother would wilt like a dying flower, and my youngest sister would be planning the arrival of our first child if either were to walk into my chambers and see us in such a state," I admitted.

He paused after wringing the water from the towel. "Yes, I imagine this would look rather damning, considering that under that flimsy fabric, you are as naked as the day you were born."

The left-over tears that had been in my eyes were completely dry now. All it took to stop my sobbing, apparently, was a handsome warrior pointing out how unclothed I was beneath a sheet.

Torben sat down in front of me this time and reached up with the warm cloth. He pressed it to my face, and my eyes closed of their own accord as he began to wipe away the evidence of my break from reality. His touch was surprisingly gentle for such a large man. His hands were probably more familiar with handling a sword than a woman's skin. But his movements were slow and confident. His face held a level of concentration that I knew from experience was not needed to accomplish such a simple task as wiping a face clean. But Torben seemed determined to do a thorough and proper job. My lips turned up in a small smile at my thoughts.

"What?" he asked as he pulled back slightly to look down at me.

I shook my head as my smile grew wider. "I was just thinking about how hard you were concentrating on your task."

He chuckled but didn't look the least embarrassed. "I believe if you're going to do something, no matter what it may be, then you should always do it to the best of your capability."

"Even washing a face?"

His own lips tilted in a roguish smile. "Certainly when washing the face of such a beautiful female."

My eyebrows rose. "Beautiful, huh? And what if she's not beautiful?"

He frowned. "Now why would I be cleaning the face of an ugly female?"

I couldn't help myself. I laughed at the seriousness in his voice and the utter dismay in his eyes. Though I could tell he was teasing, he seemed so appalled at the notion that it was comical.

"Forgive me, my lord, for assuming you would lower yourself to such a task," I said in my best aghast voice.

"Well, Princess, see to it that you do not assume such ridiculous notions again." He paused with a stern look, but then his eyes softened, and his mouth returned to its flirty grin. Torben tapped me on the end of the nose playfully. "He has no bloody clue how lucky he is," he murmured.

My breath caught as I watched the playfulness fade from his eyes only to be replaced by something else, something much more consuming. He set the towel down and shifted closer to me. My mind was screaming at me to back away. This wasn't my betrothed, this was not even a man I would be allowed to marry. He was a guard in my father's royal army. His station was below mine and yet he was one of the most honorable men I'd ever met.

As his face moved closer to mine, one of his large

hands reached up and cupped my cheek. I had to force myself to breathe so I didn't pass out. I didn't want to move. I didn't even want to blink for fear I would miss something, or that he would suddenly disappear and I would come to realize this whole thing had been a dream. His lips were mere inches from my own when he spoke again.

"Princess, I'm going to need you to tell me to back off." His voice was deep and rough.

My blood felt as though it were heating in my veins, and my heart felt as though it was going to beat up out of my throat. I swallowed and licked my dry lips, not missing the way his eyes followed the movement.

"And if I do not want to tell you to back off?" I asked, knowing I was playing with fire. Apparently, I liked the idea of being burned, because I was not about to push him away.

"Then we are both in trouble."

"Why is that?" My voice sounded breathless, and I thought maybe I should be embarrassed over the sound, but I couldn't bring myself to care. All I could see were those intense eyes and full lips. All I could think about was how badly I wanted those lips on mine. I wanted them to replace the memory of Cathal and give me the chance to have a man kiss me with passion—real, raw passion.

"Because I'm planning on kissing you. I have no willpower to stop, nor do I have the desire to stop. So, unless you tell me right now that you don't want this, I am going to kiss you."

I simply stared back at him, waiting, practically daring him to do what he was threatening. Good thing the man didn't back down from a challenge, because I might have taken the choice from him if he hadn't acted when he did.

"So be it," he whispered before slipping his hand around to the nape of my neck and pulling me toward him.

My eyes closed, and the breath rushed out of me as his warm lips pressed to my own. It wasn't a gentle kiss. It was a kiss that spoke of possession and want, desire and need. It was a kiss that would ruin a woman for any other man after him. It was the type of kiss that every woman should have as her first.

I felt his mouth part, and his tongue press against my lips, demanding entrance. I'd never willingly kissed a man in such a way, and, had it been anyone else, I think I might have hesitated. I didn't hesitate with Torben. This man, who had shown up at my chamber doors half a month ago and declared himself my new guard, had captured my attention from the first look. He'd driven me crazy, made me furious and needy in the same breath, and protected me without worry for his own safety. I opened my mouth and moaned when I felt the heat of his tongue touch my own.

Why on earth weren't people kissing all the time? That's what kept running through my head. If this was what it felt like to really be kissed by someone who you desired and who desired you, then why were people doing anything else besides kissing? *Silly and childish thought?* Probably, but then you aren't the one sitting on my bed having your mouth ravished by a handsome rogue. When that happens to you, then you can judge me on my thoughts about simply kissing every minute of every day for the rest of all time.

His hand tightened on my neck, and his other hand landed on my waist and pulled me closer. I had to remind myself that there was nothing under the sheet, because I desperately wanted to wrap my arms around him, but that would have left me a little more exposed than I was ready to be.

Torben's deep rumble only caused me to open my

mouth wider and push closer to him, as though I could simply crawl right inside of him to be as close as possible. I craved his heat. I needed his touch and at any moment, I was truly afraid I was going to start rubbing up against him the way Thomas's cat, Sir Rufus, rubbed against anything that got close to him.

I ran my tongue across the roof of his mouth and was rewarded with a deep chuckle. I did it again in hopes that he would chuckle one more time. He did. I had no idea how much time had passed when he finally pulled back. My lips were slick and swollen, and my breathing sounded as though I'd run from the stables to the kitchen and back again.

Torben looked down into my eyes, and I was afraid to put words to the emotions I saw there. I felt them, too, but it was much too soon—not to mention a tad forbidden. I could not fall for him. I couldn't... and yet I was pretty sure I already had.

"Thank you," he said softly as the back of his hand caressed my warm cheeks.

"For what?"

His eyes crinkled at the sides as he smiled. "For allowing me the honor of tasting you."

I knew my flushed skin only got darker, because his words sounded so much more provocative than he probably meant them to be.

He winked at me.

Well, maybe he had meant them just as provocatively as they'd sounded. The scoundrel.

"Would I be completely unladylike if I said it was my pleasure?" I asked him.

He chuckled. "I would consider it the highest compliment."

We stared at one another in what I could only describe

as awed silence. Our eyes ran over each other's faces, and his hands continued to pet me—my face, my back, and my sides. He was stirring up desire in me like a man stoking a fire. I should have told him to stop, seven hells, we needed to stop, and yet I could not get my lips to cooperate with my brain. How was I going to go back to treating him like just a random castle guard? How could I ever return to the way things had been?

"Allete." My name rolled off his tongue so smoothly, and I found that I loved the sound of it. "I need you to know, I did not come in here with the intentions of seducing you."

Torben sounded truly worried that I would think such a thing about him.

"I know that," I assured him. "I would have never thought that."

"I was worried about you," he confessed. "After what that horse's arse had done, I needed to see for myself that you were okay."

"Only I wasn't," I said pathetically. I gritted my teeth as I thought back to how I'd crumbled under the weight of what had happened and what was to come.

"No, love, you weren't." He leaned forward and pressed his lips to my forehead and, for the first time in my life, I felt cherished. "But that's why I'm here. To make sure that you will be okay."

My brow drew together as I looked up at him. "What do you mean? You speak as though you knew me before we met."

He shook his head. "I didn't know you, but I knew of you and knew that you would be important to me."

I was not sure how to interpret his words. I felt as though there was some hidden meaning behind them. There was something he wasn't telling me.

"I'm not going to be okay if I have to marry that man,"

I said, trying not to think too hard about the meaning of his words. "I thought I could do it. I thought I could just grit my teeth and do what I needed to do for my kingdom." I looked down at my hands that were now clenching the sheet. The tears that had fled were threatening to once again flood my face. "But I can't. Torben, I can't be with Cathal. He'll kill me, or I'll kill me."

A deep growl rushed from Torben as he grabbed my shoulders. "Never say such things," he bit out. "You will never take your own life, and I will do everything I can to ensure that you do not marry him."

"How?" The word was out before I had time to think. I knew I shouldn't dare hope, but I couldn't help myself. Could Torben really keep me from having to marry Cathal? It wasn't possible. But the steel in his eyes said otherwise. How could he do such a thing? He was a guard in my father's castle. How on earth could he prevent my marriage to a foreign king?

"I am still working out the details," he said as he stood and backed away from the bed. I felt cold at his sudden retreat and fought my urge to reach out and snatch him back to my side.

"What are you doing?"

"I'm looking for your sleep garments," he said as he glanced around the room.

I motioned toward the wardrobe directly behind him. "There should be a gown in there."

He smiled at me. "As much as I love the idea of you naked, I fear it could be damning to your reputation if someone were to come in."

I chuckled. "Yes, it would be quite damning."

Torben searched through the wardrobe until he found a gown and then walked over to hand it to me. He turned and kept his back to me as I dropped the sheet and slipped the gown over my head. I tugged it down my body until it fell to the floor, and then I resumed my seat on my bed.

"All right, I'm decent."

He turned and looked at me, his eyes starting at the top of my head and traveling down until he reached my bare feet. "No, love, I'm afraid you are far too tempting to qualify as decent."

I smiled at him. He was so handsome. And so not mine. Why was life so unfair? I would renounce my right as a princess in a heartbeat if it meant I could be with Torben and didn't have to marry Cathal. I would give up all the luxury just to have my happiness and safety and the possibility of real actual love.

"Thank you, Torben, for caring for me," I said after several heartbeats of silence.

"It is not a hardship, Allete." His eyes burned with an intensity that held me in place. I didn't want to move for fear that he would look away. For some reason, that was the last thing I wanted him to do.

"Actually, caring for another person is always a hardship. It is in our nature to care for ourselves first," I told him.

"Sometime, yes. But then, sometimes, we come across a person who means more to us than ourselves. Sometimes we do anything for that person. Then there is no hardship."

I WATCHED AS ALLETE'S eyes flickered with surprise at my words. I knew she did not intend to be insulting, but it made me want to laugh that she assumed I would not be capable of any sort of deep thought. As a lowly guard, in comparison to her station, it would make sense for me to be uneducated and simple. But she didn't know that I wasn't just a guard. Nor was I just a warrior of my clan. I was the son of an Oracle, and my mother had no intention of allowing me to remain ignorant.

"How do you know when you have found such a person?" she asked.

My lips turned up in a small smile. I retook my seat next to her on the bed and brushed some errant hair away from her face. "You know because they are all you can think about. Even when you know they should not be on your mind, they are still there. You know because everything becomes second to their wellbeing, safety, and happiness."

"What if they cannot be yours? What if it's just not possible?" Her eyes were swirling with questions as she stared up at me. Her shoulders were tense, and I could tell that she wanted me to simply walk away. Allete wanted me to make this easy on her. I wished I could do that, but even if she wasn't the woman in the prophecy, I would not be able to walk away from her. At some point, between the moment I first laid eyes on her and the moment we now shared, the moment where she sat staring at me with such need, I had realized that my life would never be complete without her.

"Who are we to decide what is possible and what is not? I responded. "We should leave the prospect of possibilities to the gods, and we should simply be the ones trying."

She shook her head at me and huffed. "That isn't the way of it, Torben. At least not for me. I don't know where you truly come from, but here, you don't just walk about trying new things. There are responsibilities, duties, and expectations. I can't just flit about like a whimsical girl with romantic notions." Her hands fidgeted in her lap, and she ducked her head, no longer looking at me.

I pressed a finger under her chin and lifted it until her eyes met mine once again. My beautiful Allete. She was smart, beautiful, and brave, and she didn't even realize just how much control she had over her own future. Would it come without pain or sacrifice? No, it would not. In fact, it would probably be more painful that she wanted to truly know. But that did not mean it was impossible. I had to somehow make her see that I was the man for her. I needed to make her realize this, not only for the hope of my clan, but for her own people as well. For both of our peoples, she would have to leave her kingdom and become part of mine.

"I will do whatever it takes to prove to you that your destiny is just that—yours. You are the master of your own life. There will be bumps and detours along the way, but at every turn, there will be a choice. Do not let yourself become a victim of your circumstances. You are too special for that fate."

How was I supposed to respond to Torben's statement? How could Torben possibly understand that, in my world, there was no choice, only duty? I was sure he couldn't possibly understand that. I wanted to scream at him to stop giving me false hope.

"I wish that I could make your words my own, but we come from very different situations," I tried to explain. I didn't know how to verbalize what I needed him to know. I was frustrated and hurt.

"What do you want, Princess?" he asked. The look in his eyes said he was daring me to be honest with him.

"I want a life that is my own," I finally admitted.

"Then it is your goal in life to make that desire a reality, not just a dream." He stood and backed away toward the door. "You need your rest, and I need to think about how to keep Cathal from repeating today's events."

I winced as I saw his entire body tense as he said these words. "I appreciate your help, Torben, and your willingness to protect me. But..." I paused and took a deep breath to steady myself for what I knew I had to say. "This can't happen again. We can't be."

I expected anger or hurt, but what I got instead was an amused smirk.

"I may be a guard, but sometimes I find that I have trouble following orders. Princes, this is happening, and it will continue to happen until you are mine." He turned without another word and walked out of the door, closing it quietly behind him.

"Ugh!" I growled. "Infuriating, bull-headed, ridiculous male," I snapped to the empty room. Frustration and helplessness threatened to overwhelm me. Why must I fall for him, the one I could not have? Why did he have to be so certain that we would be together and that I had some sort of choice in the matter? It was like talking to a cat. He stared at you while you spoke, and you might even believe for a second that he understood what you were saying, but then he just up and walked away with a confidence that made it clear he was going to do what he damn well pleased.

I stood, unable to sit still any longer, and began to pace the room. The warmth of the fire had chased away the chill on the outside, but it did nothing to warm the cold I felt enveloping my heart. To survive, I was going to have to harden myself. If I wanted to keep my sanity while being married to Cathal, then I would have to come to terms with the fact that my life would simply be about surviving. I couldn't afford to hope for anything else. There would be no celebrations, no joy, or happiness. I would know only sorrow and pain. I would constantly be surrounded by the anger and evil of a man who cared for no one or nothing but himself.

I would have to learn that genuine smiles were a thing of the past. Laughter would be foreign to me, and joy would no longer be a part of my vocabulary. Instead of light, I would be surrounded by darkness, and I was going to have to learn how to survive. I wouldn't thrive; how could I in such darkness?

By my twentieth turn across my chambers, I was ready to scream. Torben had been able to calm me down. He'd been able to drag me back from the despair into which I had been sinking. Who would drag me back from the pain of knowing I could never be with him? Who would help me heal over the loss of a chance at happiness?

"Why did you let him kiss you?" I seethed at myself. It would have been so much easier if I had never known how his lips felt or how his mouth tasted. "Easier?" I snorted. "I think not, Allete." I couldn't fool myself; kissing or not, it would be painful.

After fighting the frustration and hurt for over half an hour, I finally gave in. I let the sorrow fill me. I felt a single tear slide down my face and knew it would be the first of many. My heart was breaking for a love I would never know. Before the second tear fell, I found myself with my back pressed against the door, sliding down until I was sitting on the cold floor. It was the same position I'd found myself in once before, only then I'd been listening to Torben's steady voice as I'd sat there, breaking down. This time there were no words of encouragement, just me with my tears and sorrow. I pulled my knees to my chest and wrapped my arms around my legs. My head fell forward until my forehead pressed against them.

My shoulders shook as I bit my lip to keep the sobs from filling the room. I felt weak. My heart was broken in more ways than one, and my soul felt empty. I needed to be strong for my father, my sisters, and my kingdom, but I didn't know how to be that person. I wanted to crawl away into a hole and curl up while the world moved on without me. It would be easier to be stuck than to move forward with the future that life had for me.

"Why?" I whispered to myself. "Why does it have to be like this?" Some part of me longed for someone to answer. I wanted to have some sort of reason that might make it easier to accept, but there was no mystical voice or sudden revelation. There was only me, a cold floor and tears that could not wash away the pain that would burn inside of me until the day I died.

I closed my eyes as the tears continued to fall. Wrapped in my grief, I didn't even realize when sleep surrounded me and pulled me down. I didn't hear the voice on the other side of the door whispering words of love to me. I didn't hear the promise of protection and happiness.

# CHAPTER
## Sixteen

"I REFUSE TO BREAK MY PROMISE. I THINK LONG AND HARD
BEFORE I MAKE ANY VOW, AND IN MY SHORT LIFE, I HAVE
ONLY GIVEN MY WORD A HANDFUL OF TIMES. WHY? BECAUSE
OTHERS MUST BE ABLE TO TRUST MY WORDS. I CANNOT LEAD
IF I AM AN OATH BREAKER. I AM AN HONORABLE MAN AND I
AM DETERMINED TO KEEP ALLETE SAFE. IF I MUST SACRIFICE
MYSELF TO MAKE THAT HAPPEN, THEN I FREELY LAY DOWN MY
LIFE."

~TORBEN

"YOU KISSED HER," BRANT accused as I stood just outside
of Allete's door.

"Why is that any of your business?"

Brant's eyes narrowed. "You will be of no use to us if
you get yourself killed by that crazy arse of a king."

His words rang true. I was playing with the sharp side
of the sword and expecting not to get cut. But what else
was I supposed to do? Allete could not marry Cathal, and
truly, she should not have to spend any more time with
him. The man was crazed. I couldn't believe that Allete's
father hadn't picked up on the king's madness. Perhaps he
had and was choosing to ignore it, but I hoped this wasn't
the case. I would like to think that her father would not be
willing to allow her to wed a man capable of such abuse.

"What would you have me do?" I growled.

"You can save her without taking her virtue," he snapped back.

I clenched my jaw at the insinuation of his words. "Careful, brother. You may be my second in command, but that does not give you the right to be disrespectful."

"What about being your friend? Does that give me the right to speak up when you are making choices that will hurt your clan?"

I had to bite back my response because I knew it would have been unfair. Brant cared about me. He may have looked like a heartless warrior, but I knew differently. He was as honorable a man as they came.

"I will be honest with you, I know not what to do. She makes me feel crazy with need. The need to have her, to protect her, to hold her. Needs I've never felt before. The thought of his hands and mouth on her makes me rage on the inside. Truly, Brant, I was planning his murder in my mind as I watched him touch her." I took a deep breath as the rage returned once again. "How am I supposed to let him be near her again?"

He shook his head. "I would not want to be in your shoes, but I will stand beside you no matter what. You want to become a king slayer? I will hand you the sword and watch your back while you do what needs to be done."

My heart clenched at his words. There were few things as valuable as the trust and loyalty of the men I led. They weren't all loyal to me, but the ones who were would not hesitate to run into battle with me, even if it was one we couldn't possibly win. They would fight with me and die right alongside me.

"He's going to have to die. If I take her and leave him alive, he will pursue her and probably kill her family to punish her. But if I kill him now, I could be hung for it, and then I still wouldn't be able to take Allete as my own. Our clan would be doomed."

Brant smiled, though his eyes didn't speak of humor. "Oh, what joy we find in having so many choices that lead to death and destruction."

"You are a twisted man, brother." I laughed because if I didn't, I would probably start blindly swinging my sword, breaking everything in sight.

I knew what he meant. We had choices. There always were choices, but that didn't mean that the choices were necessarily easy or good. I was stuck between a rock and a hard place. The best possible outcome I could hope for would be to get Allete away before anyone realized that Cathal was dead. Even after that, I would have to figure out a way to deal with her father and to take out Magnus as well.

"So, did you kiss her?"

I chuckled. "I thought you knew?"

He shrugged. "You were in there a long time. If it were me, and I was alone with my woman, well...I wouldn't have walked out with anything less than a kiss or three."

"And that is why you have a line of females knocking down the door of your hut."

"Do not be jealous," Brant snorted. "The females just can't resist me. I am quite unforgettable."

"Anyone who looks like the arse end of a monkey is unforgettable. Don't read too much in to their ability to remember who you are."

"The kiss, Torben. Quit your stalling."

"Fine," I breathed out. "Yes, I kissed her. But I'm leaving it at that. I do not make it a habit to share what goes on behind closed doors between my woman and me."

Brant's stupid grin was still on his face. "Because you have had so many closed-door encounters with the fairer sex, have you?"

I waved him off. He was just trying to annoy me at that point, and I wasn't going to walk into his traps. I was annoyed enough as it was. I could tell when I'd left the Princess's chambers that she was going to try to push me away. She thought to end things between us before we could even get started, and that was annoying enough. I didn't need Brant's shite added to the mix.

The rest of the night passed quickly, too quickly. Brant and I took turns sleeping so at least we got four or five hours each. It wasn't entirely restful, considering we'd been leaning against a wall while doing it, but it was better than nothing.

"Sirs." Lidia came rushing around the corner and bowed her head slightly before hurrying into Allete's room, shutting the door quickly behind her. I strained my hearing in hopes of catching some bit of conversation, but there was nothing. I wanted to know if Allete was okay, if she'd slept at all, and if she was hungry. I wanted to check the bruises on her body and make sure there weren't any injuries that I'd missed. I wanted to brush her hair again and sit quietly in her company with no one to interrupt us. But all of that was about as likely to happen as it was for Cathal to come crawling down the corridor like the dog he was and lift his leg to piss on the wall.

"What are you smirking about?" Brant asked.

I chuckled. "You don't want to know. I'm tired, and my mind is twisted."

"How is that different from when you're not tired?"

"Piss off, Brant."

Just then the door to Allete's chambers opened, and Lidia stepped out. Her eyes were red and puffy, and her cheeks swollen.

"Are you all right?" I asked quickly and then added, "Is

Allete all right?"

Lidia nodded. "Just a bit taken aback, is all. My lady has asked that I fetch breakfast. She isn't feeling well and wishes to cancel her engagements for the day. She asked also that you and Brant remain on guard for the entirety of the day. She said to apologize, because she knows you're tired, but she would very much prefer you." She paused, and then corrected herself. "She would very much prefer both of you to stay instead of rotating off duty today."

"And if King Cathal should come to call?" Brant asked the question that had been burning a hole in my head.

"He is to be kept off her corridor for the day. Princess Allete has requested I call upon the queen after she has broken her fast."

"Lidia." I took a step toward the handmaiden. "Did Allete tell you what happened yesterday? With Cathal?"

Lidia's eyes widened. It was apparent she didn't know that I knew. "Yes," she finally whispered.

"I won't let it happen again."

Her eyes softened. "You care for her. She cares for you, too. But Cathal, he's a dangerous man with too much power. He could kill you for something as slight as an insult. Allete wouldn't want that on her conscience."

"Then it is a good thing that I make my own decisions. She cannot be held responsible for my actions."

Lidia's mouth dropped open as she stared at me and then slowly her lips turned up into a smile. "You are right, Sir Torben. It is a good thing."

I frowned. "Sir? I am hardly a knight."

"After what you did for my lady last night, you are every bit a knight and more. Thank you, my lord," Lidia said as she gave me a deep bow. It was a bow reserved for royalty, and I was honored that she would think me worthy of such a thing. What had Allete told the little hand maiden?

She stood and then gave Brant another slight bow before hurrying off.

Brant glanced in the direction Lidia had run and then looked back me. "Sir?"

I shook my head and raised my hands up with my palms out. "I know not why she would call me such a thing. All I did for Allete last night was bestow human courtesy and kindness. Nothing more."

"Keep telling yourself that, General."

Twenty minutes later, Lidia was scurrying back toward us with two other maids, each laden down with trays. I reached for the handle of the door and pushed it open quickly just as the women arrived so they didn't have to pause in their walking. They swept into the room, and I closed the door just as quickly behind them, though not before I glanced around the room to see if I could spot Allete. She was sitting in the far-right corner. Her head was pressed to the window glass, and her eyes were closed. She looked tired. I wanted to hold her and tell her to rest, that I would keep her safe, but I knew she wouldn't welcome it. Not right now. Right now, she was too busy attempting to convince herself that we couldn't be together. But soon she would see that by my side was exactly where she belonged.

I HEARD THE DOOR open, and several feet shuffled inside, but I didn't open my eyes. My eyelids felt as if they were being pulled down by tiny weights hanging onto the tips of them. I was finding it impossible to keep them open. My head hurt from hours of crying, and my nose was raw from all the times I had blown it. I simply wanted to crawl under the covers and never come out.

"My lady." Lidia's sweet voice broke through my sorrow.

"We brought you breakfast and tea."

I wasn't hungry, but I knew I needed to eat. I needed to keep up my strength, and I hoped that maybe if I got something in my stomach I would not feel as sick as I did in that moment. I had decided the minute I'd woken from the less than three hours of sleep that I had gotten that I simply wasn't up for being around company, especially that of King Cathal. I knew that if I spent any time with the vile man, I would wind up saying something that would only cause myself more pain. I did not think I could handle any more pain, at least not yet.

"Thank you, Lidia," I told her as she set the tray beside me on the table next to the chair where I sat.

"Are you sure you don't wish me to fetch the doctor?"

I shook my head. "No thank you. I think I just feel ill from lack of sleep and yesterday's events. I simply want to be alone today."

"I daresay that your sisters will make that difficult, my lady. Especially after what happened yesterday. I do not think Dayna, or even Lizzie for that matter, will want to be away from you for long."

She was probably right. There was no way Dayna would be staying away. Lizzie was more of a wild card. Not because she didn't care, but because her world did not revolve around mine the way it did for Dayna. Being the middle child, Lizzie tended to be more introspective and kept to herself. But even still, with what Cathal had pulled, Lizzie would be more apt to check in on me than usual.

There was a knock on the door. Before I could ask who it was, the door opened and Dayna came sweeping in. Her dress twirled around her legs as she turned to shut the door. I could see the tension in her shoulders. Her chin jutted out in defiance, and when she turned back to face me, her eyes were narrowed. They looked ready to shoot flames at the first person to further incite her obvious anger.

"What vexes you, dear sister?" I asked as I watched her measured movements. She seemed to be using all of her energy to maintain her composure.

After several minutes of silence, Dayna finally seemed steady enough to speak. "I ran into that pigheaded scum this morning."

There was no need to ask to whom she was referring. There was only one person in all the castle who invited such an insult. "Did he do something to you?"

Dayna laughed a humorless sound. "I'm surprised he didn't call for my hanging."

"What did you do, Dayna?" I sat up straighter and moved to the edge of my seat. My heart was pounding in my chest as I considered all the things that my headstrong little sister was capable of.

"When he grabbed my arm, I reminded him that I have no obligation to him and that I would not hesitate to tell my father of his actions. And I also told him it would be wise of him to sleep with one eye open." She held up her hand to stop my reply. "I did not threaten him. When he attempted to point out that I had, I told him that all I had done was warn him about his safety. It, after all, would not look great for Father if something were to happen to Cathal while in our home."

I let out a resigned sigh. What was done was done. It could not be taken back. Dayna always had been the impulsive one, often acting before she considered the consequences. And I had no doubt that there would be consequences for her interaction with the king today. Very few kings would put up with insults, and this king was even less likely than most.

"That is not all I have done this morning," she informed

me.

"Oh, good heavens, Dayna. What more could you have possible done?" I groaned.

Before she could answer, the door opened once again, and, to my utter surprise, my father walked in, followed by my mother.

"Let's just say that my patience and ability to be civil ran out yesterday. I am not going to let you marry that man, Allete. He would wind up killing you just as he's done his other wives," Dayna nearly growled as she stepped aside allowing our parents to stand in front of me.

I started to stand, but my father motioned me to remain sitting.

"Your sister has brought some things to my attention," he began, his deep voice was rough with an emotion I couldn't quite put a name to. "I have come to verify her claims." He moved closer and placed his fingers under my chin, raising my head so he could better see my neck. His mouth tightened, and I knew he was seeing the marks Cathal had left upon me.

"I did not want to burden you with this, Father," I told him as he took a step back. "You already have so much to deal with."

"You are my daughter. What could possibly be more important than my own children?" he asked. "I realize that asking you to marry a man you do not love, and leave your homeland, seems cruel, but I did not realize the man was a monster. Do you believe me to be of so poor character that I would approve such an arrangement?"

"Of course not," I answered quickly. "But what other choice do I have? I know the nature of our kingdom's finances. I know defending against the Viking raids have depleted our resources. I understand we do not have the manpower to repel another attack from outside invaders.

We need Cathal's protection, and we most certainly could not withstand his wrath. I have to marry him," I declared with a conviction I didn't feel. I had to make my father see reason.

He shook his head. "No. We will find another way. I will not give you over to a butcher like a lamb to be slaughtered. I would never forgive myself, and I'm quite sure your mother would kill me."

I glanced around him to her. She stood, stoically quiet, but her eyes were filled with unshed tears. She looked strong and fragile all at the same time. It hurt me to see my kind mother in such a state, but I could not change the past. My father was correct, however. If he let me marry Cathal, she would kill him, or worse, leave him, which would cause him great shame.

"You can't," I pleaded. "His men are already inside our castle. He could attack us, kill our friends and their families. I couldn't let that happen, Father."

"Perhaps we wait to make a move," offered my mother. "At least until the morning of the wedding. Then his men will be packed, their weapons and equipment loaded on the ships."

"She cannot spend any more time with him," my father growled.

I huffed. "It's only two weeks. I can manage."

"And what if he takes things further the next time he manages to get you alone? What if he attempts to rape you or succeeds at it? I cannot put you in that kind of danger."

"I will be extra vigilant to keep from being alone with him. I will keep my own guards with me always, and I will wear the thigh sheath and dagger that Thomas gave me for my birthday two years ago. I will be fine, Father." I attempted to reassure him but I could tell from his narrowed eyes that he wasn't buying it.

"I don't like it," he snapped.

My mother stepped closer to him and placed her hand on his shoulders. I could see him visibly relax. "I don't like it, either. However, I trust our daughter. And she is right. We need the element of surprise, making our move when he is least expecting it. Her strategy is a sound one, and you know it."

"The gods were cruel for not granting me one son so that I would not be outnumbered by females," he grumbled.

I couldn't help but laugh. I stood up and wrapped my arms around my father and king. He bore the weight of an entire kingdom on his shoulders, and yet he maintained the humility of a man who did not wield such power. Yes, I had been angry at him for setting up an arranged marriage. But I had always known it would happen one day. And I knew it wasn't because he was seeking more power; it was because he knew we needed protection. My father was not a selfish man, but like any king, he often found himself faced with difficult circumstances—situations when none of his options were good. This was one such situation. And it broke my heart to see him blaming himself.

"This isn't your fault, Father. You could not have known that Cathal was a beast. Please do not take on the responsibility of his actions."

"You are not a parent, dear one," he said as his hand ran down the back of my head and hair. "One day you will be, and you will understand that any time your child is caused pain, you cannot help but feel as though you could have done something to prevent it. I would never wish such a fate on any of you, and yet it has happened. I beg your forgiveness, Allete."

To my utter shock, my father, the king, knelt before me and bowed his head. My heart broke, and for a moment I was speechless.

"There is no need for forgiveness, Your Highness," I said formally. "You have not wronged me. But if it will make you feel better, I will forgive you, though I feel no ill will toward you, and I never will."

After several silent moments, he stood and leaned forward, pressing a kiss to my forehead. "Promise me you will not be alone with him," he demanded, though not cruelly.

"I promise I will do my best to keep that from happening."

He stared at me for at least a minute before finally nodding. "That will have to be enough, I suppose."

He turned to Dayna and bowed his head. "Thank you for being brave, Dayna. Your courage and loyalty to your family will not be forgotten."

She smiled at him. "I wanted to be sure you knew ahead of time that there was a strong possibility someone would call for my head. If he touches her again, I will do everything in my power to slit his throat."

My mother shook her head and pinched the bridge of her nose. "Dear child," she mumbled.

"Please attempt to refrain from committing murder. At least until after you have spoken with me first," Father said.

"I make no promises, but I will try to control my urges."

"Then we are surely doomed," I teased. "Controlling your urges isn't exactly your strong suit."

"We all have minor flaws, sister mine," she cooed. "Some more tragic than others."

"We will leave you to rest," our mother said as she grabbed Father's hand. "We love you both."

Dayna and I spoke at the same time as we repeated the sentiment. When they were finally gone, and it was only Dayna, Lidia, and myself, I let out a slow breath. "I cannot believe you went to them."

"Somebody had to. What he did could not go unpunished or ignored. He assaulted you, a princess, and his future wife. I was not about to let that go, Allete."

I was grateful for my sister, but I worried for her. She was as in as much danger from his wrath as I was now that she'd threatened him. Dayna would not keep quiet if he confronted her again. Though I did not think myself any less brave than her, I did know that she was much more impulsive than me, and I was better at thinking things through. Dayna would simply act. Despite what her actions might provoke, she would simply lash out and consider the consequences later.

"You need to avoid being alone with him, too," I told her. "He will consider your confrontation as a direct insult to him. Even though he cannot kill you, he will do what he can to punish you."

"I am not afraid of him," she said. "He is nothing but a coward."

"Even cowards can be dangerous. Please be smart about your actions, Dayna."

"I will try to think before acting. I need to tell you one more thing," she said.

I held in the groan, knowing by the hesitation in her voice that I was not going to like what she had to say.

"I might have mentioned to Thomas what happened with Cathal."

"You what!" I nearly shouted.

"He loves you. He had a right to know."

I didn't have the energy to scold her, so I decided to hold my tongue and save it for when I could tell her off properly. I didn't want her to have any confusion about my displeasure at her actions. "So he will be here momentarily? Is that what you're saying?"

She nodded. "You might want to get dressed."

I motioned for Lidia to pick out a dress from the wardrobe and quickly ate the now-cold breakfast. I gave it my best effort, but I couldn't help being anxious. I knew there were so many ways my terrible situation could get much worse, but I did not want to give fate any ideas.

# CHAPTER Seventeen

"I HAVE COME TO REALIZE OVER THE YEARS THAT NO NEWS IS
GOOD NEWS. SO WHEN MY MEN CAME TO ME UNEXPECTEDLY, I
KNEW I WOULD SOON BE FACING TROUBLE. I HAD A FEELING IT
WOULD BE A LONG TIME BEFORE THERE WOULD BE NO NEWS TO
REPORT."

~TORBEN

I HEARD SEVERAL PAIRS of feet moving quickly through the
corridor. I turned my body in the direction of the sound,
simultaneously keeping my body in front of Allete's door.

"It's our men," Brant said as he too turned to face the
direction of the approaching steps.

I almost asked how he could tell, but then I too heard
the unique rhythm of the march, something I had trained
my warriors to do long ago, a pronounced stomp every
few steps. It let us distinguish friend from foe even at a
distance. I must have missed the sound at first because of
my worry over Allete.

Less than half a minute later, Amund, Rush, and
Delvin rounded the corner and came to a halt in front of
us.

"Sir," they all three said at the same time and bowed
their heads slightly.

"What brings you from your posts?" I asked.

"We have information," Amund spoke up.

"What news?" Sometimes getting information out of them was like trying to get a mule to lead a heifer.

"Magnus," Amund answered. "His plans have changed. He has become obsessed with taking over this kingdom. We aren't sure when he is planning to take action, but it will be soon."

I cursed under my breath. It was just like Magnus to take an already-dumb arse plan and make it worse. "Do you have any idea what he is planning?"

Rush stepped forward. "It will involve killing, that much was made clear by the men he'd snuck into the kingdom."

That was not surprising. With their Jarl, any raid would involve killing, even if it was not necessary. "Do you know if there is any discord among his ranks? Does anyone else see the folly of his plan?"

They all three shook their heads. I cursed under my breath.

"Continue to keep your ears and eyes open. Bring us any information immediately."

"Yes, sir."

"What report from your assigned posts?" I asked.

"We've had the displeasure of being around Cathal's soldiers," Delvin practically spat. "They're as dumb as bricks and as mean as wild boars."

"That isn't surprising," Brant chuckled. "Their king is no better."

"I cannot believe that the ruler of this kingdom would ship his daughter off to be married to such a man," Amund said.

"She is not going to marry him," I growled. "He's too dangerous, and she belongs with me." I hadn't really planned on saying that second part out loud, but it was true. And my men should probably know that she would be accompanying us home.

Before they could respond, another body appeared from around the corner. Thomas, Allete's cousin, looked as though someone had jabbed him with a hot poker. I could feel the violence emanating from him, and I did not like the look in his eyes.

"I need to see my cousin," he declared and took a step toward me and the door behind me.

"You won't be going in like that," I pointed at his face. "You get yourself under control first."

"Have you forgotten your place, guard?"

I tried not to hold his words against him. I knew he was simply worried about Allete, but I wouldn't allow him to think he could intimidate me just because of his station. "Not at all. I am Allete's chief guard, and it is my duty to ensure that she is safe from anyone—including overly emotional family members."

Thomas's jaw flexed, and his hands clenched into fists. After several minutes, he finally relaxed, if only a little. "Fair enough. Please allow me to see my cousin."

I turned and knocked on the door behind me. When I heard Allete's voice say to enter, I opened the door and stuck my head in. "Your cousin is here to speak with you."

Her lips tightened, but she gave a stiff head nod. "Send him in."

I pushed the door open wider and stepped aside so he could pass. Before he could walk into the room, I grabbed his arm and pulled him close. "If you do anything to further upset her, I won't react kindly. She's been through enough. Remember that before you open your mouth." I released him and waited until he was inside before closing the door.

Brant looked at me with a small smile and shook his head. "You are smitten."

My men shot me a look and their eyes widened. "Not a word," I snapped at them. "Return to your posts."

They each nodded and turned, heading back in the direction they'd come.

Brant began to speak again, but I held up my hand to stop him. "No more, please. I'm just worried about her safety." He left it alone, and we stood guard in silence. My own mind wandered to the life I might have with Allete in the future—a life filled with promise. I realized that until her, I had not been looking forward to my future. But now, now I very much wanted a chance to have a life with her.

I WATCHED AS THOMAS paced the room. He hadn't spoken since he'd arrived. He simply looked at me, shook his head, and began pacing. This went on for several long minutes before I finally addressed him.

"Are you going to say something?"

He stopped and looked up at me. "What do you want me to say? Do you want me to ask you why on earth you haven't told me about the things Cathal has said to you? Do you want me to ask why you didn't come to me when he assaulted you?" His voice rose with every question, and by the last one, he was yelling. "Do you want me to ask why you kept quiet and continued to put yourself in danger?"

My mouth hung open in shock. Thomas rarely yelled. He was the patient one in the family, but today he looked anything but.

"I can try to explain, but I do not think you will understand."

"I am not an idiot, cousin. I am capable of rational thought, if what you've done is rational."

"That's not what I meant, and you know it. I mean I

don't know if you can understand because perhaps I wasn't being rational. I was trying to protect my family. I understand why Father needs this alliance."

"He would not allow this if he knew what Cathal was like," Thomas challenged.

"You are correct. He does not wish me to marry Cathal, and he is trying to figure out a way to stop it without provoking all-out war. A war that we would have no chance of winning," I pointed out.

"So, your parents do know?"

I shot a look at Dayna. "Yes, they had the same source you did."

Thomas looked at my sister and a small smile appeared. "At least one of you was using her brain."

"I understand that you are worried for me, but please keep your insults to yourself. I have no need of another man treating me like I am a dullard."

Thomas's eyes widened. "I don't think you are a dullard, and I did not mean to imply that. You are correct. I am worried about you. You are my dearest cousin, and I can't stand the thought of anything happening to you."

I stepped toward him and wrapped my arms around him. "I know that. But I need you to trust me. I have agreed with Father that I will not be alone with Cathal again. I will always have my own guards with me, not just his. But we must be careful. Cathal can never know that my parents are aware of his behavior. I fear what he would do to those I love. He has already threatened to hurt my family."

"Why can't we just kill him and make it look like an accident?" Thomas asked.

Dayna laughed. "I knew I loved you for a reason."

"I'm your cousin," Thomas said dryly. "Isn't that reason enough?"

Dayna shook her head. "Just because you're family

does not make you worthy of my love."

"Good to know," Thomas laughed.

"You two cannot go around speaking about killing a king. That is treason, and the penalty is death. I don't even know if Father could keep you from being executed, so mind your tongues," I practically barked.

"You have turned into quite the little mama bear," Thomas chuckled.

I shrugged. "I'm just telling you what you already know. You are blinded by your hate, and that can cause you to act rashly."

"I suppose you are right, but sometimes acting rashly is needed."

I groaned. There was no point in arguing with him. When he'd made up his mind about something, there was rarely any way to change it. "So, did you only come here to scold me, or have you actually missed me? I have only seen you a handful of times in the past two weeks. Where have you been hiding?"

Thomas grinned and shrugged his shoulders. "I don't know what you mean. I've been around."

"No, you haven't," I argued. "You have been noticeable scarce. Have you found a girl or something?"

Dayna's eyes widened. "Have you finally found someone who will put up with you?"

I laughed. It was true. It would take a woman with great patience to handle the likes of Thomas. Though I was sure he would make a wonderful husband. He had a kind soul and playful nature. He was sure to be a most delightful father, too because of his childlike nature. His children would never lack for adventures.

"Why on earth would I tell you two wenches if I'd found the woman of my dreams? You would just run off to warn her away from me. No." He shook his head. "I think it better to keep that secret to myself."

"You have to tell us," Dayna said as she stomped her foot. "We're your favorite cousins."

"You're my only cousins," Thomas pointed out.

"That's beside the point."

"No, I think it is the entire point. How can I have favorites when there is no one to compete for my affection?"

Dayna picked up the nearest thing she could grab, a shoe I'd discarded on the floor, and threw it at him. "Do not play games with me, Thomas Mathew. You will tell us if you have found a potential bride. We have to approve of her. That is the way of it."

He laughed, and his eyes sparkled in that joyful way that I loved. "No, Dayna, that is your way of it. Not everything revolves around you and your ways."

"Allete, tell him he is wrong," she pleaded.

It was my turn to laugh. Thomas had a point. Dayna was by no means a selfish person, but she could tend to be a tad self-centered at times. "Dayna, you can't force someone to tell you something that he does not wish to share."

"Why not?"

"Because it is his right to keep things to himself."

She sat down on the end of my bed with a plop and crossed her arms in front of her chest. She looked like a scolded child. It only made me want to laugh more, but I bit my tongue to keep from doing so.

"But..." I turned back to Thomas. "She isn't entirely wrong. A second and third opinion might be in order. After all, you can't hide her away from us forever."

"Well, look at the time. I must be on my way." Thomas ignored my statement as he walked over to Dayna and gave her a quick hug and kiss on the forehead.

"Thomas," she practically whined.

He was undeterred as he came back to me and wrapped his arms around me. "You stay safe. Promise?"

I nodded. "I promise."

He stepped back and gave me a playful tap on the nose and then headed to the door. He pulled it open and just before he closed it behind him, he said over his shoulder, "Just to drive you both bat crazy, yes, there is a woman in my life. But I will reveal nothing further." He closed the door quickly behind him.

I saw the look on Dayna's face and chuckled. "You really hate not knowing, don't you?"

"It's not fair that he won't tell us. If we had found suitors, he would demand to know who they were, and then he would want to meet them."

She was right, he would. But then, we were female and whether we liked it or not, there was a double standard when it came to male and females and courting. "We should be happy for him and wait until he is ready to tell us more," I offered.

"Fine," Dayna huffed. "I'll wait, but I won't be happy about it."

"I said you should be happy for him, not happy about waiting."

"I'll consider your counsel."

I smiled at her. "I look forward to the day you find your match. He will have to have a backbone of steel to stand up to you."

"I've already met him." She pointed at the door. "He's on the other side of that door, and everything about him calls out to me."

"A guard, Dayna?" I asked, even though I knew the answer. "You cannot marry a guard. No matter how kind he is or how good a warrior, he is beneath your station."

"That doesn't make him less than me. Just because I

was born a princess does not make me worthier or in any way better than him," she argued.

"I agree with you, but it is the way of our society. You must marry within your own class. It's the way it has always been." I didn't agree with it either, but I understood that anyone of noble birth who married a commoner would be shunned and treated with disdain. I did not want that for my sister.

"And how will that ever change if we aren't willing to take the first step?"

I returned to the chair I'd been sitting in before Thomas had arrived and looked at my younger sister. "In so many ways, you are wise beyond your years. I wish I had an answer for you. You are right, we should set the example for change. But any time there is change, there is trouble. I don't want you to have to be the one who bears that burden."

"You cannot protect me from everything, Allete."

"You certainly try to protect me from everything," I pointed out.

"That's different. You are important. You're the firstborn. You need to continue Father's lineage."

"It's a male who carries the lineage, and please don't ever insinuate that I am of more importance than you or Lizzy. We are all of equal importance, and unique in our own ways," I said, hoping she would hear the sincerity in my words. I had never thought myself to be somehow worth more than my sisters. Yes, I was firstborn, but that did not place a greater value on my life.

"Neither of us possesses the power that you have," Dayna pointed out. "No matter how unique we are, we cannot heal others. That *does* make you more valuable."

I didn't know how to argue that point, though I still did not agree. I did not know why I had been giving the ability and my sisters given none. Magic had no rhyme or reason, as far as I could tell. Some people had it, and some people simply did not.

"What are your plans for the day?" she asked.

I breathed out a tired sigh and sat back, folding my hands in my lap. "I just want to enjoy quiet and rest. Obviously, I want to stay as far away from Cathal as possible."

"No one blames you there," she said.

"I had Lidia inform Torben and Brant that they were to stay at their post and not let anyone in before speaking with me first. I know that he will be here soon, considering I did not attend breakfast."

"Do you want me to leave?" Dayna asked.

I could see that she hoped I would decline. She hated being alone. I had never been uncomfortable with solitude, but for Dayna it was almost a form of punishment. "You can stay," I said finally, not wanting to be the one to make her feel as though she was being punished.

"Would you mind if I gathered your laundry, my lady?" Lidia spoke up. Sometimes it was easy to forget the quiet servant was there. From what I had learned from Lidia over the years, when servants went through training before being allowed to work in the palace, they were taught two important things. Servants were not to be heard. Servants were not to be seen. Basically, she said it meant that they were to do their job to the best of their ability without disturbing the people of the house.

It didn't bother me to notice Lidia, and I never wanted her to feel like she couldn't make noise in my presence, but her training had been drilled into her mind. She did her job very, very well.

"That would fine. Thank you, Lidia," I said and caught the small smile she let slip.

When I turned back to Dayna, she was holding a deck of cards in her hands. "What mischief are you up to?"

"After Cathal makes his appearance and stomps off in a huff, let's get Brant and Torben to play cards with us. Maybe throw in a few wagers."

"Where did you learn to play for wagers?" Before she could answer I held up my hand. "Never mind, I don't want to know."

There was a booming voice from outside the door. I felt a sudden headache coming on, and if it had a name it would have been Cathal.

"**I** DEMAND THAT YOU open this door this instant, or I will hang you myself," Cathal snarled.

I supposed I should have at least tried to look scared by his threat, but I was too angry. It was like dealing with a disobedient child.

"The princess is not feeling well and has given strict orders that she isn't to be bothered by anyone. Therefore, I am not required to acquiesce to your demand. That means I do not have to do what you tell me."

"I know what acquiesce means, you cad."

I shrugged. "Just wanted to make sure there would be no misunderstandings. I will let the princess know that you came by to inquire about her." I nearly gagged on my own words. He hadn't come by to check on her, that was sure. He'd come by to make demands, bully her, and take what did not belong to him.

"I am to be her husband. Her orders do not apply to me. I can see my bride whenever I damn well please. Now, for the last time, open this door!" His face was turning an interesting shade of purple, and his teeth were gritted so tightly together that I was sure they would break at any moment.

I began to answer, but the door behind me opened and closed quickly. Lidia, the handmaiden to Allete, stood next to me, her shoulders pulled back and her chin up proudly.

"My lady says to bid you good morning, but she cannot see you. She has been ill this morning." She indicated the linens in her arms as if to insinuate that Allete had been vomiting on them. "She doesn't want to expose anyone else, and her chambers need a thorough cleaning."

When I looked back at Cathal, I almost laughed. His face showed a level of disgust that I had frequently observed on new soldiers in battle who've seen the belly of a man cut open and watched the intestines spill out. The man wasn't even concerned that his wife-to-be was ill.

"Very well," he said as he straightened his tunic and took a large step away from Lidia and the soiled linens. "Please tell her I wish her a speedy recovery." He turned on his heel and strode quickly away.

"Did he just say something that wasn't an insult?" Brant asked.

Lidia chuckled. "I do not think he cares about the recovery for her sake. I imagine it has more to do with the upcoming wedding. He doesn't want to have to take a sickly bride to the altar."

I nodded. "Yes, that seems the more likely motive."

Lidia stepped in the opposite direction Cathal had gone and looked at Brant and me. "My lady also said that once Cathal was gone, she wanted you both to enter her chamber."

My eyes widened. "Why?"

She leaned forward and whispered. "She isn't really sick. These linens aren't soiled. She's tired and does not want to deal with anyone today. But Dayna is spending the day with her because, well, she's Dayna. And the young princess suggested a game of cards. You two were invited to play."

She turned and moved off down the corridor while we stood staring. Allete wanted us to play ... cards? I should probably regretfully decline and explain that I needed to be at my post to keep watch, but I didn't have the self-control to do such a thing. I wanted to be near her. I wanted to keep her from attempting to put space between us because she thought we couldn't be together.

"Up for a game of cards?" I asked Brant.

"With the lovely Dayna? Always."

I knocked on the door and waited until she bade us enter. Allete and Dayna were already seated at a small table, and Brant and I joined them. I was itching to touch her. But it might look strange if I just reached out for no reason and took her hand, and even stranger still if I attempted to braid her hair the way I had the night before.

"What kind of cards do you two play?" Dayna asked them.

"I've only played a few times," Brant said. "But I do not remember the name of the games."

"What about you?" she asked me.

"Same."

Allete frowned. "I thought all guards played cards. Aren't you all notorious gamblers?"

I wished I could tell her yes, but the truth was I had no idea what guards did during their time off.

"Brant and I aren't always the most social of men," I hedged.

Allete gave me a look that said she was not convinced that my words were entirely true. She was too perceptive for her own good.

"We can teach you a new game, but I'm afraid there might be some wagering involved," Dayna said as she shuffled the cards. "I'd hate for you to lose anything too valuable."

"A little betting never hurt anyone," Brant smiled.

Allete chuckled and shook her head. "If you believe that, then you are more naïve than I would have guessed."

He pressed a palm to his heart and scrunched up his face. "You wound me, Your Highness. I have the weakest of constitutions."

The sisters snorted together.

"I will believe that when I see Cook relinquish her carving knives," Dayna said.

"Deal the cards, Dayna, and explain the game," Allete ordered. It was obvious that she was trying to keep her sister on task. Dayna seemed to be distracted by Brant, and the young girl couldn't quite keep her eyes on what she was doing. Brant was simply grinning at her, knowing full well the effect he was having on her. He would be insufferable to be around for at least a week.

I was surprised that the day continued without any disturbances. In between games and talking, Brant and I would step out into the hall and walk up and down the corridors to make sure no one was hiding, and to talk about the girls, of course. Then we'd returned to Allete's chamber for more cards and pleasant conversation.

Everything felt natural and relaxed. At one point, I felt less like a guard and more like a companion, an equal to the two women. I wondered if Allete felt it. By the time the moon had replaced the sun in the sky, and the darkness at last lay like a blanket over the kingdom, I knew we needed to call it a night.

"While I have had had a wonderful time," I began as I stood from the small table. "I think it is time we returned to our posts. You both need rest."

"You need rest as well, Torben," she said gently. "You've been up all night and all day."

"I need to guard you," I said, knowing that it would be very difficult to entrust her safety to someone else.

"Please choose two men you trust and have them take your place at least for a few hours so that you may sleep," she said, the tone of command in her voice.

I nodded. "As you wish."

I glanced at Brant who was busy whispering to Dayna and grabbed his tunic. "Let's go, lover boy. We must not overstay our welcome."

Before we could close the door behind us I heard Allete's quiet voice and turned to look at her.

"Thank you, Torben, for being here."

I bowed my head and made sure my eyes held hers. "There is no other place I would rather be than by your side."

# CHAPTER Eighteen

"NO MATTER HOW LONG YOU'VE KNOWN SOMEONE—EVEN IF
YOU'VE GROWN UP WITH THEM, KNOWN THEM THEIR WHOLE
LIFE—THEY CAN STILL SURPRISE YOU. SOMEWHERE ALONG THE
WAY, THEY GREW AND CHANGED AND YOU MISSED IT."

~DIARY OF ALLETE AUVRAY

IT WAS LATE WHEN a knock on my chamber door woke me
from a light slumber which I had not fallen into easily.
I wiped the sleep from my eyes and sat up, attempting to
tame the hair that had escaped my braid.

"Come in," I called, not wanting to climb out of bed. I
suspected the identity of my visitor, and I knew Torben's
man would not allow entrance to anyone who would do
me harm.

The door made a creaking noise as Lizzy pushed it
open. It was a small thing, something that went unnoticed
during daylight hours, but now seemed to echo throughout
the castle, causing me to irrationally wonder if it would
wake the entire house.

My sister stuck her head in. Her face was lit by the
glow of a lantern as she held it out so she could see into
the dark room. "I'm sorry to wake you, but I need to speak
with you."

I motioned her to come in and grabbed the dressing

robe that Lidia had laid on the end of my bed. Once I'd slipped it on, I pointed at the chair. "Have a seat, Lizzy, you look dead on your feet. What have you been doing? We haven't seen hide nor hair of you in a couple of days."

"I am sorry that I had to leave after what happened to you," she said. "Dayna stopped me on my way in and gave me a good scolding for not being around."

I smiled. "She is overly protective."

"And rightly so. I should have been here for you. I just don't understand how that man could do such awful things to his future wife? He has no shame. No sense of honor."

"No, he does not. He is a vile man ruled by his wants and desires and the pursuit of power. Father was not aware of his true nature when he promised me to the monster."

Lizzy's eyes widened. "Is he aware now?"

I nodded and explained that Dayna had told our mother and father. When I was finished, relief flooded my sister's face.

"What is he going to do?" she asked.

"I'm not sure. Dayna and Thomas want to assassinate him," I said, rolling my eyes.

"Good," my sister spat. "It's what he deserves."

This took me aback. It would be something I would expect from Dayna, but not Lizzy.

"Father has not spoken of violence. Since when were you so comfortable with the taking of a man's life, sister?" I asked as I watched her face carefully.

She shrugged. "Any assault on a royal family member, especially the eldest princess, would be grounds for a hanging. Why should it be any different with Cathal?"

"Because he is a king. His death would bring terrible consequences." I knew she had not come only to speak about Cathal. I could tell that something else was agitating her, but she was stalling. For some reason, she was avoiding the topic.

"Where have you been, Lizzy?" I asked again. "Have you been tending the sick?"

After several minutes, she shook her head. "No," she said softly.

"Are you going to voluntarily tell me where you've been and what you've been up to, or am I going to have to drag it out of you?"

She took a deep breath and then looked up from where she'd been staring at her fidgeting hands. "I've met someone."

This was a declaration I had not expected. I kept my face relaxed as I spoke. "And I assume this is someone that we do not know, otherwise you wouldn't need to sneak around."

She nodded.

"Where did you meet him?"

"While walking out around the castle grounds."

Okay, so Lizzy was going to make getting this information as difficult as getting Thomas to behave like a grown man.

"Who is he?" I asked.

"He is from Cathal's court," Lizzy admitted

I wasn't sure what I should say to that. I had imagined Cathal's men as nameless, faceless monsters, following the example of their vile leader. But it wasn't fair to judge an entire kingdom because of its king's actions. Still, the news was unsettling.

"What do you know about him? What is his name? How long have you been seeing him?" A barrage of questions flew from my mouth. I tried to keep an accusatory tone from my voice but feared that I was unsuccessful.

"I met him in the tavern one day when I'd gone in to get lunch with Mrs. Topper. I'd been gathering herbs, hoping

Quinn Loftis

to find something that would help her cough. He was sitting at a table alone. He looked so troubled, I couldn't ignore him. After Mrs. Topper left, I admit that I lingered in the common room." She paused, and her eyes seemed to become unfocused. "He caught me staring at him and came over and said hello. We sat and talked for an hour, and I agreed to meet again the next day."

"And how long ago was this?"

"Almost three weeks," she answered.

"With no chaperone?" I tried not to sound upset, but I clearly was. A single maiden alone with a man was not proper, and I didn't want anyone gossiping about my sister. It wouldn't matter if Lizzy had not done anything inappropriate with the man; the implication of what could happen would be enough for people to condemn her. "Did you consider what could happen? You, of all of us, are the one with good sense, Lizzy. Why would you behave in such a manner?"

"I don't know." She sighed and leaned back in the chair. Her hair was windblown and dark circles adorned her eyes. "Something about him just makes me forget my surroundings. I get caught up in our time together. He hasn't been forward with me, and he's never acted like anything but a gentleman."

"He should have asked to speak with Father and to have a chaperone. That is what a gentleman who cares about a woman's virtue does to protect her," I pointed out. I could tell she was disappointed in herself, and I hated to see her hurting.

"Maybe, but it doesn't matter now," she said. "There's something more important I need to tell you. It's urgent."

"What?" I asked, now truly perplexed.

"Something is going to happen, but I can't tell you about it yet."

"What are you talking about?" Butterflies were forming in my stomach.

"If I wait to tell you until the last moment, then you can honestly say you knew nothing about it. You won't be able to be accused."

"Okay, now you're beginning to scare me, Liz. What is going on?" There was a prickling sensation running down mine spine, and a voice in my mind yelling, 'Danger!'

"I truly can't tell you now."

"What does it involve? Is it dangerous?" There I went with the bombardment of questions again. But I had this desperate need to know that she would be safe.

"It is dangerous, yes, very dangerous. But—" She held up her hand before I could interrupt. "It is also going to solve a lot of our problems, especially for you." She reached over and grabbed my hand, clutching at it like a lifeline. "Everything is going to be okay, Allete. Please trust me, okay?"

I wanted to trust her. I wanted to believe that what she was saying was absolute truth, and all of our problems would go away. I didn't want to be stuck with Cathal. I didn't want to move away. I didn't want to be away from Torben. I scoffed at myself. Even if I could be near Torben, I could never marry him.

"It is not you that I don't trust, Lizzy. It's this man you've met. He's an unknown factor. How do we know he is being truthful? Whatever he's told you could be a lie."

"He is telling the truth. I know it," she said. The certainty in her voice was a little shocking. She truly believed this man would help us. I had no idea how.

"Then please tell me what's going on."

"I can't." She shook her head violently. "It would be too dangerous for you. I'm asking you, sister to sister, please trust me."

There was nothing I could do in that moment. I could see in her eyes that she felt she was doing the right thing, not just for me, but for our entire kingdom. Perhaps a couple of days' consideration would help me decide on how to move forward with the additional information.

"I know you are tired, and I do apologize for interrupting your sleep," she said as she stood and headed toward the door. "I love you, Allete, and it pains me to see you endure so much agony because of a sense of duty."

She was gone before I could respond to her words. I knew that she loved me. It wasn't something we just went around saying all the time, but I knew it. Lizzy wasn't emotional, and she was rarely affectionate, which made her words tonight even more poignant.

I lay back in my bed and pulled the covers up around me. Sleep would be difficult to come by after what my sister had told me. But I guessed I was more tired than I'd realized, because I managed to drift off after only a few minutes.

My dreams were filled with a hideous monster wearing a bloody crown. Wolves carrying sharp swords and biting axes chased the monster. Suddenly, another monster, stronger and more terrible than the first, appeared. This one wore a black sheep's skin over his body and a boar's head on his skull like a helmet. He was quiet as he hunted, ignoring the other monster and the chasing wolves. His narrowed eyes were cunning but also crazed, like a starved beast given a banquet of meat. He was too wary to eat, though his hunger gnawed at him. The chaos suddenly stopped as a glowing light appeared in the middle of the battlefield. At first, it was just a small ball of illumination, but then it began to grow, larger and larger, until finally it was blinding. Then a woman appeared, standing alone. The wolves were bowing to the woman. Both monsters simply watched her, salivating as they stared at her. Then they looked at each other and each had venom in their eyes. Suddenly, with a mighty roar, they lunged at one another, fangs bared and slavering. I didn't see what happened next. The dream winked out, and I was simply sleeping.

Even in my sleep, with the dream gone, I still wondered at the second monster that slunk around the battlefield. I understood the monster with the crown, of course. That part of the dream was all too clear. But the second monster and the army of wolves was a mystery to me. Why were the wolves chasing Cathal? Whether correct or not, I saw myself as the woman, the light around me representing my healing ability. Both monsters terrified me. The second monster, however, seemed even more terrifying because I didn't know his identity. Just before I felt myself beginning to wake from the restless sleep, I heard a woman's voice inside my head.

"I will be coming soon. It is time we talked. It is time you know what fate holds in store for you."

"Who are you," I asked the voice.

"I am the Oracle."

"THIS IS THE THIRD day she's not left her room," Brant said, as if I was unaware.

I nodded.

"Cathal isn't going to put up with it again today. Yesterday, he was even more aggressive. If Allete's father hadn't stepped in and told Cathal that his counsel was needed, who knows what might have happened?"

"I agree, he is going to be angry. I know that he will have a temper tantrum right here in this corridor. And I know there is nothing I can do so stop him."

"You could suggest to her that she simply take a walk around the garden," Brant said. "Perhaps he would be appeased."

"I don't want her around him. Better I face his wrath than Allete." The idea of him anywhere near my princess produced a kind of rage in me that I had never known was possible. I was not about to suggest she spend any time with him, no matter how brief.

As if on cue, Cathal rounded the corner.

"Speak of the devil, and he shall appear," Brant muttered under his breath.

I didn't bother to acknowledge the king. I simply stared straight ahead like a silent sentry. There was no point in me wasting my breath. Cathal would do enough talking for the both of us.

"I have left her alone for two days. I am not leaving here without seeing my bride." His voice was surprisingly calm, but his clenched fists and stiff shoulders spoke volumes about what he was feeling on the inside. Cathal was livid.

"I will check with the princess," I told him and knocked gently on the door. Her voice called out for me to enter, and I pushed the door open, slid inside, and closed it behind me in a nearly seamless motion.

"How are you today, princess?" I asked as I looked her over, trying to determine how she was feeling simply by observing her body language. She seemed resigned, and it troubled me.

"I am fine, Torben. Thank you for being so diligent in your job. I know you must be tired."

My lips lifted only a fraction. "I've gone longer without rest and spent time in far worse conditions than a palace corridor."

Allete sighed and turned to fully face me. She wore a simple blue dress that was alluring and concealing at the same time. She was beautiful, even as worried and tired as she looked. She was the most beautiful woman I'd ever seen.

"I suppose Cathal is waiting on me? Is that why you've come in?" Her voice held a weariness to it that made me want to fix anything and everything in the world just to see her smile for a moment.

"I came to see you because the corridor is dull and cold. You, lovely Allete, are the opposite. You are bright and shining, with a warmth that fills any room. You are my sun." I do not know at what point in my life of raiding and plundering that I suddenly became a master of words, but there it was. If Brant had heard me, he would have laughed until his huge body laid sprawled on the floor, belly up, twitching like a spider that was taking its last breath.

Her eyes were wide, and her mouth had dropped open. Her chest was rising and lowering a bit faster and she was wiping her palms on her dress. I'd made her uncomfortable. I'd shaken the ground beneath her feet, and she didn't know quite how to handle it.

"But, yes you are correct, the other reason I came was because Cathal is demanding to see his bride." I felt my own heartbeat increase, loathing the idea that Cathal believed Allete to be his.

"I've allowed myself two days," she began, choosing not to acknowledge my poetic words. "I will not get away with another." She took a deep breath and then several steps toward the door. She stopped and looked at me. "You will be with me?"

"I will. Whether the heavens collapse and the mountains descend into the depths. Whether the gods curse all humans and wipe us out. Whether the great abyss and Hades himself takes over the world of the living. For as long as you want me, I won't leave you." She couldn't possibly know all the ways I meant those words. She couldn't know that I'd just chosen her as my mate, the woman I would build a life with. She couldn't know that the words I'd spoken were the very same words used in the ceremony of joining a man and woman in my clan.

# CHAPTER Nineteen

"THERE ARE TIMES IN OUR LIVES THAT PAINFUL THINGS HAPPEN. DURING THESE TIMES, WE REALIZE THAT NOTHING COULD HAVE PREPARED OURSELVES FOR SUCH PAIN. OUR HEARTS ARE NOT PREPARED FOR IT, OUR MINDS CANNOT GRASP IT, AND OUR SOULS ARE LEFT BROKEN FROM IT. I HAVE FELT SUCH PAIN, BUT I REALIZE THAT BROKENNESS IS NOT THE END. I REALIZE THAT I CAN LET THE PAIN DESTROY ME, OR I CAN RISE FROM THE RUBBLE THAT HAS BECOME MY HEART AND BE ALL THE STRONGER FOR IT."

~DIARY OF ALLETE AUVRAY

I HAD ONLY BEEN expecting a simple 'yes'. The question was certainly simple enough. I just needed to know that I would not be facing Cathal alone. But deep down I knew that the question wasn't that simple. I needed to know that *Torben* would be the one to keep me safe. But he had said so much more than yes. The words were beautiful, but something in my gut told me that they were more significant than I realized. The words were far more than a simple statement. They felt like a covenant. Whatever the words had meant to him, for me they were a lighthouse. They were a beacon of hope. Maybe he realized I needed something hopeful to stand on because I felt so uncertain about my future.

I took a deep breath and then nodded at Torben to open the door. I kept my eyes on the ground, unable to look at the man who had stripped me of my dignity. But of course, he wasn't about to let me protect myself.

I felt his fingers under my chin, and I had to swallow back the bile that was threatening to make an appearance. As he put pressure on my chin to raise my face, I bit the inside of my lip in order to keep myself from crying. I would not shed anymore tears because of the monster before me. He was not worthy of my tears. But when my eyes finally met his, my resolve nearly crumbled. If it was even possible, Cathal looked more eager and lustful as his eyes roved over my body.

I felt like I needed to scrub myself with lye soap after his eyes perused me. He was no doubt removing every piece of clothing as he stared. The anger invoked by that thought kept the tears at bay. I was simply a brood mare to him. He did not want me for any other reason than to look pretty and bear his children. I would not cry, no matter how it hurt my soul.

"How are you feeling, my love?" Cathal asked. His voice was sickeningly silky. He leaned closer and took a deep breath. "You smell divine. You must no longer be sick."

"I am better. Though I'm still tired."

"I have missed you." His hand dropped from my face and grabbed my hand. He wrapped it in the crease of his elbow and began to lead me away from my chamber. "Instead of spending time with my lovely, tasty bride, I have had to endure boring talks with your father concerning your dowry and the protection of his kingdom."

"I apologize, my lord. I'm sure that must have been quite unpleasant." No matter how unpleasant he thought his time with my father had been, I knew it would be nothing compared to the time I was about to spend with him. My skin was crawling, and my stomach was threatening to climb out of my throat. His touch alone was enough to make me want to dunk myself in a vat of scalding hot water.

"I would like to take you on a ride today," he said. "And I wish you to ride with me."

It was the 'ride with me,' comment that snapped my attention to how close our bodies were. Riding with him on the same mount would mean being even closer. I was not sure that I could tolerate being closer.

"Forgive me, Your Highness," Torben said. "But propriety demands that the princess ride her own horse."

I started to let out a sigh of relief, but it was cut short when Cathal answered.

"*I* demand she ride with me," he snapped. "And you are to hold your tongue, or I will cut it out."

I didn't miss the way Brant put a firm grip on Torben's shoulder once Cathal had turned away. He whispered something to his comrade, and I could see the battle raging in Torben's eyes. He looked at me, and I tried to give him a reassuring smile that I was fine. The short shake of his head told me he wasn't buying my false bravado.

Once we were at the stables, I did not bother arguing when Cathal demanded one horse for the pair of us. There was no point. I would simply make sure to ride behind him. If I was behind him, he couldn't get his filthy hands on me.

I walked over to the first stall and found one of the younger mares named Delilah. She was a beautiful red with a dark black mane. She shook her head at me and whinnied.

"Sorry, girl," I whispered as I ran a hand down the front of her face. "I cannot take you this time." I motioned over my shoulder to where Cathal was arguing with Geoffrey, the stable master, about which horse would be best suited for two riders. "Unfortunately, he is in charge."

Delilah snorted.

I smiled and laughed. "I know, I'm not too impressed either. But perhaps another day soon we will go out." She nodded her head as though she understood my words, and then nudged my face with her soft nose. With one last pat and a kiss on her nose, I turned back to face Cathal and the others.

I felt eyes on me as I watched Cathal complain about the fact that his own horse couldn't be used. When I turned my head slightly to the right, I saw Torben. His intense gaze was burning over me, and I felt myself blush. I shook my head at him as if to tell him to stop. His lips turned up in a smirk, and he shook his head back at me. He wasn't about to do what I told him. Stubborn man, I mentally growled.

"Allete," Cathal's voice bit out.

I turned back to him. "Hmm?"

"We will be riding this beast. Come here, and I'll help you mount. I can ride behind you."

"I would prefer to ride in the back, my lord," I said in a voice that I hoped sounded docile and unchallenging. "I've not ridden with another rider before. I would feel more comfortable this way."

His jaw clenched as though he were trying his very hardest not to growl at me. He stared at me for a long time, and I got the impression he was waging some sort of internal battle. Cathal must have seen the determination in my eyes because he finally sighed. "Fine. I'll mount first and help pull you up behind me."

He climbed up onto the large horse and then moved his foot from the stirrup so that I could put my foot in it. I bit back a gasp when I felt a hand on my waist and another grasp the back of my thigh.

"It is not necessary for you to help her, guard." Cathal leaned down to grab my arm and would have jerked it out of socket had not Torben been there helping boost me up.

"I have to disagree, King Cathal. And since Allete is my charge and responsibility, it is my duty to make sure she is safe at all times."

I couldn't see Cathal's face as I sat behind him on the horse, but I could feel his trembling form. The rage in him was going to erupt like a volcano, and the gods save any who were near him when that happened. I just hoped I was far away when it finally did. Though if Torben kept poking the beast, we would be the immediate collateral damage when the explosion came.

"I'm eager to get started," I said, trying to break the tension. "Shall we go?"

I could see Torben and Brant clambering onto their own horses, and I tried not to laugh when they both had to scurry to mount to keep up with Cathal, who had suddenly pushed the horse forward into a fast trot.

As he picked up speed, I turned my face up to the sun and closed my eyes. I wanted to forget who I was riding with and simply enjoy the fresh air. Thought it seemed Cathal's presence was casting a pall over the whole of nature, I could still feel the familiar countryside singing out to me. The trees were clapping their leaves, and the grass was swaying to the music of the birds. The sun shone down on it all as though it were giving light to a magnificent performance. How I wished I could be a part of it, but with a different rider in front of me.

I felt my hair beginning to fall from the bun into which Lidia had placed it. I loved feeling it fall down my back while the wind flowed through it. It was the best I had felt in several days, but it all came to a screeching halt when I felt Cathal's hand on my thigh.

He squeezed, and it was so painful I knew he must be leaving a bruise. He was marking me again, as if he hadn't already done enough damage. The bastard, I growled in my mind and mentally kicked him. Oh, how I would love to kick him for real. I imagined it would give me great satisfaction, but the consequences would likely be deadly.

He tilted his head so that I would be able to hear him as he spoke.

"Only a week until we wed," he told me, though it sounded more like a warning. "You will be all mine, and then there will be no guards between us."

I didn't say anything. How was I supposed to respond to such words? It wasn't like a man telling the woman he loved that he was excited about being alone with her. It was more like a butcher telling his prized hog that soon enough the crowds would no longer be watching, and he would be able to cut the poor beast apart. *Think pleasant thoughts, Allete*, I chastised myself. No matter how hard I tried, I couldn't find the resolve to remain positive.

We rode even faster and, after at least an hour, he stopped at a stream. Torben and Brant were there less than a minute behind. We all dismounted and set our horses to graze.

"Stand watch over there," Cathal told them. "The princess and I have things to discuss."

He took my hands and pulled me away from them, drawing me closer to the stream. For a fleeting second, I entertained the thought that he might be about to drown me. A few weeks ago, I might not have minded if it meant I didn't have to spend my life with him, but now there was Torben. The escape of dying no longer held the appeal it once did.

"We need to discuss your transition to my kingdom," he began. He turned me so that his back was to the guards, and I could not see them past his broad shoulders. "You do not need to bring your lady in waiting, or any of your help for that matter."

"What?" This got my attention fully. "But why wouldn't I bring my lady?"

"Because I have sufficient servants to ensure you are taken care of. There is no need to bring in more mouths to feed."

I considered making a comment about his inability to feed an additional single servant but decided I would simply be asking for a fight. I didn't want to provoke him when we were so far away from any witnesses.

"And you will not need to bring any of your things."

"What?" I interrupted. "Forgive me, but it sounds like you want me to just leave every part of my life behind. Am I to accompany you home with no clothes on as well?" So much for not provoking him.

His brow rose, and his eyes sparkled with wicked intent. "A naked bride in my carriage. I am sure that can be arranged and would be most enjoyed."

My heart nearly stopped. *Good job, Allete,* I scolded myself. Bringing up the absence of clothing around Cathal was as stupid as waving a piece of raw meet in front of a starving tiger, and just as dangerous.

"I do not understand why you wouldn't want me to take some of my own things. It would make me feel less homesick," I argued. When he simply stared at me, I realized what an imbecile I was being. I wasn't going with him anyway. None of what he wanted mattered. So why was I intent on quarreling with him like it did?

"I think a fresh start will do you good. You are going to be my queen. I want you to have the mind of a queen, the manners and look of a queen, a regal woman—not a girl." He glanced down at my body and then back up to my face.

"I know there is a woman underneath that fabric, and I want you to look the part."

I screwed my face up into one of disgust. "Why do you desire me to wear such revealing clothing? Does it not bother you that other men may stare?"

He glanced over his shoulder at Torben and Brant as though I somehow meant those two. "I won't have to worry about that. The men in my kingdom know I would scoop their eyes out with a spoon and feed them to the crows if they so much as glance at you."

I swallowed down the bile that rose in my mouth. That was a bit disturbing.

"Just do as you're told, Allete, and your life will be much easier with me. Now." He paused and then stepped closer to me. "I haven't seen or touched you in a few days, and I will not refrain any longer."

Before I could stop him, he'd wrapped an arm around my waist and pulled me tight against his body. His other hand ran up my back until it was at the nape of my neck, his thumb and fingers brushing beneath my ears. I tried so hard to think of Torben's hands and imagine it was him who held me.

Cathal tilted my head back and made me look up at him. After simply staring at me for a little while, he leaned down and pressed his lips to mine. It was surprisingly gentle. I gasped as his full lips caressed my own, coaxing me to respond. When his tongue slipped out and licked across mine like velvet, I gasped again, and he took advantage by slipping his tongue into my open mouth. His soft groan was as surprising as was my own reaction.

I didn't want to enjoy what he was doing and I certainly didn't, just because of who was performing the actions. But I could not deny that what he was doing was very, very different from the way he had kissed me previously. This time it was as though he were savoring me. He pulled me closer, and his hard body molded my softer one to him.

I was lost. I didn't understand what was happening or why I was allowing it, but I couldn't stop him from kissing me or deepening the kiss. I couldn't even stop my own sensual moan, and it made me want to vomit. I was moaning into Cathal's mouth while Torben, no doubt, watched on.

Cathal's hand ran down my back and grasped my waist. But it didn't stop there. He continued down until he was grasping the back of my thigh, right where Torben's hand had been when he'd helped me up onto the back of the horse.

He pulled back then, all the while still holding my thigh. "You are mine to touch. No one else's. Do not allow that guard to touch you in such a way again, or I will cut his hands off while you watch."

My mouth dropped open even further, and I stared up at him, seeing flames dance in his eyes. Only seconds ago, he'd been kissing me as though I was a precious lover, and now he was threatening me. I was about to say something, but the sound of hooves running mercilessly across the ground caused me to step back and look past Cathal.

Torben hadn't bothered to look behind him to see what was coming. He was too busy staring at Cathal. His face was contorted into a level of rage that I had never seen before. When his glance flicked to mine, I flinched and took a step back. He looked ready to kill someone, anyone, and I wondered if I was on that list.

"Allete!" I heard Dayna's voice before I saw her. She and Thomas were riding up through the trees. They both looked breathless, as if they'd been the ones to run instead of the horses. Both of their eyes were wide with fear.

"What's happened?" I asked, pushing past Cathal,

# Quinn Loftis

Torben, and Brant. I knew it was something bad, as all the blood had drained from Dayna's face.

"We need you back at the palace," Thomas spoke for her. "Now."

When I caught the inflection of his voice as he said 'you,' I understood he meant that they needed me specifically. Someone had been hurt; they needed my ability. I nodded and looked back at Cathal. "I'm sorry, my lord, but I must cut our time short for now."

"You can ride with me," Cathal said as he started toward the horse, which had wandered a few paces from us.

"Like hell," I heard Torben growl as he grabbed my hand. He pulled me to his horse and lifted me by my waist effortlessly. "I'm her guard, and I can get her back quickly." He called over his shoulder, not even looking at the king. "Where?" Torben asked Dayna.

"The gardens, by the pond," she said quickly, and I didn't miss the tears in her eyes.

Torben hopped up behind me and wrapped a strong arm around me. He pulled me back against him and squeezed the horse's flanks. The animal took off in a huge lunge moving smoothly into a fast cantor.

"I need to warn you now that I will be kissing you later," Torben murmured in my ear. He pulled me tighter against him. "It took everything in me not to kill him right then and there."

My breath caught, and my heartbeat flew at an unnatural pace. Not only was I worried about what I was going to find at the pond, I now had Torben threatening to kiss me. A threat that I was all too eager to endure. *Stupid woman*, I thought to myself.

He didn't say anything more; he simply pushed the horse harder, almost as if he could sense my own urgency to get there. When we were finally drawing close, I turned my head so that Torben would hear me.

"We cannot let Cathal, or anyone, see if I'm needed to heal."

"I'll protect you," he said gently. "You don't have to worry about using your magic. I will always protect you."

And I believed him without question. I didn't know why, but I had no doubt that Torben would do everything in his power to keep his word.

As we rode around the back of the castle and approached the gardens, I pointed around a large wall of bushes indicating where he should go to find the pond. When we cleared the wall of shrubbery, we came upon a small group of people. I recognized most of them as servants from within the castle. They were crowded around a tiny form that lay motionless on the ground.

My hand rose to my mouth as I realized it was a young child. There was a woman leaning over the girl, wailing and pressing kisses to her forehead. I didn't pause for Torben to stop. I jumped from the horse, heedless of the fact that I might injure myself. By the gods, I landed on my feet with only a slight jarring in my legs. I was in motion before I had time to really consider whether it had been painful.

When I reached the crowd, I tried politely pushing my way through, but I got nowhere. That was until a large hand wrapped around my own and pulled me forward. Torben's wide shoulders and impressive height sent people reeling back as though they were barefoot and standing on hot coals. They practically jumped out of his way. If I hadn't been on my way to help a child, I might have been offended by how they moved for him and not their own princess. As it was, I had more important things on which to expend my energy.

Quinn Loftis

Torben stepped to the side. Once his larger body was out of the way, I moved quickly, kneeling next to the mother and child. Before I said anything, I glanced up at Torben. He gave me a single nod, letting me know that he understood my unspoken message. I needed him to clear out the people. I didn't need anyone to see my gift in action. I was surprised by the gentleness in his voice as he asked people to step back and give the woman privacy. A second later, I heard Dayna and Thomas's voices as well. With them tending to the crowd, I could focus on the child.

"Ma'am," I said softly. "Will you let me help?"

The woman lifted her head. Her eyes were screaming at me, begging me to do something.

"If you will allow me, I will help her. I will heal her," I said. I didn't explain how I would do that, nor did I think about what might be wrong with the child. It was clear that she'd fallen into the pond, so it was likely the child was drowning. But it might be more complicated than that. It might be that something had caused her to fall in, like a sudden seizure or headache. I had no knowledge of the child's history, so I would not know—not until I touched her.

Finally, the woman nodded. I wasted no time getting my hands on the girl. I closed my eyes, shutting out everything around me. The people around me slipped away, their voices simply becoming a humming background symphony. The smells of the air, grass, and salty ocean faded away. The touch of the breeze on my skin was nothing more than a soft feather gliding ever so lightly. I was lost to my ability, to my magic, as I allowed myself to sink deep into the consciousness of the girl.

I felt her spirit stir, but it was very weak. I moved my own spirit through her form, finding the source of the problem. I began calling on my power. Her lungs were full of water, and I knew that I needed to get them empty in order for her to breathe, but that wasn't the only damage. There was something wrong with her brain. Something pulled at me there, but I decided breathing was more important, so I focused on the lungs first.

> "Little spirit hear my plea,
> Draw near and do not flee.
> Flowing lungs that have filled,
> Overflow let all be spilled.
> Push the water inside, out,
> Use my power like a spout.
> Breathe deep precious child,
> For life, play, and being wild.
> Your days are not done,
> You've only just begun.

Once the lungs were clear, I sent a pulse of magic into her heart and began to chant.

> "Pumping blood, life giving heart,
> Respond to my magic and restart.
> Pumping blood, life giving heart,
> Join with this body, be a part."

I chanted until, once again the heart was pumping rhythmically, sending out blood into the body. Finally, I moved to the brain. I wasn't sure what I was looking for. I had never had to heal a brain injury before. I search out every part until I finally found the small area that was covered in blood. I pressed my power tightly against it and let the warmth flow into it as I began another chant.

"Mind of body, mind of spirit,
Listen to me, really hear it.
What is broken, let it heal,
To my will, come and kneel.
Do my bidding and restore,
What had been just before.
Become what needs to be,
Heed this command, hear me."

I felt the magic and power flowing out of me. It was more than I had given before, and I wondered if I'd even be able to bear weight on my legs when it was finally done. When I was sure that whatever had been wrong with the brain was now repaired, and things in the body seemed to be working again, I began to pull back. As I drew away from her, I felt her spirit growing stronger.

By the time I was back in my own body, I heard coughing and a small voice.

"Mama, what happened?"

"Shh, child. Peace, you are fine now," the mother said gently.

I opened my eyes, unsure of what I would see when I looked at the woman. Would she be fearful? Would she be disgusted? When I finally built up my nerve, I looked up and met the woman's gaze.

I sucked in a deep breath as I watched the tears fall silently from her face. She leaned forward so that she was just inches from my face and then leaned her forehead down until it was touching my own.

"Bless you, child of the gods. Bless you for your selfless sacrifice." Her words rushed over me like a soothing oil, and a calm filled my spirit that I had not felt in a very long time. It was as though the words were necessary, like they ended the healing process that had just taken place.

And then words suddenly filled my mind that I felt compelled to say in return. "It is my honor to serve."

"I will not mention this to anyone if that is your wish, Your Highness." The woman spoke again. She was continuing to stare at me, her eyes full of sincerity.

"I would be in your debt if you could keep this a secret."

She gave me a slight bow with her head and then began to stand. Torben suddenly appeared and helped the woman up, while at the same time picking up the small child who looked tiny in his large arms. I had a flash in my mind of a different time, a different child, and a different set of circumstances as Torben held our own child. It was so real that I gasped and had to shake it off.

"Brant," Torben called over to his comrade. "Please escort the child and her mother home."

Brant nodded and smiled down at the woman. I think he meant it to be reassuring, but he looked more pained than gentle. He was going to have to practice on that if he was to court my sister. And why I was ever considering such a thing that was preposterous, but also seemed strangely inevitable. That was something I was just going to have to set aside for another time.

Torben stepped closer to me, pulling me from my disturbing thoughts. He reached down and took my hand, pulling me to my feet. I swayed on my feet and wished desperately that he could pick me up and carry me back to my room, but I knew I couldn't allow the people around to see me that way.

"That demon king is riding up on his horse," he whispered as he leaned closer, lending me his frame to hold for support. "What do you want to do?"

"Get me out of here," I said quickly. He nodded.

"Dayna," he said in a sharp voice.

"What do you need?" she asked from my right.

"Distraction," Torben said and motioned in the direction from which Cathal was riding.

"Why, Torben, I never thought you'd ask," she said in a syrupy sweet voice.

I rolled my eyes and let out a small groan. There was no telling what she would come up with.

"SNAKES!" Dayna's voice cracked through the air and felt like a slap across the face. "SNAKES! Not just one, there's a bloody village!"

I turned to look over my shoulder and saw her hopping about like a child, pointing wildly to a spot in the grass growing near the pond. Some people were rushing away while those who liked to put on a brave face were hurrying over. Cathal was cut off by the people fleeing the so-called snake infestation.

"Come," Torben said firmly. He placed his hand on my lower back and led me in the opposite direction of Cathal. "We only have a few minutes before her ploy falls through."

We walked quickly, though Torben was practically carrying me as he wrapped an arm around my waist and hoisted me to his side.

By the time we reached my door, I was about to pass out. I had never been so tired after a healing. It was more than being tired; it was like the life had been sucked from me.

"Maybe it has," Torben said as he steadied me and shut the door behind us.

"Did I say that out loud?" I asked. I took a step toward the bed and almost fell. If Torben hadn't been there, I'd have likely fallen face first onto the floor and just stayed there until someone found me. As it was, he snatched me up and carried me to the bed. He pulled the covers back and laid me down gently and then pulled the covers back up to my chin.

"Rest," he said softly as he leaned down and pressed his lips to my forehead. "I will keep watch."

Before he could walk away, I reached for his hand. "Torben?"

He turned back to look at me. "Yes?" His voice was just as soft as my own.

"Thank you." I paused. "For taking care of me."

A small smile tilted up one side of his mouth, and his eyes lit up, yet still managed to smolder. "It is what I do."

"What? Take care of women in need?"

He shook his head. "No. I take care of *my* woman in need. It is my honor and pleasure."

I didn't know how to respond, but he didn't give me a chance. He slipped from the room while my eyes were already betraying me as they slipped closed. I couldn't help but wonder if bringing the child back to life—because I was pretty sure that is what I had done—had taken some of my own life away.

As I slipped deeper into my dreams, I wondered if the power I possessed could somehow lead to my own demise. Did my power come from magic, or did it come from my own life-force, the power and spirit inside of me that gave me breath? And if it did, what did that mean for me each time I used it to help others?

# CHAPTER Twenty

"MY BODY FEELS WORN THIN. LIKE A GARMENT THAT HAS
BEEN WASHED TOO MANY TIMES, THE THREAD OF MY LIFE IS
BEGINNING TO WEAKEN."

~DIARY OF ALLETE AUVRAY

"IS SHE ALL RIGHT?" I asked, for what felt like the
hundredth time when Lidia came out of Allete's room
carrying a basket full of dirty linens and clothes. The last
time I had seen Allete, she'd looked exhausted. No, she'd
been more than exhausted. The strain of bringing a
drowned child back to life had sapped all of her strength.
I'd put her to bed after the ordeal and, almost three days
later, I'd yet to see her again.

I was not the only man wanting to see the princess.
But I was the only man who had the right to be by her side.
At least that was how I felt—rational or not.

"She is just resting," Lidia said gently. She said it just
as kindly this time as she had the ninety-nine times I had
previously asked.

"Can—" I began, but she interrupted me.

"As soon as she says she wants to see people, you will be
the first to know," she assured me and then, with a slight
head bow to Brant, the girl scurried off.

I was about to speak, but I clamped my lips together

when Allete's door was jerked open. Dayna stuck her head out and glanced at me, then grinned at Brant, causing the big mountain to smile back.

"Allete asked me to inquire about the child," she said, looking back at me.

I stared back at her blankly. If she thought I was about to leave my post in front of her door, she'd gone mad.

Brant let out a loud sigh. "I'll see about the child. Do you know where I would need to go?" he asked Dayna.

"The kitchen," she said and started to shut the door.

Brant's large hand moved swiftly and met with the door to keep her from closing it. "You mean the mother works in the kitchen, or the child is there?"

"Neither," Dayna said as if it should be completely apparent. "Everyone knows that if you want to know anything about anyone, then you go to the kitchen. Just pop in and listen for a few minutes. You will probably come back with more information than you need."

"You want me to pop in?" Brant asked, a small smile playing on his lips.

"Could you both refrain from dallying in front of me?" I huffed. It was childish of me, but I did not want Brant to get to see the object of his affection, if I was being kept from seeing mine. Brant glanced at me from the corner of his eye with a raised brow. He knew exactly why I was acting like a pouting child.

"I will be back," he told Dayna, and with one last amused look at me, he walked away.

I turned to say something to Allete's sister in the hope that I could somehow talk her into letting me see the princess, but the door was shut before I could get a word out.

I leaned my back against it and thudded my head against the wood as the frustration that had been growing inside of me rose to a dangerous level. I did not understand my driving need to see her. I loved her, but did that mean it would be my demise if I was unable to make sure she was well? Would I survive if I was not the one caring for her, ensuring that she was healthy and safe? I didn't want to answer those questions. I already knew the answers. I'd never been tied to anything so tightly as I was to Allete. She was the weakness I'd never had. But she was also what made me stronger in so many ways. I smiled to myself as I thought of how challenging she could be at times and yet how compassionate she was at the same time. She was stubborn and yet she was funny. She made me want to do anything for her, to be anything she wanted me to be, and that meant she was also dangerous. There was no one I wouldn't destroy, no country I wouldn't crush, no god I wouldn't challenge, if it meant keeping her safe, or if she even asked me to, for that matter.

"You can only hide for so much longer, Allete," I muttered under my breath. "Before the 'morrow, I will see you again."

I TOOK A DEEP breath as I sat on the edge of my bed. "How'd he look?" I asked my youngest sister as she closed the door.

"Thoroughly put out," Dayna chuckled.

"You enjoy torturing him way too much," I told her.

"Maybe, but he's a big strong warrior. He can handle it. And if he can't handle it, then he is not worthy of your affection." She paused and took the seat next to the bed. "Speaking of affection, dear sister, are you ever going to tell me what happened between you two?"

My eyes widened. "What are you talking about?"

"Don't play coy with me," Dayna tsked. "It's written all over both of your faces. Something more than words has been exchanged between you two. You've kissed him."

"That is quite an accusation against an engaged woman," I said as I brushed invisible lint away from my night dress. It was the third one I'd worn in the past few days because I'd been too tired to get up and dress myself properly. Saving the little girl had taken much, much, more out of me than I'd realized it would. For some reason, I just couldn't seem to bounce back like I usually did. Even after three days of rest, I felt just as exhausted as I did when Torben had put me to bed.

"You aren't engaged," she snapped. "What you have is a farce. Cathal isn't worthy to be the groom of a prize hog. Actually, he isn't worthy to be the groom of a regular hog, much less a prized one."

I shook my head at her. "One of these days that tongue of yours is going to get you into trouble that you won't be able to get yourself out of."

She waved me off. "When that day comes, I'm sure I'll deserve whatever happens. I rely on my cleverness to function, sister. If I haven't got that, then I don't have anything."

I laughed, and even that simple action seemed to zap what little strength I had been able to regain over the past three days. I lowered myself back and she jumped up to help me. "You are a silly woman," I told her as she helped me pull the covers up.

"Ah," she said as she tapped me gently on the nose. "But you are finally admitting I'm a woman, and not a kid."

"That you are, sister mine. And I will admit you are turning into quite an amazing one." My eyes felt heavy, but even through the small slits I was holding open, I could see the worry on her face.

"You should be better by now," she said, not for the first time. "I don't understand why you aren't getting better."

I shrugged. "I don't think I have ever brought any one back to life before. The girl's spirit was almost gone, Day. Much longer and I don't think I would have been able to help." My words felt heavy in my mouth, and I could no longer hold my eyes open.

"Just rest, Allete. We will keep watch," I heard Dayna whisper and felt her warm lips against my temple.

"Don't let him see me like this," I managed to whisper back. She knew I meant Torben. I hadn't let him into my room in three days because I knew his reaction would be severe. If he saw how pale I had become, and how I shivered as if it were snowing in my chambers, Torben would demand I see a healer. And a vain part of me didn't like the idea of him seeing me in such a mess, although he'd already seen me as such. I would prefer to keep such things to a minimum if possible.

Sleep swept over me and I knew nothing that went on around me as the darkness consumed me. My sleep was far from restless. Fire, screams, and roars filled my mind. I felt as though there were so many injured, so many sick, and there was nothing I could do. There were many more than I was capable of healing. But I had to try. I kept searching in the darkness, hollering out for them to tell me where they were but there was no reply to my questions. There was only more yelling and more cries for help. Eventually the dream changed, and I was no longer surrounded by the screams. Instead, I was faced with Torben, a very angry, very large, Torben.

"Why didn't you tell me?" he asked, his voice sounding strange to my ears.

"What are you talking about? Tell you what?" I asked quickly, confused by his anger. I did *not* want him angry with me.

"I could have helped you; I could have fixed this."

"I don't understand," I tried again. "What didn't I tell you?"

"You needn't have done this on your own, princess. That is why I was made for you. I was created to help you. You should have let me help you."

*Help me with what*? I wanted to scream, but I was suddenly unable to speak. I reached for him, but Torben began backing away from me, the pain in his eyes becoming a mirror of what I knew he saw in my own. He was leaving me. I kept reaching for him, but he just kept getting farther and farther away.

I woke with a start, sitting straight up in bed with my hands fisted into the duvet. My heart was beating painfully in my chest, and I felt as though I couldn't get enough air into my lungs. Gradually my eyes adjusted, and I realized how dark the room had grown while I'd been asleep. I wasn't sure of the time but, judging by the lack of light and the silence that filled the castle, I judged it to be the middle of the night.

I took several deep breaths, attempting to gather myself. No matter how hard I tried, however, I couldn't seem to calm down. I felt a shiver run down my spine as I slowly began to scan the darkened room. I wasn't alone. I didn't know how I knew, but with a certainty that matched the inevitability of the rising sun, I knew without a doubt that there was someone else in my chambers. Whoever was here was someone like me—someone with magic.

"Show yourself," I spoke as firmly as I could, willing the shakiness from my voice. I was not sure what I expected, maybe a shimmering light and then a magical pop of some sort? But what I got was simply an old woman, seeming to emerge from the shadows as if she were a part of them.

"You have grown into such a beautiful woman since I last saw you," the woman said in a voice full of warmth and familiarity.

I was confused. Not only by the fact that there was a strange woman in my room, but also by the fact that she seemed familiar with me, and yet I had not a clue as to her identity.

"Why am I not calling for help?" I asked her before I could stop myself.

"Because you know that I am not a danger to you," she said simply. "And because I do not want you to.

"I do?"

She nodded. "Your magic would recognize if I possessed ill intent."

"And why is that?"

"Because I have my own sort of power about me. And magic recognizes certain things, even when we do not."

"And our magic..." I motioned to myself and then to her. "It's alike?"

"Not exactly."

I started to shift to sit on the edge of the bed, but my body felt sluggish and heavy. Although I could still feel the fear inside of me, my body seemed to be all out of fight. "I really feel like I should be afraid right now," I said to the woman as I eased myself back onto my pillow to keep from falling like a pile of rocks. "But I just don't have it in me."

She walked slowly over to me, her movements stiff from age. When she reached me, the woman gingerly took the duvet that was still clasped in one of my hands and tugged it free to then pull it up and cover me. "You have no need to fear me, Allete," she said soothingly. "My name is Myra, and I'm here to help."

"Do I know you?" I asked.

Myra shook her head. "No, but I know you, and that

is what is important. You brought a soul back from the netherworld, and the action has left your spirit wounded. It is tearing your soul in half."

"How do you—" I began, but stopped when she held up her hand.

"I wish there was more time, child, but there is not. I was not aware that this was going to happen. Magic can have a mind of its own. And news of your illness did not get to me until late this evening. Little Amelia was eager to tell me of how an angel saved her, but her mother had made her rest before she could come tell me."

"Amelia?" I was trying to make sense of her words, but my mind was sluggish. She sounded muffled, as if I were listening to her from the bottom of a well. I tried to concentrate, but it seemed that she was speaking so quickly.

"I am not speaking quickly, Allete, you are fading. Shush now and listen. You need the one who calls to your soul. You need your anchor. Every seer and every healer must have a counterpart. The anchor keeps your soul tethered to his soul. This, in turn, keeps you tethered to the living. Without your anchor, your life will slowly begin to fade, with each piece of it you give away to those in need. And with one like Amelia, who needed so much, it fades even faster."

"Anchor? My soul? I don't understand," I tried to say, but I wasn't sure if my words made sense. Was I dying? Was that what Myra was trying to tell me?

"You will die if you do not allow Torben into your presence. He is your anchor. He can help you," Myra said, her voice growing more urgent. "You have to be willing to let him help. Are you willing, child? Will you let Torben of the Hakon Clan, future king of his people and father of your young, to tether your life to his?"

I stared up at the old woman, wondering if I was delusional. Had I imagined this woman? Was my mind slipping into oblivion? Had I subconsciously, as an act of psychic self-defense, conjured the specter of an old woman whose words could give me hope? I could no longer tell if she was real or simply a figment of my imagination. When my breathing became even more difficult, I decided that, real or not, I was going to allow myself to believe that her words of hope were true.

"Yes," I answered simply, and to my own ears, my voice was breathy and barely audible.

"Thank the gods, finally," I heard her mutter. There was a loud bang, and then I heard Myra yell. "Get in here, Torben of the Hakon Clan, if you want your woman to live."

I COULD SEE HER shattered face as she stared back at me, begging me to understand why I was saying such things to her. I wish I knew why I kept telling her I could help. But the problem was, I did not understand my own words. I didn't know what was wrong and had no clue how to help and it was maddening. She was sick. I had no idea why and no idea how to fix her.

"Get in here, Torben of the Hakon Clan if you want your woman to live."

The familiar voice woke me from sleep that I hadn't eve realized had captured me. Brant was across from me, wide awake.

"You needed it," he said by way of explanation at my, no doubt, irritated face.

Then it registered that someone had called my name. I turned and grabbed the door handle and pushed it open without even knocking or announcing myself. Myra stood by Allete's bed, hovering over the princess's too-still form.

"What have you done?" I snarled. The anger in me rose swiftly as I lunged toward the witch.

"Peace, warrior," Myra said and held up a hand freezing me in place. "I mean her no harm. I am here to help her, and you."

"Release me," I snapped, irritated that she had ensnared me so easily. She did immediately and I was in motion once again. But instead of heading for Myra, I moved to the other side of the bed and climbed onto it, walking across on my knees until I was beside Allete. "Tell me," I demanded.

"She needs you," the witch said simply.

"What do I do?" When she did not answer right away, I lifted my head and looked at her. She was looking back at me with a pleased gleam in her tired eyes.

"You are a good match for her."

"I am no match for her if she is dead. Tell me what to do so I can fix this." I looked back down at the woman that the gods had given to me and felt my chest tighten at the sight of how pale she was.

"A blood oath needs to be struck, and your souls need to be bound."

"Do it," I said without pause.

"Just like that?" she asked. "No explanation as to why?"

"Will it save her life?"

"Yes."

"Then I don't give a shite as to why, just do it."

Myra began a slow, melodic chant, and as the room warmed and filled with the smell of incense and wood fire. I had to look away from Allete to see what was happening. The old witch was bathed in a golden light, and her hair floated around her as though she were suspended in water. Her eyes were closed and her hands out, her palms toward the ceiling. As I watched, a dagger with an intricately adorned handle appeared. The sight of something so deadly so close to Allete caused my need to protect her to surge forth, but I kept it in check. Myra had helped us before, and I needed to believe she was helping us again.

The witch's eyes opened, and she held out her hand to me. "Blood is powerful. It gives life and the lack of it takes life away. Blood oaths work in the same manner. They give life to the joined pair, and they can take life if broken. You must truly want this and be unwavering in your commitment to her. Can you do that?"

"I can and I will," I answered, using the oath binding language of my own clan.

"Expose the skin above your heart."

My eyes narrowed on her. "Why?"

"Because the blood closest to the heart is the purest and cleanest. It is this blood that will be joined with hers," she explained.

I did as she asked. Myra ran the dagger across my flesh, just over my heart. The blood welled up instantly, the bright red like a beacon against my tan skin. She coated either side of the edge of the blade in my blood and then looked down to Allete.

"You may turn your head to protect her modesty, as she is not yet your wife, but witnessing the blood binding is powerful. As she cannot observe the ceremony, perhaps you should."

I leaned over Allete and positioned the duvet so that it would keep as much of her covered as possible while still exposing the creamy flesh over her heart. I ignored the fact that her skin smelled like lilacs and looked as soft as silk. And I bit back a growl as Myra ran the blade across that beautiful skin.

She laid the blade on its side across the cut, wiping my

own blood on the wound, mixing the two liquids.

"Do you, Torben, accept your place as the soul anchor of Allete, Seer and Healer of the Hakon clan, committing your spirit to hers for all eternity? Do you agree to care for her, shelter her, and provide for her needs so that she can perform the task the gods have given to her? Do you swear to protect her from all threats? Do you bind yourself to these oaths with your life, knowing it is forfeit should you fail to keep the covenant you speak here today?"

"I do and I will."

"Help me wake her," she commanded.

"How?"

"Your blood is giving her strength as we speak. The magic of the bond you are forming between her now should be enough to wake her."

"Allete. Princess," I said gently as I shook her shoulder. "Wake up for me. I need to see you."

She didn't stir.

I leaned closer and pressed a kiss to her neck just below her ear. "Hear me, Allete. I am yours. I've pledged it. I need to know that you are mine. I need you. Hear me," I whispered pushing every ounce of that need into my voice.

After several heartbeats, she finally began to move. Her eyes shifted beneath her lids and then gradually began to flutter until they were open. She was looking directly up at me. Her brow drew together as the realization that I was in her room, on her bed with her, washed over her. Then her face scrunched up, her lips pulling tightly together.

"Ow," she grumbled as she reached up and rubbed her chest where the cut had been made. Then, several remarkable things seemed to come to her mind all at once. "You have long hair and a beard. You're in my room." She turned and looked at Myra. "With a woman who claims to have magic. And you let her cut me." Her eyes began to blaze with the heat of the anger that made me want to poke her more just to see how far I could push her. "What is going on, Torben, and why do you look like that?"

"Do you trust me?" I asked.

She nodded without even thinking. "I don't know if I should any more since you allowed someone to carve me like a holiday bird."

I smirked. "Being a bit dramatic, don't you think, princess?"

"I woke up bleeding. I am entitled to dramatics."

"I told you that you needed your anchor to survive," Myra interrupted. "Do you remember that?"

She nodded.

"Torben is your anchor. He is the match for your soul, and without him, your ability to heal and continuation to do so will take a piece of your life with every attempt."

"What?" I growled. "You didn't say any of that to me, witch."

"Did you want me to take time to explain while she slipped further into oblivion, or did you want her to live?"

I pursed my lips. "All right, you have sound reasoning."

Myra turned back to Allete. "We have begun the bonding process by the joining of his blood with yours. Hence the cut." She pointed to the wound. The bleeding had slowed, but not fast enough for my liking. I tore a piece of my tunic and pressed it to the wound. Allete slapped my hand away which made me chuckle.

"One day, princess, you won't be pushing my hands away," I said, knowing it would ignite her temper.

"Want to bargain on whether you can hold your breath longer than I can keep pushing your hands away?"

"Would you two please stop acting like kids with crushes and complete this bond so you both can be stronger?" Myra snapped.

# The Viking's Chosen

I was too busy grinning down at the woman I had fallen for, loving that she always rose to the challenges that I threw at her. She was my equal in every way—my soul match.

Allete shot me one more glare before turning back to Myra. "Am I marrying him?"

Myra shook her head. "One day I'm sure you will marry in the way of your people. But what we are doing is more permeant. It is a merging of souls. There is no bond that is its equal. Soul matches are a rare occurrence that only happen with those who possess magic. This is not to be taken lightly."

Allete turned and looked up at me. "You truly want this? We've only known each other a short while, and I still have no idea why you look so barbaric at the moment."

"I am a Northman, a Viking. Myra put a spell on me and my men to make us look like Englishmen so we would be easily accepted as guards. What you are seeing now is what I truly look like."

"Why did you come here and pretend to be my guard?" she asked.

I rubbed the back of my neck. "That's a bit complicated."

"I'm about to bind my soul to yours. Un-complicate it, and do it quickly."

# CHAPTER
## Twenty-one

"THE FEAR OF REJECTION WAS NOT SOMETHING WITH WHICH
I HAD EVER CONTENDED. I AM A WARRIOR. I PROTECT THAT
WHICH IS MINE, I DESTROY MY ENEMY, AND I LEAD MY PEOPLE.
THAT IS WHAT I HAVE ALWAYS BEEN. BUT WITH HER, I AM
MORE. AND EVEN AS A WARRIOR, WITH ALL THE TIMES I STOOD
ON A BATTLEFIELD STARING DOWN DEATH, I WAS NEVER AS
AFRAID AS I WAS THEN. STARING DOWN AT MY LOVE AND
PRAYING SHE DID NOT DESTROY ME BY REJECTING ME."

~TORBEN

"MY CLAN CAME BECAUSE our Jarl wanted to raid the
ships of the king that was coming to marry you,"
Torben said, then added reluctantly. "And your father as
well."

"And why did you come?" I could tell by the sound of
his voice that his answer was not the complete story.

"I came for you," he finally admitted.

"To abduct me?" I asked.

He shook his head. "No. I came to court you, but the
only way I could do that was by getting close to you. We
came across Myra, and she agreed to help us."

"Why would you want to court me? How did you know
me?"

"You were part of a prophecy that my mother received.

She is an Oracle. She saw that our futures were intertwined. In order to save both of our people, we must be joined."

I started to argue. I was already in a betrothal that was based upon the benefit of two kingdoms. I did not want a marriage based upon political alliances. Before I could say anything, Torben held up his hand to stop me.

"I know what you are going to say, and I understand it," he said. "I would not want a marriage that wasn't based upon love. I did not want to be forced any more than you did, I promise you. That is why I wanted to court you. If we are meant to be, wouldn't it stand to reason that we would be in love? I would never have forced you. And I still won't."

I believed him. From what I'd learned about him over the past month, despite not knowing his true background, his actions had proven his character. And, right or wrong, I loved Torben, a Viking warrior.

"And how do you feel?" I asked him. Perhaps I was pushing for something I already knew. He'd expressed his feelings before, but if we were doing something so permanent, then I needed to hear it.

"I love you," he said simply. "I knew the minute I saw you that you were created just for me. The past few weeks have just confirmed it."

As I stared up at him, at a future that I wanted to grasp with both my hands, yet seemed so very far out of my reach, I wondered if we could make it happen. Could it be as simple as just trying, as he'd said a couple weeks ago? Did we really have the power to choose our own destiny?

"You need to choose." Myra broke the silence that had filled the room.

My jaw clenched tightly as I made my choice. I sat up and reached for Torben's hand. "I need you to understand why I'm about to make this decision." I could tell that he thought I was rejecting him. It was obvious in the way his body tensed, and his mouth drew out in a tight line. His eyes narrowed and seemed to flash with a near uncontrollable anguish.

"Listen," I encouraged him and gave his hand a gentle squeeze. "I am not choosing you because I can't survive without you. I am not saying yes to us because of some prophecy. I am not choosing us simply because the gods ordained it. I'm not even choosing you simply to avoid Cathal, even though that would certainly be reason enough. I'm choosing you because my heart is yours. Even if every army from every kingdom stood between us, I would still choose you and fight to be with you."

I didn't wait for his response. I turned to Myra and nodded my head.

"Will you, Allete, Seer and Healer of the Hakon Clan and soul match to Torben, pledge yourself to him? Will you stand beside him as his equal? Will you support him as his queen? Will you be his helpmate and share your insights, encouragement, and advice to ensure he stays on the path intended for him? Will you let him protect you, lift you up when you need it, carry you when you cannot walk, shelter you when the storms of what is to come become too much? Will you bind your soul to his and take his into your keeping as well?"

"I do and I will," I answered, the words seeming to simply flow from my mouth like the chants that came when I was healing. As soon as the words passed my lips, a soft glow and feeling of warmth surrounded Torben and me. The light grew brighter and brighter, and the heat felt as though it was trying to meld us into one being. I felt a tugging deep inside of me, as though a string was attached to my heart and was being pulled gently, the force directed at Torben's chest.

I looked up at him, and my lips curved up to match

the smile that was glowing on his face. His eyes were filled with a contentment that I felt deep inside of me. As the light and heat slowly faded, I knew it was done. Torben, my soul match and anchor, was bound to me and me to him.

"It is done," Myra said and took a deep breath. "There are things coming that I cannot speak of, but it is imperative that you let nothing come between what has been joined here today. The gods have blessed this union, and nothing in heaven, in hell, or on earth, can destroy it. Be prepared, a fight is coming your way."

She melted into the shadows of the room and was gone in a matter of seconds as if she'd never been there.

"That did not sound very encouraging," I said as I sat back in the bed. Torben sat next to me, his hand resting on my thigh.

"We will face whatever is coming, together," he said with a certainty that I trusted because he believed it, even though I didn't feel such assurance myself.

"What now?" I asked.

"Now we pretend as though nothing has happened until the morning of the wedding," Torben said.

I really did not like the sound of that, but I understood why it was necessary. As he stood from my bed and walked around to the other side, I felt a sudden urge to grab onto him and never let him go.

"I feel it, too," he said as he looked down at me, his handsome face exhibiting a tenderness that I only saw when we were alone. "I don't want to leave, not even to be just outside. But I have to keep you safe."

I nodded. "I know."

He leaned down and kissed me, a sweet, lingering kiss that had my toes curling under the covers. I kept my hands to myself, knowing that if I wrapped them around his neck

I would try to pull him closer.

"One day left," he whispered against my lips. "The banquet is the evening after tomorrow. Then we will make our escape. I will be honest, I'm still trying to devise a plan."

I smiled. "You infiltrated my father's castle as a guard and captivated my heart. I have every confidence in you."

"Sleep well, princess." With a final kiss, he stood and walked to the door.

"Torben," I said quickly. He turned and looked back at me. "I'm glad it is you. I'm glad you are my soul match."

"As I am glad, Allete Auvray, that you are my everything."

The door shut quietly behind him, and I laid back in my bed no longer feeling as though I was at death's door. In a matter of a few hours, my life had veered off one path and been placed on a completely different course, one with a considerably better outlook. I was sure in that moment the smile on my face could not get any bigger without my face splitting in half, and my heart could not swell with any more love without bursting.

Torben was mine, and I was his. For once I felt as though I was exactly where I was supposed to be and that my life finally had a purpose.

WHEN MORNING CAME, I still couldn't wipe the stupid grin off my face.

"Are you going to tell me what happened in there?" Brant asked as he motioned with his head to the door behind me.

"I made her mine," I said simply.

Brant's eyes widened. "She allowed that without any vows?"

I shook my head. "Does your bloody mind always

jump to the ditch, man?"

"You said you made her yours," he argued. "How else should I interpret it?"

"We bound our souls."

"Oh, well," he nodded. "That's good." He scratched his head and narrowed his eyes on me. "What the hell does that mean exactly?"

I could not help but laugh. "Remember Myra?"

He nodded. "Of course. Why you think I look like this?" he said, motioning to his face.

"She was here last night. She explained some things about what it means to be a healer and a seer. Apparently, Allete is both, though she's never had a prophecy. Myra explained that a seer did not begin to have the sight until she was united with her soul match, her anchor. I am Allete's match. We took a blood oath last night and bound our souls. She's mine in every way but one. And as soon as we are off this damn continent, I intend to marry her and make her mine in body as well."

"And she's on board with all of this?"

I nodded and the grin I'd had only moments ago returned. "She loves me."

Brant shook his head. "I really thought she was smarter than that."

"Shut your mouth, you horse's arse. You're just jealous."

"Why should I be jealous? I've got my eye on the future mother of my offspring as well. She will admit her undying love soon enough. Just wait."

"I don't doubt she will admit her undying love. And I'm anxious to learn who the object of her affection is," I jested.

Brant scoffed. "I am not worried, brother. I can simply kill anyone who thinks he can have her."

"I'm sure murder will endear her to you."

The object of his affection rounded the corner only

seconds after his words had left his mouth.

"Good morning, dashing brutes," Dayna said with a grin.

"Princess," Brant said bowing his head. Apparently, he thought that this formality was what would endear her to him because he reached for her hand and tugged her closer. He lifted the hand to his mouth and ran kisses across her knuckles. Dayna looked shocked for a moment, but quickly recovered herself.

"You are sure of yourself, Brant," she said in a tone that she probably intended to sound severe. Instead it came out husky and breathless.

"No, beauty. But I am no fool when fate drops a gem in my lap. No man finds riches and turns away. He grasps it with both hands and holds it close to protect it from those who might steal it."

"And you have found such riches?"

"I have found something far greater than riches, lovely Dayna. I have found the one my soul cannot live without."

My brow rose as I stared at my long-time comrade. When had he become such a poet? When I looked at Dayna's face and saw her flushed skin, I knew his words were having a profound effect. I coughed, adding some words that I hoped would break his spell. "Too young."

Brant dropped her hand but didn't look away from her. "Not for long she isn't," he said, responding to my prodding.

Dayna stepped back from Brant and then surprised us both. "I am inclined to think you are full of horse droppings ... but ... I do not think you are so dense as to try and seduce a princess into your bed while in her own home and under the eye of her father. So I guess you will just have to prove your words to me. You do that, Brant, and I'm yours. Of course, you will have to wait until I come of age. Which means no playing about with other women until then. I know there are many who are much too eager to lift their skirts for a handsome warrior."

I choked as I swallowed. She was young, and yet she spoke her mind with such decisiveness. I could see why Brant was smitten with her.

"I wouldn't dare," he murmured, his eyes taking her in as though she was the first piece of a land he'd seen after being on the ocean for months.

Dayna pulled her shoulders back and raised her chin. Her eyes danced with the same fire I'd seen in Allete. "I am not jesting, Brant. You want me?"

"You know I do."

Well, damn, these two weren't going to just continue to flirt. Then again, I knew that once Brant made a decision, he never wavered. There would be no changing his mind. If he said he wanted her, then he meant it with everything in him."

"If I even hear of you setting those eyes on another woman, then I'll cut them out and feed them to fish. I won't allow my heart to be toyed with."

"So you want me as well?" he asked her. "You do not think you are too young to be making such a declaration?"

"I may be young, but I know my own damn mind, and when I see what I want, I am not afraid to take it. My own ability to wait for you does not need to be a question. I am a female and one of high ranking. Even if I did not respect myself and took a man to my bed before taking him as my husband, I would be disgraced. But a man..." She laughed, but there was no humor in it. "A man can take as many women to his bed as he pleases before taking a bride, and everyone turns a blind eye. Your past is your past, but if you are telling me that I am what your soul wants, then you had better be ready to show me the truth in your words."

She turned and reached past me to grasp the handle

to her sister's chambers.

"Dayna Auvray," Brant's voice came out in a low growl.

She looked back at him over her shoulder.

"I have no problem proving anything to you, and I am not an animal in rut, needing to satisfy my every urge. But hear me, female. You expect my devotion, and you have it. I expect the same."

She began to speak, but he held up his hand to stop her. "I am not talking about your body. I've no doubt you will keep your skirt down and your beautiful legs closed. I am talking about you. You want me to be yours, then you had damn well better be mine. None of that flirty shite that you do so well. No casual touches from other males, I don't care if they are a member of your father's court. We clear, little princess?"

Dayna's lips tightened. She obviously did not care for the endearment.

"We are clear. But, Brant, if you ever call me little princess again, I won't have to worry about you ever lusting after some barmaid. I will make sure you are cut to be a eunuch, and I will be the one doing the cutting." After a moment of intense staring between the two hotheads, she grinned and blew him a kiss.

When she was behind the door, Brant let out a sigh. "Damn, I want that one. She's perfect for me."

I cleared my throat. "She just threatened to cut your balls off, and you think she's perfect."

"Hell, yes," he grinned stupidly. "A woman who can handle a blade can no doubt handle other things just as well."

"Bloody hell, man," I said shaking my head. "I suppose you're right. She's just as crass as you are and doesn't blink an eye at your crude comments. *And* she's just as violent as you. I have a feeling there will be blood drawn many times before you two make it to the marriage bed."

Brant nodded. "Of that I've no doubt. Too many of those pansy, court males look at her as though she's a trophy to be set on their mantle. I've no doubt, if we stay here much longer, I will have to kill a few. She's the type who will flirt with them just to piss me off."

"And you love it."

"Aye, I do. Doesn't mean I won't beat the shite out of the males she flirts with."

"Don't you think that's a bit unfair to those males?"

Brant shrugged. "Wrong place, wrong time. Not my problem."

I pinched the bridge of my nose. I had a feeling Allete and I would be constantly intervening where those two were concerned. Brant was like rolling thunder, and Dayna was a bolt of lightning. Put them together, and you've got the makings of a volatile storm.

We stood there in silence, both of us lost in our own thoughts. The more time that passed without the appearance of Allete from her chambers, the more I fought the need to barge into her room and see her. I needed to know that nothing had changed in the light of day. I needed to know that she wasn't panicking over what had taken place the night before. Just when I was about to lose my patience, the door opened, and Dayna stepped out.

"She's asking to see you," she said with a knowing smile.

"I suppose she filled you in?"

She nodded. "Just so you know, I was all for you being her beau."

I smiled. "Well, thank you for your blessing."

She stepped out of the way so I could walk past her. Before I closed the door behind me, I turned and looked at Brant. "Behave. That's a direct order."

As the door shut behind me, I heard Dayna say in a

playful voice, "'Tis a good thing he can't give me direct orders to behave."

I chuckled as the door latched behind me. My eyes found her immediately. She stood across the room, looking out of her window. I'd noticed that this was a place she seemed to be when she was thinking. I walked over to her and stepped close behind her. My hands found her small waist and slipped around her sides until they rested on her stomach. She leaned back against me as though she'd done it a thousand times before.

"Did you get any rest?" I asked as I leaned my head down and buried my face in the place just behind her ear. Her hair was soft against my skin, and she smelled like home.

"A little," she answered, and her voice ran over me like a warm summer rain. "I suppose you didn't."

I chuckled. "I'm used to it, princess."

When she turned to face me, her brows drew together. "You still look like a Viking."

"I suppose once you've seen past the magic, you won't see the illusion any more. Or it could be our bond. I do not know."

"But everyone else still sees you without the long hair and ..." She motioned to my face which had grown a nearly full beard.

"Your sister didn't notice, so I assume they still see me with the spell on me."

Allete studied me for a few minutes and then reached up and ran her hand across my cheek. "It's softer than it looks."

"Did you prefer me before, without it?"

She shrugged. "I don't know yet. Give me some time around you now, and then I'll make my decision."

I smiled down at her. "Bossy little thing." As my eyes

held hers, I finally gave in to what I'd been wanting to do since the previous night. "I can't wait any longer." I leaned down and pressed my lips to hers. She felt so good against me, and the warmth of her mouth urged me to deepen the kiss. I wanted to be selfish with her. I wanted her to feign being sick so she could stay in her room with me, but I knew that wasn't a possibility, not with the banquet happening the very next day.

When I pulled back, there was a small smile on her face. "That was nice."

I shook my head. "If the only compliment I get from kissing you is *that was nice*, then I'm not doing it right." I leaned down and put my hands beneath her thighs, hoisting her up into my arms. She gasped and then laughed. I walked her back until she was pressed against the stone wall. Her hands cupped my face and when she simply sat there staring at me, I closed the gap between us. Gentleness fled. Consumed by my passion and need for her, I took possession of her mouth and devoured her. My love's hands ran through the strands of my hair, and it felt so good. Allete felt so very good.

I pulled back to let her take a quick breath. "Torben," she gasped. But that was all I allowed her before I was on her again. Her small hands moved to my shoulders, and she pulled herself closer to me.

"How am I supposed to be around you all day and not touch you?" I asked her as we both attempted to slow the rising and falling of our chests.

"Consider it a game," she said with a grin.

"And what do I get if I win?"

"Guess you'll have to wait and see."

The flirty smile on her delectable lips had me groaning. The woman was going to be the death of me. I let her slide down from my arms and pressed a final kiss to her forehead.

"So no regrets?" I finally asked the question that had been burning a hole in my brain.

Allete shook her head. "None."

I noticed an errant hair that had fallen loose from her braid, and I gently tucked it behind her ear. "Have you considered that we will be leaving your family, at least for a while?"

She nodded. "I was leaving anyway, but at least now the circumstances are much, much improved. I will have to conceive a way to let my father know that I left with you on my own volition. I don't want him to think that you took me against my will."

I had considered the very same thing. "After the banquet, we will talk to him, together."

After several seconds, she nodded. "All right."

"Will you be ready to go down for breakfast soon?"

"Yes, just give me a few more minutes."

I gave her one last lingering kiss and then left her chambers. With every step, my gut clenched tighter. It was going to be a very long couple of days.

I STARED DOWN AT my food as I listened to the forks and plates clinking around me. I was afraid if I looked up, I would seek out his eyes. The feelings welling up inside of my spirit seemed so strange to me. I wondered if it was some sort of reaction to the bonding, this driving need to be close to him, to touch him. But I knew that we must be careful not to exhibit any strange behavior. We didn't want to draw any attention to ourselves. I had to pretend that he was just my guard, nothing more.

"Forgive my tardiness," Cathal's voice carried across

the room.

My stomach hit the floor, and I had to swallow back the bile that threatened to make an unwelcome appearance. When I'd arrived in the dining hall to see that he wasn't present, my anxiety was momentarily lessened, but the reprieve was short lived.

"Good morning, Allete," he said as he took the empty chair next to me.

I took a small breath and steeled myself before looking up at him. I plastered a smile on my face and prayed it seemed genuine. "Good morning, my lord."

"You are looking especially lovely. Your skin is flushed, and you're glowing. It seems the thought of our pending nuptials is agreeing with you."

"Certainly," I agreed. Although I knew exactly the real reason I appeared flushed and glowing. The memory of Torben's kisses this morning was enough to have me nearly panting. I daresay that would not have been very ladylike. Which almost made me want to do it, just to see the look on Cathal's face, and Torben's, too, for that matter. I smothered the smile that wanted to break free. I was acting like a school girl with a crush. Ridiculous, really.

The rest of breakfast passed in an uneasy silence. My father and mother no longer went out of their way to make small talk with Cathal, and I hoped he hadn't noticed a change in their attitude toward him. I kept shooting them glares, trying to silently implore them to keep up our charade a bit longer.

"If you'll excuse my queen and me," my father said suddenly as he stood and reached his hand out to my mother. "I've not been feeling well this morning. Considering the importance of the coming occasion, I think I should take every opportunity to rest until then. I'd hate to be sick during my eldest daughter's wedding banquet."

Cathal looked over at them and a small smirk appeared. "Certainly, Albric. It is good you have a queen to wait on you."

My father's jaw tightened, and I held my breath, hoping he would keep his temper in check. For some reason, it sounded like Cathal was baiting him.

"It is my pleasure to care for my husband," my mother said, her tone genuine, leaving no doubt that their love for one another was sincere. She turned to me and smiled. "Do not forget to come find me when you are done, Allete dear. Lidia and your sisters have the final preparations to go over with you for the banquet."

"Yes, Mother," I said and then watched as they left the room.

"I am to spend another day apart from you?" Cathal asked, the barely contained anger boiling beneath the surface of his carefully controlled façade.

"What is a few days when we will be married soon, and I will be with you every single day for the rest of your life?" I asked, giving him my most innocent smile.

He stared at me, trying to gauge my tone. I could see him contemplating whether I was being sarcastic. Finally, he shrugged. "I suppose you are correct."

I had no appetite whatsoever, owing mostly to the fact that the distracting memory of the feel of Torben's lips on mine refused to leave my mind. Still, I finally managed to clean my plate. I set down my fork and pushed my chair back. Cathal stood as I did.

"I will bid you good day, my lord," I said.

Before I could turn to go, he wrapped an arm around my waist and pulled me close to him. It was extremely forward in such a public setting, and I resisted the urge, barely, to shove him away from me.

His head leaned down until his mouth was next to my ear. "I see how your guard looks at you. If you do not tell him to back off, I will cut out his eyes."

I wanted to look at Torben, but I made myself continue to stare at the wall just past Cathal's shoulder.

"Do I make myself clear?" he asked as his hand squeezed my side painfully.

I smiled and tried to look as though his advances were most welcome. I knew that I couldn't let my eyes betray me in that moment. Not only was Cathal scrutinizing my face, I could feel Torben's eyes boring into me as well. There would be no way I could look in his direction at that moment and not betray some sort of emotion. And I couldn't let him know Cathal was causing me pain. Torben might just kill Cathal right then and there if he saw me wince. If that happened, he'd be arrested on the spot. I had to protect him because I knew he would not protect himself. His concern would be for me alone.

"Of course, my lord," I said as pleasantly as I could.

He released me, after a final warning squeeze and stepped back giving me a warm smile. The look in his eyes made my skin crawl. "I look forward to seeing you at the banquet. I have, of course, provided an appropriate dress for you. Your mother has it. It is a gift." Cathal took my hand and lifted it. He pressed a kiss to the back of it and then released me. As he strode from the room, I forced myself to inhale so I would not pass out. I hadn't realized my breath had been caught in my throat.

Once I'd gathered myself, I glanced around the table and gave a smile to those who remained. Lizzy and Dayna were there, a few members of the court, and Thomas, who was glaring daggers in the direction Cathal had just departed.

"I bid you each a good day," I said with a small curtsy.

Knowing Brant and Torben would follow, I walked from the room without looking back. Dayna would come find me soon enough. Lizzy I wasn't sure about. She'd been gone so much lately that I did not know what to expect from her. And I'd been so caught up in my own problems that I had not been a very attentive older sister. Thomas would, no doubt, have something to say to me at some point. Yes, my day would be filled with concerned family who meant well, and yet would not understand what had taken place between Torben and me.

Honestly, Thomas was the one I worried about the most. He was so protective of me, and I wasn't sure how he would feel about Torben being a Viking. Regardless of what he thought, however, he'd just have to accept my new situation as is. It was my life, and I wouldn't live it without Torben.

We were half-way to my mother and father's chambers when I felt Torben's hand on my waist guiding me to my right. We entered a small sitting room, and the door closed behind us. When I turned to face him, I saw Torben staring at the ground. I could imagine Brant standing sentry outside the door.

"Torben," I said gently. I felt as though I was approaching a wild beast ready to pounce at any moment. "Are you all right?"

His shoulders rose and fell with each heavy breath. One hand was clenched into a fist at his side, while the other rested on the hilt of his sword. "I did not realize how difficult it would be to watch him touch you. That was agony, but it wasn't the worst part. The worse part was knowing he was hurting you and not being able to immediately hold him accountable for it. That is not the way things are done in my clan."

I bit my lip. Clearly, I hadn't succeeded in hiding the

pain Cathal had inflicted. "How did you know?"

When he finally raised his head, the rage in his eyes caused me to take a step back. "I felt your pain."

I covered my mouth with my hand as a shocked gasp escaped. "What? How?"

He shook his head. "I do not know. But as soon as you felt it, I did, too. The sensation in your side, where his hand was, I felt it all. But that's not everything. I also felt you trying to keep me from knowing about it. I wanted to cut his hand off."

I didn't know what to say to that. Had Myra known that the bond between us could cause something like that? Neither one of us had any idea of what to expect, and I felt like a new foal learning to walk. We were simply stumbling along together, hoping to stay upright.

"I know. But it's only two more days, Torben. We must keep our secret. I will not have to be around him until tomorrow evening. I can make plenty of excuses. It will certainly be understandable that I'll be terribly busy preparing for the banquet. You cannot attack him. That would ruin everything. Please."

He stepped closer to me, close enough that I could feel his breath on my face. I knew we were playing with fire. Even with Brant guarding the door, it would not look good if someone caught us alone like we were.

"I won't attack him. But if he hurts you again, I cannot guarantee that some ill fate doesn't befall him in the middle of the night," he warned.

I suppose I had to give him that much. If it were the other way around, I would not like to see Torben hurt either. I understood his frustration and anger. I do not know what I would do if someone caused him pain. "Fair enough."

We stared at one another for a few seconds longer

before he sighed and stepped back. "If I touch you now, we might not leave this room for two days. Your mother and sisters are no doubt waiting for you." He grinned roguishly as he grasped the handle of the door. "I must insist we be on our way now. Otherwise you will arrive a bit disheveled. I can't have anyone thinking you've been ravished by a madman in the halls of your own castle. What kind of guard would I be?"

My mouth dropped open. I might have had a response ready had I not been so distracted by his handsome face and smirking lips. Instead I simply followed him, attempting to will away the blush that was covering my face. The man was going to drive me crazy for the rest of our lives, and yet I could not wait for forever to begin.

Three hours later, I had been poked and prodded to the point that I was ready to stab someone with the sharpest object near me. Cathal's "dress," if that is what you could call it, was so ridiculously revealing that my mother was unwilling to allow me to wear it. So she, along with my sisters and Lidia, had spent that last several hours adding material to it to make it appropriate.

The funniest moment of the entire time had been when I'd first arrived with my guards in tow. We'd walked into the living area of my parents' chambers to find Dayna strutting about in the dress. Upon seeing us enter, she'd stopped midway through ridiculously throwing her head back and flailing her arms and said in a snobby aristocratic tone. "Sister dear, I do believe your future husband wants to whore you out like a common woman in a brothel."

I was pretty sure my mother was going to choke to death. Lidia had to beat her on the back to help her collect herself. Lizzy, whose presence had surprised me, had covered her mouth to keep from laughing. Brant had cussed a blue streak under his breath and Torben had muttered four words: "Over my dead body."

I could not believe the King of Tara had the gall to expect his bride to wear such a spectacle. And I wasn't too proud to admit that I couldn't wait to see Cathal's reaction when he saw our alterations. He would not be able to scold me in front of those people. He would be fuming inside.

After the dress was finished, we each took places on the couches in the sitting area and relaxed. It felt good to just sit.

"It feels like forever since we've all been together," our mother said, looking at each of us.

"There has been much going on," I pointed out.

"I know what Allete has been up to," Dayna said. "But Lizzy, you've been absent much lately. Don't think I haven't noticed. Where have you been sneaking off to?"

Lizzy blushed. "I've been out with friends."

"Friends?" Dayna asked. "Are these female friends?"

"Dayna," Mother gasped. "Really. Don't be crass."

Lizzy glanced at our youngest sister and then looked at our mother. No one said anything for a few moments. Dayna eyed Lizzy with a scrutinizing stare. She seemed to be on the verge of pressing the issue when Lizzy appeared to come to a decision. "I have been seeing someone, Mother," she said and then quickly continued. "He's a member of Cathal's court. He's a good man."

The eyes of everyone in the room widened, and a couple of mouths dropped open. My mother said nothing for several seconds. "Then why has he not addressed your father and me to request permission to court you?" she finally asked through tight lips.

"Because it isn't that simple," she explained. "Cathal would have to approve the courting as well, and that would never happen."

"What?" I asked. "What do you mean?"

"Because Cathal's third queen was the woman this man courted when he was younger. Cathal took her, and then after a year of marriage she died suddenly."

"What is your beau's name?" Mother asked.

Lizzy shook her head. "I am sorry, Mother, but I promised I wouldn't say. Cathal isn't aware that he is here."

"Why did he come?" Dayna asked.

"I can't say that, either."

The three of us stared at her, shocked that she was willing to keep secrets from us, her family.

"Are you in danger? Is someone threatening you? Is *he* threatening you?" Our mother spoke up.

"No, it's not like that at all. We have been careful. No one knows him, and we go to the small tavern on the edge of the village to meet. I'm never alone with him," she quickly added.

I didn't like what she was telling us, but Lizzy was eighteen. She was of marrying age and had the right to choose who she wanted to marry, provided his class was suitable.

"So, is he planning on staying here after Cathal leaves?" Dayna asked.

Lizzy's hands were trembling in her lap, something I'd never seen in our calm middle sister. "I do not think he will be going back," she answered.

"If he stays, he must speak to your father."

Lizzy nodded. "I'm sure Father will be speaking with him soon."

I tilted my head as I looked at her. She seemed sad. Why would she be sad if the man she had been sneaking around with was staying in our kingdom?

"Wouldn't that make you happy?" I asked. "For him to stay?"

Lizzy finally looked up at met my gaze. There were

unshed tears in her eyes, but they were pleading me not to ask why they were there. "I'm asking you to trust me, as your sister." She turned to Dayna. "And yours." Then she turned to our mother. "And as your daughter. Trust me that he is no danger to me or my father."

The stunned silence in the room wasn't surprising. Lizzy didn't do emotions. She was calm and collected, and yet every time I'd seen her since she had started seeing the mystery man, she'd been anything but calm. How was I supposed to trust her when she seemed so broken over a man we did not know?

"Fine," Mother said. "I will leave it alone for now. But after everything is settled, then he must speak with your father about courting you."

I noticed she didn't say after the wedding. My mother was making it clear that she had no plans for there to be a wedding and by the seas I wanted to throw myself at her feet and thank her for supporting me. I had no doubt that my parents loved me, but they were leaders of an entire country. The people depended on them for protection and provision. By making this choice, they were essentially choosing me over their duties as king and queen. I wished I could tell them not to; I wished I was that selfless. But now that I'd met Torben, everything had changed. I couldn't see my life without him, and I couldn't see my life with Cathal in it.

We spent the rest of the afternoon simply talking. It was so strange to live with people who you loved and yet see so little of them. We were in this palace every day, and yet there were days that went by that I didn't even cross Lizzy's path if she did not come to breakfast.

We reminisced about our childhood and how so much had changed. But most of all, we avoided completely the topic of marriage, Cathal, and anything that might remotely pertain to him. No matter how much I enjoyed my time with my family, Torben was ever-present in the back of my mind. I knew he was just outside the door, and I hated that he had to act like my guard instead of my equal.

The door opened then, and in stepped the object of my thoughts. To me, he was a handsome, longhaired, lightly bearded Viking warrior, but to my family they were seeing him as an English guard with short hair and clean-shaven face. He was huge in either regard, and he was also mine.

"Ow," I growled as I rubbed the shin Dayna had just kicked.

She leaned over close. "You were looking at him like he was the last dessert on the table. Pull yourself together, woman."

I glanced back up to see Torben watching us with a smirk on his face. I wondered if he'd been able to feel my attraction for him, as he had felt my pain earlier. I felt my face flush when I realized just how embarrassing such a thing would be.

"Forgive the interruption, Your Highness," Torben said as he bowed to my mother. "Your nephew is here and wishes to speak with Allete."

"Of course," my mother said as she motioned with her hand. "Let him in."

Thomas walked in and gave Torben a pointed look. Whether it was a look of good or ill, however, I couldn't decipher. Torben turned to close the door and winked at me just as it shut him out of the room. I received another kick from Dayna for the grin I couldn't suppress.

"Dayna, quit kicking your sister, and Allete, quit doing whatever it is you're doing to illicit such a response," Mother said, her voice sounding so much like it had when we were children doing much the same thing.

I started to say something, but Thomas cut me off.

"What exactly happened this morning at breakfast?" His clenched jaw made it perfectly clear that he knew what happened, but he wanted me to confirm it.

"Cathal was simply asserting his dominance," I responded.

"Allete, he was hurting you. I could see it in your face. Why would you—"

"What?" I suddenly said as I stood up. "Why would I what, Thomas? Why would I let the king of Tara, a man who I am subject to and betrothed to, speak to me in such a way, handle me in such a way?" I was nearly yelling as the anger and humiliation built inside of me. I knew that Thomas simply cared about me, and this was his way of expressing his sorry. I knew that he did not mean his question to be insulting, and yet I was insulted. "I may be a princess. I may be next in line to be queen in my own country, but that holds no value to Cathal. The only value I have for that man is what I can do for him. The alliance I represent to Britain and the sons I can bear him. To openly disrespect him in front of others, especially in front of the court, would be throwing Father at his mercy." My breathing had increased, and my heart was racing in my chest as I pointed my finger at my now-helpless looking cousin. "I am simply a woman, Thomas. Royal, yes. But still a woman. I have pushed the boundaries that hold my sex back as far as I can push them without causing Father disrespect. I will continue to do what I can, but I could not speak out against Cathal this morning. He would have done more than bruise my side."

When I felt the steam seep out of me, my shoulders sagged forward. I felt bereft and tired, as though I'd been working in the fields all day instead of sitting on a cushioned chair, calmly conversing with my family.

"Forgive me, cousin," Thomas said after several

minutes. He walked over to me and wrapped his arms around me, pulling me tightly against him. "I just cannot stand to see you hurting, physically or otherwise."

"I know," I said as I patted his back. "I am the one who should apologize. I shouldn't have yelled. I think I am simply tired and have too much on my mind."

Thomas released me and stepped back. He wiped the tear from my cheek that I hadn't realized had fallen and smiled at me. "And just so you know, there is nothing such as 'simply a woman.' The statement itself is an oxymoron. There is nothing simple about any woman and certainly not you. Remarkable? Yes. Unique? Most definitely. Passionate, good, honest and beyond lovely? Without a doubt. But never simple."

He pressed a kiss to my forehead and bowed to the rest of the room. "I'll take my leave, good ladies. And plan to see you all tomorrow evening at the ball. I'm sure it is going to prove to be an interesting evening."

I snorted out a laugh. Interesting indeed.

To my surprise, Mother insisted we eat dinner in her chambers instead of dining with the court. It was the first time in a very long time that we'd eaten as a family. Even Father joined us. My heart was overflowing with love by the time the evening was ending. As we each said our goodnights, Father came over to me and hugged me tightly to him.

"I want you to sleep tonight, Allete. Do not stay up worrying about everyone else. Do no worry for our kingdom and do not worry for yourself." He pulled back to look at me. "Tomorrow evening will be the last time you have to see or deal with Cathal. You have my word."

I kissed his cheek. "Thank you, Father. I will do my best not to worry."

He chuckled. "Liar. You're too much like your mother.

You care too deeply, even about things you have no control over." He paused and brushed my hair from my face. "But then I would rather you care too much than too little."

# CHAPTER
## Twenty-two

"SIMPLY A WOMAN. COULD SHE REALLY BELIEVE SUCH NONSENSE? WE ARE MALE AND WE ARE FEMALE AND WE ARE BOTH NECESSARY TO THE CONTINUATION OF HUMANITY. HOW COULD ANYONE THINK THAT ONE SEX WAS GREATER THAN THE OTHER? MEN ARE NEEDED TO CREATE LIFE, AND WOMEN ARE NEEDED TO CARRY, NURTURE, AND BRING FORTH LIFE. ONE COULD NOT EXIST WITHOUT THE OTHER. WHEN TWO THINGS NEED EACH OTHER TO SURVIVE, IN MY MIND, THERE IS NOTHING MORE EQUAL. MEN NEED WOMEN AND WOMEN NEED MEN. WHY WAS THAT SUCH A DIFFICULT CONCEPT FOR SOME TO GRASP?"

~TORBEN

ALLETE WAS QUIET AS we walked back to her chambers. I had heard her laughter throughout the day as I stood guard at the door to her father and mother's chambers. There were a few times that I caught the king and queen's guards attempting to hide their own smiles when they heard her laughter as well. It took all of my control not to pull my sword on them and claim her like some barbaric warlord and demand that they cover their ears, as if I was the only one who had a right to enjoy the sound of her joy. So many times, I had been tempted to open the door just so I could see her. I wanted to see the light that shone in her eyes. I could imagine how the light intensified when she found something humorous. I wanted to listen to her voice as she spoke. I wanted to be at her side, where I belonged.

"Did you have an enjoyable time with your family?" I asked when we reached her door. My voice seemed to startle her from her thoughts as she blinked several times and then looked up at me.

"Forgive me, Torben, my mind is a bit of a mess."

I leaned around her and grasped the handle of her door. As I pushed it open, she backed up to keep me from bumping into her. I glanced over my shoulder at Brant. "Give me fifteen minutes. If I'm not out by then, come in and get me."

"Do I look like I want to die?" he balked. "I'm not ready to challenge you for the position of hersir just yet."

I thought about what I'd just asked him to do and then nodded. "You're right. I'd kill you. Fine, send Dayna in if I'm not out."

He grinned. "That I can do. Any excuse to talk to her."

When the door was finally closed and the rest of the world was nowhere in sight, I shed the pretense that she was simply my charge. With that door closed, we were now back on equal ground. She was my mate, my bride, and I was her warrior. I took her in my arms and chuckled at the breathless squeak that rushed out of her. It didn't last long because my lips covered hers before anything else could come out.

I needed to hold her. I needed to taste her. I just needed her. Being so close to her and unable to touch her had been torture. Watching Cathal touch her, as if he had a right to her, had nearly driven me to kill. And then knowing he'd hurt her and there was nothing I could do about it made me want to destroy him, raise him from the dead, and destroy him all over again. There would be no honorable death for Cathal. There would be no quick passing from this world into the next. When he died—and he would by my sword—it would be slow and agonizing.

"Are you all right?" Allete asked breathlessly as she pulled back. She cupped my face in her small hands and tilted it until she could look directly in my eyes. "Where did you go? You were with me, kissing me and wanting me, and then you were gone."

I closed my eyes and leaned my forehead against hers. This new ability between us was going to take some getting used to. "I'm sorry," I said as I sighed and rubbed my hand down her back. "I was just thinking about what happened at breakfast."

She pressed her finger to my lips to stop me. "He is not welcome in this space," Allete whispered. "Not in thoughts or words. In here, it is just you and me."

When she stepped back from me and smiled, it felt as though everything that was wrong in my spirit was suddenly right again.

"Just you and me," I repeated.

She nodded. "And I think you're down to about ten minutes before Dayna comes bursting into our bubble."

I undid the belt that held my sword to my side. Her eyes widened, and I couldn't help but laugh. "Wishing your sister would show up early?" I asked, my voice dropping an octave as I saw the rise and fall of her chest quicken.

"Of course not," she said as she glanced down to straighten her already straight dress.

"First rule of battle, princess, don't take your eyes off your opponent," I said as I lunged for her and tackled her onto the bed. Her laughter filled the room and the rightness of it settled into my soul. For the next ten minutes, my world consisted of Allete and nothing else.

"I didn't realize we were in a battle, Viking," she said

and halfheartedly attempted to get away.

"I have a feeling you and I are going to have lots of battles, love. But I'm okay with that."

She frowned. "Why would you be okay with us fighting?"

My grin widened. "Because every battle we have will end with an equally passionate reconciliation."

"And what if we are at an impasse?"

"Then it will be a passionate impasse."

She laughed again and tapped me on the end of my nose. "You, sir, are incorrigible."

I shrugged. "Maybe." I kissed her cheeks, her nose, her chin, and finally her lips. Her skin was soft under my fingertips as I ran them down her neck and the shiver that rushed through her body told me she was equally affected by me as I was by her.

"Who would have thought that a mighty Viking warrior could be so gentle?" Allete said softly as she sighed and pressed her cheek to my palm.

"For you, I can be anything."

By the time I stepped back into the castle corridor and shut Allete's door behind me, much longer than fifteen minutes had passed.

"What happened to sending in Dayna?" I asked Brant.

He shrugged. "You needed time with her."

"And what if someone had come along and asked where I was, namely, Cathal?"

Brant shrugged again. "I had a plan."

I narrowed my eyes on him. "What exactly did that plan involve?"

"Let's just say a wild boar, some rope, and expertly placed cuts were all included."

I rubbed a hand down my face and leaned back against the door. "Leave it to you to have a wild boar as your accomplice."

"I have a rule. Always be able to murder your murder accomplice."

"Remind me to never assist you with murder."

He chuckled. "I've already picked out my partner if the boar doesn't come through, and she'll be even tastier."

I frowned at him. "That is not even funny. That's her sister." I pointed behind me. "And eating ... and ... just—"

"Oh, come one, it is a little funny."

His stupid chuckling caused me to chuckle right alongside him. "Okay, fine, if I don't think of her as the sister to the woman I love, then yes, it's a little funny."

"If you have the same policy, we both know the boar wouldn't be your first choice, either."

That earned him a fist to the gut, which he took in good humor.

Brant held up his hands in retreat. "All right, all right. I won't go talking about you and your female's dining habits."

"If you weren't the best warrior I knew, I'd tell Dayna I saw you flirting with a linen maid." I paused for effect. "While she was making a bed."

Brant's faced wiped clean of the smile. "Don't even jest like that. You know what she said she'd do if she heard I was flirting."

I nodded. "Aye, I did. Now I finally have some leverage to keep you in line."

He grumbled, but his grin was fast to return.

"What are you smiling about?" I asked him.

"Just looking forward to when this is over, and we're back home with our women."

Home. That was the one word that always puts a smile on any warrior's face. But home had a whole different meaning to me now. Home was simply wherever Allete was.

I DIDN'T KNOW WHY I awoke. One minute I was sleeping, dreaming about a small but inviting home with a warm fire and the smell of fresh bread wafting through the air. The next minute my eyes were blinking open. It took several seconds for them to adjust to the darkness in the room. I sat up and pushed my messy braid over my shoulder.

Just as I had the night Myra had come to visit, I felt the otherness in the room, the power that only came from one who had magic.

"Show yourself, Myra," I said into the dark.

A small woman stepped out of the darkness. She was standing across the room next to my window. "Who are you, and how did you get into my chamber?" I asked.

"I scaled the wall and climbed in the window," she answered without hesitation.

I was so shocked that I didn't speak right away and then my senses returned. "Really?"

She turned and looked at me, her silver eyes dancing with mirth. The small smile on her lips made her resemble a child who'd just gotten away with mischief. "No. That would be ridiculous. I walked in through the door like any other old woman would. Could you imagine me, with my frail bones and stiff joints, climbing up the side of a wall?"

"Forgive me, but I do not believe you are as frail as you would like me to believe," I told her as I took a step sideways, keeping myself close enough to make it to the door if I needed to escape.

"Then you are not as dumb as I first thought," she chuckled.

Now that was just rude. "You never answered the first question; who are you?" I asked again, this time with a little more bite in my tone.

The woman's eyes widened as her smile grew larger. "Yes, I think you will do just fine," she muttered. "I am the Oracle of my people," she said with a voice much stronger than the one she'd been using. "I am the seer and the teller. I am the healer of the sick and injured. And I am the woman who will teach you to use your magic, as well as hone other abilities you do not even know you have." She paused. "Oh, and my name is Hilda, and I will also be the grandmother of your offspring."

"I have no offspring." The words tumbled out before I could think about how ridiculous they sounded.

"Hmm," Hilda said as she narrowed her eyes on me. "Perhaps I spoke to soon."

"What?" Now I was just confused.

"You aren't dumb. A little dimwitted might be a better description."

"Bloody hell, woman. I am not dimwitted. I am confused, and maybe in shock. Yes, definitely in shock. But I am not so confused as to know that I don't have any offspring."

"Of course, you don't have any offspring. You still have your maiden head." Hilda shot me a sharp look. "You do, don't you? Because I have a feeling my son would be a tad irritated and likely to kill whoever took it if he finds out otherwise."

I rubbed my hands over my face and let out a groan. At no point during the day had I thought I would be entertaining an Oracle and discussing the matter of my womanhood. "First of all, I do not appreciate my virtue being questioned," I said, raising a finger. Then, raising a second, I added, "And I have no idea who your son is, nor do I have plans to share a bed with him and bear his children. And third..." I held up another finger. "What do you mean you are going to teach me to use my magic? How do you know what I can do?"

Hilda walked slowly over to one of the chairs next to the small table where I often took my meals when I did not wish to dine with the court. She kept her eyes on me while she took a seat. The woman leaned back as though to get comfortable and then motioned for me to take the seat across from her. When I had done so, she began to speak.

"As I said, I am an Oracle. I come from the North Country, the clan of Hakon."

I sucked in a breath. "You're a Viking?"

"I'm a Norsewoman," she corrected. "But really, I am simply a woman—a woman from another part of this world, child. I am not a foreigner from another world. Like you—a woman from this land—I have all the necessary parts that make me a woman and nothing more. We are no different."

When she explained it like that, I had to admit it made the differences we claimed to be so unsurmountable see ridiculous. What did it matter if we were from different parts of the world? Did that somehow make one of us better than the other? Did the fact that I was born in to a family that was royal make me worthier of life than one who was not? If anything, Hilda's life was more valuable because of her abilities. I might have been able to heal others, but I could not see into the future.

"You said you could help me understand what I can do?" I reminded her.

"Get comfortable, it could take a while."

I glanced at the door, a motion that did not go unnoticed by her keen eyes.

"He is aware that I am here," she told me.

"You mean Torben?"

# Quinn Loftis

She nodded. "It is driving him crazy that I won't allow him to come in and listen."

"You can keep him out?" I asked hesitantly.

"Of course, I can," she said indignantly.

"How? Do you have more magic than just the healing and seeing?"

She chuckled. "It's called being a mother and teaching respect. He will not enter because I have asked him not to, and he respects and trusts me."

My shoulders dropped. "Oh," I said simply.

"Magic," Hilda began. "This is an old power that is passed through the blood. It lives in the very cells of a person. It is not exactly clear why some people inherit it in a family while others do not. I would presume to think it is like the fact that some siblings have blonde hair while others have brown. Certain traits are past to certain children. Perhaps the gods know who will be better capable of wielding something that can hurt or help those they encounter." She paused, looking as though she was anticipating questions. I simply stared right back, waiting for her to continue.

"I'm sure that you have learned certain things about your magic through trial and error since you have not had a tutor. For instance, you've learned to chant to use your magic. Your words help draw out the power that lives inside of you. Words are powerful, especially words that are spoken out loud. You must never forget that. Your words not only have the ability to heal, they also have the ability to destroy."

"Wait," I held up a hand to stop her. "You mean I could hurt someone?"

She nodded. "Of course. Every action has an opposite reaction. So if you are healing someone who has a tear in his skin, you can either make it better and close up the skin and repair the tissue, or you could increase the tear and damage to the tissue."

My mouth dropped open. I felt my chest tighten as I considered the horror of such an ability. How could I ever use my magic for something so evil? Could I destroy someone if I had to? Would I use such power against someone such as Cathal? I didn't know because as much as I abhorred the idea, I would not deny the secret comfort that came in knowing that I was not completely helpless anymore, especially when it came to the king that had treated me so cruelly. If I needed to hurt, him I could.

"But you need to understand," Hilda continued. Her face grew serious as her lips tightened and her silver eyes narrow on me. "Every use of magic has its consequences. When you use it to heal, it depletes you of your strength for a time. You are essentially using your life force to heal another. When you use your magic for damage, the consequences are even more detrimental. Using magic for a dark purpose removes a part of your soul along with the magic. It can tie you to that person forever because you imprint a part of yourself on them. It is impossible to do ill to another without dire repercussions. It is imperative that you remember that before you act in such a way. Also, the more you use your magic for ill, the more you will crave the surge of power you will feel later, after the exhaustion has worn off."

"Have you ever used your magic in such a way?" I asked the question before I could consider just how personal it was.

Hilda's eyes became thoughtful, and I wondered what memories she was considering. Judging by the haunted look that came over her face, I guessed they weren't pleasant.

"I have," she admitted. "One hopes to never find

herself in a situation that requires she act in a way that requires her to defend herself or those she love. But despite having magic, we are still limited in how we can affect the outcome of what we see. And there are consequences if we do attempt to intervene."

"What would drive someone to use her magic for harm?" I asked. I knew in my spirit that the woman before me was not evil, so I knew that she must have had a justifiable reason for her actions. Regardless, I felt compelled to ask her motivations.

Hilda seemed reluctant to tell me exactly what she'd done, but after several minutes, she finally gave in. "I have been under the thumb of the jarl in our clan. He is basically the equivalent of your king. He knows what I can do. Those in my clan only know that I am an Oracle. They do not know about my healing ability."

"You don't use it for your clan?"

She shook her head. "The jarl will not let me use it on anyone but himself. He keeps me by his side wherever he goes. He doesn't, however, know of my ability to do harm with my magic. I have had to make sure to be subtle over the years, lest he deduce that I have had something to do with any of his health problems. Over time I have been drawing his life force from him any time I have been required to heal him. But despite my age, there is still much I do not know about magic. For instance," she held up a finger. "By drawing his life force, I have caused a kind of madness in him. He has become more and more paranoid over the years. He has insane grandiose ideas and has convinced himself that he is invincible. My intention was to shorten his life, but I did not know in what way that would happen."

"You want to kill him?" I asked, not hiding the shock in my voice. Murder just seemed so extreme. But then again, hadn't that what my family had essentially been planning for Cathal if it came to that?

"You do not understand how evil this man is."

I snorted out an unladylike sound. "Oh, I bet I have a clue."

Hilda's eyes softened in understanding. "Yes, I am sorry about that. Torben explained to me what that monster did to you. You've been able to keep him from doing it again, I trust?"

"Thanks to your son," I said. "Tomorrow is the engagement banquet. So far, Torben has managed to keep me from being alone with King Cathal."

"Magnus, that's our jarl, has no concern for anyone but himself. If he continues to lead our clan, he will drive us into extinction. There is only so much war a country can endure. Eventually, there are no more men to fight. Young boys cannot continue to assume the duties of those that have perished. They simply do not have the strength or experience to do such things."

"And this is the man who has come to my home?" I asked.

"I told you, he is going mad. He must be removed from his place of leadership, and it is clear that the gods are making a way for that to happen. The prophecy makes it clear that Torben is to lead, but he can only do it with you by his side. You bring him balance, and he keeps your power grounded."

"Myra explained some of what is happening between Torben and me," I told her, suddenly needing to get as much information about my soul match with Torben as possible. "You have a soul match and an anchor?" I said as I tilted my head slightly. "Right?"

She nodded. "Torben's father." Her voice was full of love. "He was my anchor and my perfect match in every way. I am not as old as I look," she chuckled. "Did Myra explain why you need Torben?"

I nodded.

"Well," Hilda motioned to herself. "This is what happens when you continue to heal but don't have an anchor. Every time I heal Magnus, I lose more of my life. I am aging much more quickly than I should. Part of me is glad. I am tired and ready to join my husband on the other side. But then, the rest of me still has a lot of living to do."

"What about the bond?" I took a deep breath. "Torben and I bonded." I said it as though we'd been caught doing something were ought not to have been, which seemed ridiculous. "And now, we can sort of sense each other, I guess."

Hilda nodded. "That does not surprise me. Each anchor and his healer have unique abilities that evolve after their bonding. Some can read each other's minds. Some can feel what the other feels. And some have the ability to soul speak."

My brow furrowed. "Soul speak?"

"It is a very intimate communion where the souls are able to communicate with each other without the conscious effort of their owners. The best way I can explain it is that even when you do not realize it, your soul may need the comfort of its mate. Those who can soul speak, well, their souls reach for one another when they need it without you choosing to do so."

The breath whooshed out of me as I considered her words. The level of intimacy that something like that would bring seemed mind boggling.

"How will we know if we have that ability?" I asked her.

She shrugged. "Everyone is different, and abilities appear of their own accord. It is not an exact science."

"Thank you," I said after a few moments. "For telling me all of this."

She smiled at me. "I like you, Allete, but then I knew that I would."

I chuckled. "Must be weird to know how you're going to feel before you feel it."

"I'm used to it."

"Oh," I said quickly when I noticed she was heading for the door. "One more thing. Myra said I will have the ability to be a seer. When will that start?"

Another shrug. "Depends on many things."

When she said nothing more, I tilted my head at her, and my brow rose. "You do realize how frustratingly vague that is, right?"

Hilda shrugged. "I am an Oracle. It is my place to be vague. Otherwise, people would not think for themselves. I will not take someone's free will to make something happen that is supposed to happen. It will either happen, or it won't."

The Oracle stood and gave me a warm smile. "You are a good match for him. The gods knew what they were doing when they chose you for him and him for you."

I wasn't sure how true that was, considering how much we bickered with one another.

"I must be on my way before the jarl realizes that I'm missing. I gave him the slip back on the beach. Men panic when you start talking about the flow of a woman. Little did he know that I am much too old to even have such a problem anymore." She laughed as though it were the funniest thing ever. And I couldn't help but smile.

She left quickly, giving me a brief hug, and I wanted so desperately to ask her to stay. For some reason, she made me feel as though I could handle anything and everything that was headed my way as if I was easily capable. Hilda's presence had reassured me that I was not in this alone; she was like me and understood what I was going through with the new bond with Torben. But I knew I could not come to rely on the comfort and strength of another too much. There might come a day when I would need to stand on my own two feet, just as she had done for so many years without anyone to aid her.

# CHAPTER
# Twenty-three

"I have fought many battles, few of them worth the effort.
But now I have found a battle worth everything. For Allete,
I would destroy any enemy, cast away any darkness, and
willingly lay down my life. Winning her heart is worth all
of that and more."

~Torben

I SPENT THE REST of the night pacing in my room, thinking
of all the things the Oracle had told me, especially my
ability to use my magic to harm others. The idea still rested
uneasily on me, but I couldn't deny the usefulness of the
power, should I ever need it. Every time I considered the
possibility of using my magic to cause pain, Cathal's face
seemed to subconsciously jump to my mind.

It was early the next morning when I suddenly felt the
pull. I was just about to change out of my sleeping gown
when my heart sped up and my soul began reaching for
the injured being outside the castle walls. Somewhere
out there, in the early dawn hours, someone was hurt. I
slipped into a light overcoat and hurried to my chamber
door. I paused, unsure of what I should say to Torben
and Brant. But as the urgency in me intensified, I knew I
could hesitate no longer. I pulled the door open and met
Torben's eyes.

"I have to go," I said as I hurried from the room. I rushed past him and felt the heat of his body as he followed closely behind me

"What do you mean you have to go?" he asked as he followed close behind me. His long legs had no trouble keeping pace with mine and I could hear Brant next to him, stepping in time with us.

"Something is wrong. I need to help someone," I explained.

"Wait. This could be dangerous," he growled. "You don't know what you're walking into."

I shook my head. "It doesn't matter. I can't ignore an injured being. I have to help; it is a part of who I am," I explained.

I could sense that he wanted to tell me to stop. I could feel his need to keep me safe, but he knew that I was a healer. There was no changing that. I couldn't stop being a healer any more than I could stop being a woman.

"Do you know where you're going?"

"No, but my emotions, the magic inside of me, has connected with the person. I do not feel any maliciousness or evil. Just pain—a lot of pain," I explained, wondering if I was making any sense whatsoever.

I rushed through the castle corridors until I reached the kitchen where I hurried out the side door. My mind was being swamped with the emotion of the one calling out to my magic, which was something I'd never felt before. The cool night air caressed my skin and the quiet, stillness in the air seemed to hold its breath as it waited for me to act. I was shocked when I turned a sharp corner and my feet led me straight to the door of Cook.

I knocked on the door as fear overwhelmed me. I didn't want anything to be wrong with Cook. She was not only a worker in my home, whom I'd known my entire life, but she was a friend. I knocked harder and there was still no answer. I attempted to push open the door but it held fast, locked from the inside.

"Step back," Torben said suddenly and gently pushed me aside. He reared back, pulling his leg with him, and then slammed his foot onto the door putting all his force into the kick. The door splintered as it flew inwards and there was a collective shriek from inside.

"Cook!" I called out as I entered the dim room. "It's just me, Allete," I reassured. "Is something wrong?"

"Allete?" A shaky voice came from the back of the room, beyond the small kitchen. "Is that you, child?"

"Yes ma'am. I felt something wrong. Who is injured?"

"Come back here quickly. We have need of you."

I followed the sound until I reached the rear of Cook's small living quarters. She sat beside a bed that held the body of a small boy. He couldn't have been older than twelve summers. His eyes were glazed over, and his breath was very shallow. He had a sheet pulled all the way up to his chest but I could see a red spot staining the linen, growing larger as I looked down at him.

"What happened?" I asked, moving forward to the other side of the bed. I pulled the sheet back and gasped. There was a gaping wound on the right side of his chest. I could only see part of it through the tear in his tunic. I glanced up at Torben who looked ready to jump into action. "I need clean water and dry cloths. I will need to clean it before I heal it so there is no infection afterward," I told him. He nodded and then proceeded to search out the things I needed.

"He was running an errand for me," Cook began explaining. "He was in the castle grounds, I don't worry about him none when he stays in the castle grounds, with all the guards and such walking about."

I nodded at it her to continue while I gingerly moved the tunic around, trying to get a better view of the gash in his chest.

"He was attacked. He said it was a savage. A large man dressed in animal skins with a crazed look in his eyes. He spoke a strange language, and my boy could not understand him. He said the man just attacked him for no reason. He only got away was because the man was slow, as though he were drunk on mead."

When Torben returned with the basin and rags, I rinsed my hands in the water. "Dump this and get me more clean water," I ordered. Then I ripped the tunic away from the boy's body. He cringed but didn't move or make any noise. That wasn't a good sign. He was going into shock.

"Forgive me, Cook, but both of your boys look similar. Which one is this?" I motioned to the child.

Despite the situation, Cook smiled. "This is Evan," she said affectionately. Her hand reached out and ran across his forehead, and I could see the fear in her eyes though she held it behind her familiar iron will.

I took the towels that Torben had brought me and pressed them to the wound in an attempt to staunch the blood flow, then I soaked one of them in the clean water and squeezed it over the opening and watched as the blood and small amounts of debris flowed out. When the wound finally appeared clean, I laid my hands over it and closed my eyes.

"Damaged cells and jagged skin,
Listen to my words, heal from within.
Mend the nerves and muscle and tissue,
Fix it all so it is like new.
Gather my power and use what you will,
Let nothing slip by and any disease kill.

Prevent infection, wash out any sickness,
Make flee the evil and wickedness.
Heal this child, heal his flesh and mind,
Show him not all who are unknown are unkind.
Let there be no damage or pain,
I, Allete, so speak this and pull power from my name.

I felt the energy flowing from my body and into Evan's. I felt the blood flowing from his body abate, and the skin begin to knit itself back together, but it wasn't enough. I wanted to erase the horror that the young boy had faced. How scary it must have been to stand before a strange warrior who was hell bent on killing you. How would a young boy recover from that without nightmares? I hated what he had been through. I could only imagine how Cook was feeling.

Once I was done and I was sure the wound was completely healed, I stepped back and nearly collapsed. Had Torben not been there to catch me, I would have sprawled out indignantly on the floor like a tossed towel.

Cook pointed to a chair. "Rest, child. You have done much, and I am so very thankful."

"You aren't scared of me?" I asked her.

She shook her head. "Why should I fear someone with a heart as pure as yours who gives so selflessly of herself? No, I am not scared of you. I am humbled that you would take your time to heal my boy, and I will be forever grateful."

Torben brought me the bowl of water and allowed me to wash the blood from my hands and then handed me a clean towel. After a half hour of rest and several cups of water, I finally felt that I had the strength to return to my chambers. "If you need anything at all, please let me know. Send your other son to my room and I will back in a heartbeat," I told her. I wanted to stay, but she refused to allow that and Torben was not too keen on the idea, either.

We left her small home. Once outside, I took a deep breath of the cool air. It felt good to be outside, free from confining walls. "Would you mind if we walked to the gardens?" I asked him.

"As you wish," Torben said and walked beside me with Brant trailing just behind us.

"You don't have to pretend you are my guard anymore," I told him, finally having the nerve to tell him that I knew about him.

"Perhaps not for your sake, but for the sake of everyone else, I need to appear as though I belong here," he explained.

We walked the rest of the way in silence. In the garden, I found my favorite spot to sit beneath one of the large trees. Dawn was slowly breaking, and the light from the morning sun was illuminating Torben's handsome face. He appeared deep in contemplation, and I wondered at the thoughts swirling in his head. I couldn't feel his emotions as I had before. A sudden sense of loss overcame me. I hadn't realized it fully at the time, but having the privilege of feeling what he was feeling, with no words spoken between us, was an intimacy the likes of which I'd never experienced before. We sat there in silence, and I considered how frustrating it was not being able to have free access to his emotions when it was convenient to me. I was curious to know if he wondered about what his mother had told me. Did he care about whether she approved of me? I wondered if he would ask me if she'd told me things that maybe he didn't know.

He chuckled and sat across from me, leaning against the base of a stone statue that portrayed a great bear. He motioned for Brant to keep watch and then set his eyes back on me. "Go on and ask," he said with a small grin. "I know you're dying to, so might as well get it over with."

"Ask you what?" I asked, playing coy. It was ridiculous of me, but I was embarrassed that he read my face so easily. "My mother came to see you. I can only imagine all the interesting things she shared with you. Not to mention, I am curious as to how she acted. My mother can have a wicked sharp tongue," he laughed.

I couldn't help but laugh with him. "She does at that," I agreed. I paused to gather my thoughts. "When did you find out about the prophecy?"

"A few months ago," he admitted without hesitation.

"How did you feel about it?"

"I was shocked, naturally. We have never had a foreign queen," he explained. "My people have always believed other races to be beneath them. We have always been the better warriors. I am still unsure how they will accept you."

"Do you still believe others are beneath you?" I asked.

He shook his head. "Not after meeting you. You are every bit, if not more, worthy than a Norsewoman to be my queen."

My insides quivered at the mention of me being his queen. It felt so real when he said it, and I had to admit that I liked the way it sounded. Part of me really wanted to be his queen, wanted to be his, but another part of me dreaded the idea of leaving my family. How could I possibly leave them? But that was the way of it, wasn't it? Young girls grew up, were courted until one of their suitors met their father's approval, and then they married and left the home to start their own families. It made sense, but it did not make it any easier.

"I did not expect to like you," he said as his face grew serious. "I did not have any idea that I would be able to love you."

My pulse picked up, even though he'd said the words

before, it was still so new and I really liked hearing him say them. But then I considered exactly how he'd worded it and wasn't sure if I should be offended.

"I just mean that I didn't know what to expect. I had assumed that all princesses were spoiled brats, but you surprised me."

A single brow rose on my forehead. "Spoiled?"

He shrugged sheepishly.

"I will admit that I have met my fair share of spoiled princesses. I, however, was not raised to take what we have for granted. I also know that wealth cannot make happiness. Happiness is something we choose, regardless of the circumstances in which we find ourselves. I cannot deny that I have had a tough time finding happiness over the past month as I have dealt with Cathal. In the beginning, I truly wanted to try and find the happiness in the situation, and I feel like I've failed at it. But then there was you and you became a bright spot in the darkness that had become my days. I can't imagine how much worse this could have been had you not been here."

"Well, you fought against this bright spot pretty hard," he said. His voice was full of frustration but not of anger.

"Could you blame me?" I asked. "I didn't know how we could possibly have a relationship as a princess and a guard."

"And what about now?" he asked.

"I still don't know how it is going to work, not because I don't want it to, but because we are both so very strong-willed." I took a deep breath.

"But you love me?" he asked.

The bluntness of his question gave me pause. I had already told him I did. But then, just as I needed to hear the words from him again, perhaps he needed that every bit as much as I did. "I do," I said with a small smile.

He scooted closer to me until I could feel his warm breath on my face. "I can't walk away from you, Allete," he said in a deep, sure voice. "Now that I've met you, and I see what an incredibly beautiful person you are, inside and out, I know that I do not want to face life without you. Bond or no bond, I am yours. I want you to marry me, as soon as we reach your new home. I want you to become my wife."

He ran a finger across my lips and I found myself leaning into his touch. "We barely know one another."

He chuckled. "You were on the way to the altar with a man you'd never even met, princess. I don't think that is a fair argument.

*True enough*, I thought. "How will your clan feel about you taking a foreign bride?"

"Those who trust my mother will not question it. Those loyal to the jarl are on their way out of this life; they just don't know it yet."

"You're going to kill them?" I asked with wide eyes.

He shook his head "I won't have to. If Magnus moves when I think he will, your father and Cathal will take care of that problem for me. There was a time that my jarl was a great strategist, but his greed and madness have made him careless and impulsive. He is going to get himself and all those who follow him killed."

"And you will be taking his place?"

Torben nodded "That is what the gods have decided for me. I don't know exactly what it will look like or how I'm going to change things, but I do believe that you will play a huge part in it."

"Me?" I asked as I pointed to myself. I didn't see how I could possibly make any difference to the health of his clan.

"Yes, you. You are strong and humble. You are smart

and innocent at the same time. You have great compassion and discipline. You are a mighty warrior, Allete."

His words made me feel so much more special that I truly was. I wanted them to be true. I wanted to be this woman he saw, but all I felt like was a teenager on the cusp of adulthood, scared of facing the future and afraid of death.

Little Evan was brought to my mind as I thought about death and how all beings face it eventually—some sooner than others Evan was so very young and had his whole life in front of him. It angered me that there was someone out there who thought they had a right to take another's life. "Was it a Viking that attacked Evan?" I asked him.

Torben nodded, and his lips tighten. "I heard the description Cook gave. It sounded like it was Magnus himself. That would surprise me. He isn't usually one to wander too far from camp. He prefers to hold court in the center of his warriors, sending others to do his bidding. If it was Magnus, he could be growing even more unpredictable.

"Why would he attack a young, defenseless boy? Is he truly that evil?"

"Power will do things to a man. It will change him from the inside out. It twists him and makes who he once was become unrecognizable to those around him."

I thought about his words and realized they applied to more than just Magnus. Cathal too had been corrupted by power. I didn't know at what point in his life he had been changed, or if it had simply started at an early age because of an example set by his parents, but it was more than apparent that he lived for power. Sitting there with Torben, talking about the future I could have, I knew without a doubt that I could not settle for Cathal. There would be no way to find happiness in life with him.

"What are you thinking about?" Torben asked.

"That I need to go begin getting ready for this dreaded ball."

His jaw clenched, and he nodded. "And don't forget to pack. After the ball, we will speak with your father and mother and then we will be on our way."

*Home* was the word he left unspoken at the end of that sentence. Although we were headed back to his home and for good reason, he was sensitive enough to understand the pain that I would feel leaving my own land.

"HOW ARE YOU HOLDING up?" Dayna asked as she helped lace up the back of my dress. It was the dress Cathal had given me, with the alterations my mother and sisters and I had added. I was ready for the night to be over and it hadn't even begun.

"I'm just ready to get this started so we can be done," I admitted.

"There's something else bothering you," she prodded.

Yes, there was. I had yet to tell Dayna everything that was happening between Torben and I. I needed to, but I dreaded telling her I was leaving.

"You might as well tell me because I won't leave you alone until you do."

"You might want to sit down for this," I finally said with a sigh.

She sat on the bed and I took the seat across from her. Dayna's feet dangled from the side and she began to gently kick them, reminding me of how she used to do that very thing when she was much younger and much smaller. The years had flown by, and now I was leaving my home forever.

"After the ball tonight, I will be leaving with Torben," I

said and felt as if the weight of the world had been lifted off my shoulders. There was still so much to tell, but it was a start and that was what I had needed. From that moment on, everything poured out of me. I paused a few times to answer her questions, but Dayna listened quietly in rapt attention.

"That is all," I finally finished over half an hour later.

"Well," she said, straightening her dress as she stood from her perch on the bed. "I suppose I had better get Lidia to come help you finish getting ready. I need to go pack."

My eyes widened. "What?"

She grinned at me. "You didn't really think I was going to let you go on this grand adventure without me, did you?"

"What about Father and Mother? And your home here?"

"The kingdom isn't going anywhere, Allete. We can always come back and visit. I was already determined to accompany you to Tara. This will be no different. Besides, Lizzy will still be here. That's what middle children are for," she winked. "The oldest goes off to do her duty for the family, the youngest rebels and does whatever she wants and the middle child picks up the slack."

"You can't come." I tried being bossy instead of reasoning with her. Reasoning had never worked on Dayna.

She laughed. "I always find it adorable, sister, when you attempt to tell me what to do and then always seem surprised when I do not obey."

I wanted to growl at her. "I'll tell Mother to put Clay on you as your guard this evening."

She waved me off as if it was a meaningless threat. "Clay refuses to come near me. The last time he was ordered to guard me, I told Cook he didn't like her meatloaf. She wouldn't let him eat her cooking for a month. He has learned not to mess with me." She reached the door, and I realized I was out of time and out of threats. "And it's not just you I need to keep an eye on. Don't you remember what I told Brant? How can I make good on my threat to snip, snip if I'm not there to witness his indiscretions?

She waved her fingers at me and shut the door behind her. I wouldn't lie, I was secretly ecstatic over the thought of having Dayna with me, but I also felt selfish. She couldn't really understand what it was going to be like living so far away from our parents, in a strange, possibly hostile land. But, for some reason, Dayana had always felt it was her duty to protect me, as if she was the elder sister and I was the younger.

Lidia entered a few minutes later and finished what Dayna had started. By the time the dreaded knock came, I was ready to chew off every finger nail I had and then start in on my toes.

When Lidia opened the door, I had to force my eyes to stay on Cathal and not seek out Torben. I could feel him there, tense and ready to pounce on anyone he perceived as a threat, namely Cathal.

"Good evening, my bride," Cathal said in a deep, rich voice. "You look," he paused and I could see him taking in the alterations we'd made. His jaw clenched, as did my own to keep from smiling. "You look stunning," he finally finished.

"Thank you, my lord," I curtseyed, but didn't return the sentiment, no matter how true. Cathal was stunning, but he already knew it and did not need me to remind him.

As I took his offered arm and walked past Torben, I felt him brush his hand discretely against my side and took comfort in knowing he was right there with me and would be no matter what.

WATCHING MY LOVE WALK beside a serpent masquerading as a king was like stabbing myself in the heart. I hated Allete being so close to him. I hated knowing that I'd have to keep even a little distance between us tonight, especially after the disturbing news I'd received earlier that day.

After I'd dropped Allete in her chambers, Amund had come to inform Brant and me that Magnus would be making a major move tonight. He and a large group of his men would be infiltrating the banquet dressed as English guards. I had no idea how Magnus expected to pull it off, but then, mad men sometimes seemed to be capable of things that normal men were not.

As we entered the grand ballroom, my eyes immediately began to scan my surroundings. I kept close to Allete, as close as Cathal would allow me without causing a scene. Brant was just as alert as me, but I didn't miss the way his eyes continually drifted over to Dayna. He would be ensuring she was safe, and I would not fault him at all if he dropped his guard position to protect her if need be.

The room was filled with quiet chatter and music as the orchestra played. I knew, at some point, they would formally introduce Cathal and Allete, and I wondered if that would be when Magnus would do ... whatever it was he was planning to do.

My hand continually moved to brace against the hilt of my sword as if assuring itself the weapon was still within ready reach. I would much prefer to be carrying an axe on my back in addition to the sword. I liked having two weapons, if not more on me, but the royal guards only carried a sword. Of course, I had a few small daggers in hiding under my tunic and in boot sheaths, but they didn't quite carry the punch an axe did. Wielded properly, however, they could be just as deadly.

"There he is," Brant murmured softly. "As the clock tolls high noon." This was his way of communicating to me Magnus's direction without having to point or motion with his head.

My eyes landed on our jarl, and I was shocked at how well he'd managed to disguise himself. His guard uniform was immaculate, and his beard had been clean-shaven. I wasn't sure if his hair, which usually hung well past his shoulders, was cut, or if he'd managed to hide it under the helmet. Regardless, the wild mane was out of view. He was casually glancing around the room, appearing as though he were simply watching for trouble, ready and willing to intervene if necessary to ensure the safety of the partygoers.

Only a few minutes later, I spotted several more Norsemen. I was still unable to deduce their plan. What did they hope to accomplish here? I wracked my brain, hoping to understand their intentions. If I couldn't figure out their next move, I might not be able to get Allete out of harm's way.

Suddenly the music stopped, and the trumpets began their royal call. Once they were silenced, the herald stepped forward to the side of the stage next to the orchestra.

"Lords and ladies, I present King Albric and Queen Alease."

The king and queen stepped forward and nodded to the applauding crowd. Then King Albric held up his hands and the applause died as he turned his attention to Allete. "Tonight, we celebrate the engagement of my eldest daughter. She has grown into a beautiful young woman and we are so proud of her." He motioned for Allete and Cathal to step forward. "Please join us as we congratulate her and her fiancé, King Cathal."

The room became an uproar of applause as the two came forward. The clapping continued for several minutes as the seemingly happy couple waved to the crowd. Finally, the room began to quiet, everyone anxiously awaiting an address from King Cathal and his soon-to-be queen. All of a sudden, I heard a thrum, followed by a distinct whooshing sound. I knew immediately an arrow had been loosed. Instinctively, I dove in front of Allete. In doing so, I caught a brief glimpse of the arrow in flight, zipping through the air like a death sentence, headed straight toward us. She fell back but I didn't see if she'd been injured. I was too busy taking an arrow to the chest.

The pain was immediate. I hit the stage with a thud and landed on my back. There was a sharp scream, and the room erupted into a melting pot of confused people moving in different directions. Men and women alike shouted and ran for the exits. Confused guards yelled to one another, pulling their swords from their sheaths. Tables and chairs toppled, spilling wine, food, and dishes onto the floor.

I tried to sit up, but as soon as I put pressure on my arm, it collapsed under me. Suddenly, like the image of a beautiful Valkyrie, Allete's face, was hovering over mine.

"Don't you dare die," she growled.

I smiled. "It's good to see you too, love. And yes, I did just take an arrow in the chest to prove my love for you."

"Shut up," she snapped. "This isn't the time for jokes, Torben. I've got to pull this out and then heal you quickly."

"Don't," I said, attempting to keep her hands back. I was too weak to stop her. *Why was I so weak?*

"You're losing too much blood. I think the arrow tip is close to the heart," she answered. I guess I must have asked my question out loud.

I bit the inside of my cheek as she grasped the arrow and jerked it free, with a strength I wouldn't have guessed she was capable of. I could hear Brant arguing with Cathal, restraining him, trying to convince him that Allete was a trained healer—albeit, not a healer of the magical variety—whose help was vitally important in that moment. Cathal was giving him a thorough cursing, demanding him to move. My loyal friend was having none of it.

"Do not heal me, Allete," I ground out through my teeth as the pain radiated through my body. "There are some who do not need to know what you can—" A hand slapped over my mouth, effectively shutting me up.

Allete leaned in close to me, her nose nearly touching my own. I needed to focus, but in that moment, all I wanted was for those perfect lips pressed to my own—to taste her one last time.

"I am not going to sit by and watch you die just to keep myself safe. So you listen up, warrior, you are not going to die because I am going to heal you, right here, right now. Are we clear?"

"Kiss me," I said, ignoring her words. Apparently, that was not the correct response.

"Stupid, stubborn ...," she began mumbling but I missed the rest of it because she firmly pressed her hand to the wound, and the pain was excruciating. I heard her begin to chant but I couldn't make out what she was saying. All I could hear was the blood rushing through my ears as the pain and agony threatened to steal my consciousness.

I did not know how long it was before the pain began to ease, and the sounds around me slowly returned. There were shouts echoing throughout the ballroom. I could see legs stumbling around us and heard screams accompanied by the ringing of steel on steel as swords clashed. I was still a bit foggy, but I could guess that my people had attacked the guests and the palace guards were fighting back. I wanted to move now to get Allete out of the room, but I didn't yet have the strength to lift myself.

Just then I saw Magnus' face appear over Allete's shoulder. My eyes widened as I recognized the greedy look in his eyes. He knew what Allete was doing. He'd seen my mother do it many times. I could almost see his lust for power as a tangible thing. He knew the kind of power Allete could give him. He wasn't going to let that go.

"Allete," I said her name, but she was lost in her trance like state. She had no idea that a wolf was behind her, hunting her. I tried again to get her attention, to shift or move, anything to keep Magnus from being able to take her, but nothing worked. As I laid there, every cell in my body focusing on knitting itself back together in response to Allete's healing, I was powerless. I could do nothing as Magnus wrapped his large arm around her waist and jerked her back against his body.

Allete's eyes went wide, and her mouth dropped open. Shock held her paralyzed as she stared back at me. Then instinct kicked in. She screamed, kicked, and fought to get free, but she was no match for Magnus' strength. His madness only made him that much stronger. She called my name, and I was helpless to respond. It was as though the arrow had been reinserted and pressed all the way into my heart this time. My brain was telling my body to move, but a twitch and a weak groan was all that came in response. No amount of internal screaming at my limbs did any good.

"Brant!" I croaked when I was finally able to speak. "Go get her!"

"Can't do that, comrade," he barked back. "You'll die if I leave you here."

"GO GET HER!" I roared, but the mountain refused to

move.

"He won't kill her, Torben, you know that. He won't even harm her. She's too valuable. But you're barely hanging on, you dolt. Now, act dead until things get sorted."

"Brant, I swear by the gods if you don't..." It was the last thing I said before everything went dark.

THE ARM AROUND MY waist was like a steel band. I couldn't move so much as an inch, no matter how hard I fought. I looked back to where Torben lay just in time to see Brant knock him over the head with the hilt of his sword. My mouth opened wider, if that was even possible.

Why would Brant attack his commander? Torben was injured badly. Why would—my thoughts froze. "No," I whispered to myself. "Brant wouldn't betray Torben."

The giant who had grabbed me turned to where Brant stood and commanded, "Finish him." Brant was looking right at us. He gave a small nod. Was he nodding at me or my captor? What in the seven hells was going on?

"ALLETE!" Dayna's loud bellow reached across the room to me, and my eyes met hers. She was attempting to run to me, fighting against the stream of panicked people moving the other direction. Swords had been drawn and pockets of men fought one another all over the large room.

"Magnus, what do you want us to do?" A tall man, dressed in an English guard uniform, asked the one holding me. I realized then my attacker was none other than the jarl himself.

"Change of plans," Magnus growled. "Get the men and meet at the boats. I've got a prize I did not expect. We can come back and claim the rest after we've regrouped."

The man gave a nod and hurried off. As soon as he was

away, I resumed my fight. "Let me go!"

"Sorry, pet, but I can't do that," Magnus said as he moved quickly, weaving in and out of bodies that had fallen, some still writhing in pain. "You are exactly what I need. I had no idea you were within my grasp. And to think Torben had been keeping you all to himself."

"I don't understand; why do you need me?" Terror was rising in my chest. I was just beginning to realize he'd grabbed me during a healing. He wanted me for my abilities.

"Don't play dumb, little one. You're a healer. You must know how valuable you are."

"Why would I ever help someone who's kidnapped me?"

"You will do more than help me. You will be my personal healer," he said as if I was the most privileged woman in the history of ever.

"I will never heal you," I sneered at him.

"You will. Everyone has a breaking point, Princess Allete," he warned me. "We will simply have to find yours."

"Allete!" Dayna's voice rang out, close behind us.

"In fact, I think we just found it," he said as he grabbed the shoulder of one of his warriors. "Take that one," he said, pointing to my sister.

"NO! Dayna, stay back! Run!" I yelled as loud as I could. We clambered out of the palace and across the courtyard under a moonlit sky, my feet kicking all the while. I couldn't believe how fast the man could move all the while maintaining a grip on my waist with one arm. We were nearing one of the smaller side gates that led to outside the castle walls. Not only was he fast, but his feet were surprisingly silent despite his added load.

I heard a commotion behind us, and I lifted my head. I saw Dayna being carried over the shoulder of another large

Norseman. She was flailing like a dying fish and screaming every obscenity known to man. And I was proud of her. *Give him hell, little sister*, I thought as I debated whether to save what energy I had left. Despite Magnus' strength, surely he couldn't run forever. Perhaps, when we finally stopped, an opportunity for Dayna and me to escape would present itself.

Magnus held me tightly and I could scarcely breathe. My ribs felt as if they would break under the strength of his arm. We cleared the castle walls and headed into the trees. Magnus didn't slow; he just kept running, never breaking stride. Did the man ever tire?

I wondered if anyone was giving chase. There had been so much confusion that I didn't even know if anyone realized what had happened to us. If they hadn't, it might be awhile before my father even knew to send a search party after us.

The man carrying Dayna had caught up to us. She was still cursing, though she'd quit flailing.

"Just let my sister go," I finally said to Magnus. "I'll do as you ask. Just let her go."

"Sorry, but I am not inclined to believe a woman who I am in the process of abducting. Your sister is coming with us."

"You do realize that Torben is going to kick your flea-bitten arse, right?" Dayna yelled. I rolled my eyes. She had a death wish.

"Torben is dead, or if he isn't he will be soon," Magnus said without a single drop of doubt.

He was wrong. I would know if Torben was dead. I would feel it. *Wouldn't I?* Our bond was so new. I had no idea of its intricacies. Oh gods, what if he was dead, and I had no way of knowing? Why on earth did I have to think those thoughts in that moment? *Pull yourself together, Allete*, I snapped inwardly. There was a time and place for panic, and this was neither.

"Torben isn't dead you moron," Dayna laughed. "It will take a better man than you to kill someone like Torben."

"The archer did the job just fine, and my man will finish it."

My heart hit my toes. He was talking about Brant. He had to be talking about Brant. *Finish him*, he'd said, and Brant had nodded as if in answer. Magnus had told Brant to kill Torben. I tried to absorb the information, but it just wasn't sinking in. I couldn't reconcile the Brant I knew doing anything to betray Torben.

When I heard the deep thud of footsteps, my eyes snapped open. I hadn't even realized I'd closed them. I looked down and saw that Magnus was crossing a planked walkway. When I looked up, my eyes widened at the massive ship upon which we were boarding.

Magnus shifted me and threw me over his shoulder. "Oomph," I groaned as my stomach was squashed.

"You might want to hold still," he warned and then began climbing. By the time he made it to the top of the ladder that was strapped to the large ship, he was finally sounding winded.

He set me down, and I was lightheaded, momentarily seeing stars as the blood rushed back down from my head. My eyes refused to focus. "Dayna," I said her name as I cry of self-defense and found her standing next to me.

"Yep, I am here. Just trying not to vomit."

I swayed on my feet and began to realize how weak I was. "Why," I started, but then realized I had been healing Torben when Magnus snatched me. That was why I was weak, from the healing. When my eyesight finally sorted itself, I couldn't see much. Only a few lanterns dim lanterns were lit at various intervals along the ship. But I did not miss for a second that the ship was getting farther from the shore. We were already moving.

"Are you okay?" Dayna asked.

I nodded.

"Turn around," a man said as he walked up to us with rope in his hands.

"Where would we go?" I asked.

"Can't jump if you can't swim," he said as if he was talking about the weather.

We both did as he commanded. Once our hands were tied, he moved us to a bench. "The jarl said for you two to sit there and not to move."

Dayna started to say something, but I stomped on her foot and she snapped her mouth closed.

"If we give them reason to think we are going to run, they'll put us in a more secure location. For the time being, appear complacent," I explained.

"Torben and Brant will come for us," she said with a nod.

I cringed. I didn't want to tell her that Brant might be the reason I never saw the man I loved again, mostly because I did not want to believe it myself.

I turned at the sound of Magnus's voice. "Come and see what I've found, old crone." He was standing in front of someone I couldn't see. "I want you to teach her everything you know."

He finally stepped aside, and Hilda was staring right at me. "Oh, I will definitely teach her everything," she responded. "Do not worry, Jarl. She will be the best, even better than me."

I held a look of surprise and unrecognition on my face, as if I'd never met the woman. But my conversation with Torben's mother came rushing back to me, including everything she'd said about using my magic for harm. I understood immediately. She would teach me, all right. She would teach me how to kill Magnus using the magic that he thought would be healing him.

"Did you see Torben while you were at the castle?" She addressed him, but never took her eyes off me.

"Briefly," Magnus answered. "He was engaged in battle. The castle guard was much stronger than we anticipated. I cannot guarantee that he will make it back."

Hilda's lips twitched slightly. "Don't count your best warrior out just yet, Jarl. You know, as well as any, that he has a way of surviving impossible situations."

# Epilogue

"SOME THINK DEATH IS THE WORST FATE THAT CAN BEFALL
A MAN. THEY THINK THAT THE ABSENCE OF LIFE IS THE
ULTIMATE LOSS. THEY CANNOT FATHOM THE POSSIBILITY OF
SOMETHING FAR WORSE. WHEN THE PERSON WHO HOLDS THE
OTHER HALF OF YOUR SOUL IS TAKEN FROM YOU, DEATH IS
MERE CHILD'S PLAY IN COMPARISON."

~TORBEN.

"WAKE UP."

Brant's voice seemed to be coming from a long
distance away, but the tapping of his hand on my face
made it clear that he was right next to me.

"That's it. Wake up, comrade. Wake up so we can go
hunting."

At that my eyes snapped open. "Hunting?" I rasped.

"Allete."

Her name had barely left his lips and everything came
rushing back.

"And Dayna," he added, his voice dropping an octave.

"Magnus took her, too?"

Brant nodded.

I tried to sit up.

"Easy," he said as he grasped my forearm and helped
me into a sitting position. To my surprise, I was still on the

floor in the ballroom. The room was mostly clear now, with only a handful of the palace guards remaining behind to clear the bodies from the room.

"I will find her," Cathal bellowed from behind Brant.

I motioned for him to move aside. Cathal was standing in front of Allete's visibly upset parents. Her mother was covering her mouth with her hand, attempting to hold in the sobs that were threatening to overcome her.

"It is because of you that she was taken," King Albric roared back. "It was the arrow that was supposed to be for you, by an assassin from your very own court that started this whole mess. Forgive me if I do not trust *you* with the rescue of our daughter."

"What are these lies you spew?" Cathal snarled.

"My daughter doesn't lie," King Albric said, his jaw was clenched so tightly I wondered how he didn't break any of his teeth. "Do you recognize that man?" He pointed to a body I hadn't noticed at first. There was a pool of blood beneath him large enough to make it clear that the man had not survived his attempt at the assassination. Too bad he hadn't been a better shot.

"He is of no consequence," Cathal answered.

"He was betrothed to the woman Cathal took as his third queen," Lizzy said as she stepped out from behind her mother. "His name is Luther. He came with your court with the intention of killing you."

"You would believe the word of a girl over that of a king?" Cathal asked Albric.

"I would believe my daughter over you." King Albric took a step closer to Cathal and his guards moved with him. "This is your doing. What kind of man takes another's betrothed? Have you no honor?"

"I am no mere man," the king of Tara said, puffing out his chest like a prancing peacock. "I am a king, and I will have what I please. I will have Allete. She is my wife."

"No!" Queen Alease said sharply. "She is not. She is my daughter, and she and her sister have been taken by a Viking warlord. They are *our* responsibility, and we will get them back."

"Allete is mine. I will have her. Mark my words. I will take my army and track her down. When I find her, she will be taken back to my kingdom. And if you get in my way, I will wipe you out." He turned and motioned to his men. They stormed from the room, and Albric made no move to stop him.

"Help me up," I told Brant, unable to remain on the floor any longer.

Brant helped me walk over to the small group. King Albric and Queen Alease's eyes widened. "You're her guard," she said. "But your hair, your face..."

"Before you start screaming, please let me explain." I held up my hands in peace. "My name is Torben. I am a Norseman, but I did not come here with the intent to harm your daughters."

"Why did you come?" Albric asked sharply, his eyes narrowed.

"Because of a prophecy given to my mother. She is an Oracle." When they started to interrupt, I held up my hand. "Forgive me, but there is not much time. You must listen now. Magnus, the leader of my clan, is the man who took your daughters. He is a madman who refuses to see reason. Our people are in danger, threatened with extermination because of Magnus' tyranny.

"The prophecy states that I will destroy him and become king, and that my bride will rule by my side. The prophecy goes on to say that the woman destined to be my bride will be from a foreign land and that her people are also in danger. The fate of both of our peoples depend upon our union, and our wise rule. My bride, the woman prophesied to rule beside me, is your daughter, Allete. I came to meet her, to spend time with her, and to find out if the prophecy was indeed true."

When neither of them spoke, I continued.

"Over the past month, I have fallen in love with your daughter, and she has fallen in love with me. Her powers are much more extraordinary than you can imagine. But they require that she have a soul match—another whose fate is bonded to her own. I am that soul match, and we have completed the bonding ceremony. We've been forced to act in secret because of Cathal. But if anyone can find her, I can."

"And what if you do find her?" asked the queen.

"Magnus will not give her up without a fight, of that I'm sure. My mother is gifted with powers similar to that of Allete. He has kept her captive my entire life. I could never purposely hurt the woman I love. I will bring her back to you."

They both stared back at me, and I knew they were fighting the distrust they had for my kind.

"I know you have no reason to trust me. But hear this: when I bring Allete and Dayna home, if she refutes anything I've said, I will willingly die by your hand. I swear it by the gods." I pulled out a dagger from beneath my tunic and ran it across my palm. "By the blood of my forefathers, and the blood of my future heirs, I swear I mean you and yours no harm."

Albric's eyes widened. A blood oath was not taken lightly by any people, regardless of how different they might be.

"Are you even well enough to pursue her captors?" he asked finally.

I met his eyes and held them. I needed him to

understand how serious were the words I was about to speak. "On deaths door, or at the peak of health, I am capable of anything it takes to save your daughter. I will get both of your daughters back, and I will destroy Magnus and Cathal. You have my word."

"Cathal?" he asked with a frown.

"His actions have not gone unnoticed. I have been by Allete's side for a month. I've seen him hurt my mate, my soul match, my future queen. His life was forfeit the moment he laid a hand on her. And there are some things I cannot forgive. Cathal will die, and I will be the one to kill him."

After several minutes of silence, Queen Alease rose and wrapped her arms around me in a tight embrace. I bit back a groan of pain. Apparently, I was not completely healed just yet.

"Please bring them home. We can deal with anything else when that is done."

She stepped back, and Albric nodded. "I will trust you. But if Allete speaks one ill word against you when you return, I will hang you. And if you do not return with her, I will hunt you down myself."

"Fair enough." I bowed and then turned, walking as quickly as I could with Brant at my side.

"Do you have a plan?" Brant asked.

"Of course, I do."

"Would you like to tell me what it is?"

"Rescue the damsels, kill the villains."

Brant cursed. "I was hoping for something a little more thought out."

"That's as far as I've gotten. You think of something better, feel free to share." As we left the castle and raced to the beach, all I could think about was her. Nothing else existed but her. Until she was safe beside me where she belonged, nothing else would matter. She was no longer a faceless woman foretold by a vague prophecy. She was the woman my soul had bonded with, the woman my heart had chosen.

"You have that look in your eyes," Brant said as we hit the tree line at a run.

"What look?"

"The one that makes me wonder if you still have a soul."

My jaw clenched. "I still have a soul, but it is not my own anymore. It is Allete's, and if I lose her, then I will no longer have a soul. Do you understand what that means?"

"Hell on earth?"

I nodded. "Exactly, my friend. Hell will reign on earth, and I will be the one to throw open the gates."

# Acknowledgements

S O MANY PEOPLE TO thank. Thank you to my husband for his continued support and pushing me to do what I love even when it's hard. Thank you to Clean Teen for giving me this opportunity and being very patient with me. Thank you to The Fetching Mrs. Hill (she knows who she is) for staying up til two in the morning helping me hash out the plot…multiple times. Thank you to Angie for being willing to Beta read for me and listen to me complain. Thank you to Candace for your continued encouragement. Thank you to Jamie for being a fantastic sounding board and source of encouragement. And especially to the readers. You make all of this possible and there are no words that can truly show my gratitude.

# ABOUT THE Author

QUINN LOFTIS IS THE author of 20 novels including the USA Today Bestseller Fate and Fury. Her writing passion is fantasy and paranormal though she has dabbled in contemporary at least once. Her books are character driven, filled with humor and highlight the struggles that come in any relationship. She believes in happily ever afters, but she will make sure that you have felt every emotion she can possibly pull out of you before she gets you there. Ultimately she is a woman who gets to live out her dream of being an author because of the amazing fans who have taken a chance on her books and she is incredibly thankful to God and them. She lives in Western Arkansas with her husband, three sons, two dogs and cat that thinks he's a dog.